"The hell with Maxwell, Colonel! He's as guilty as you are for what will happen."

"Damn my eyes, but you're a stubborn Scotch ba—" Brodhead caught himself at the last moment, shook off anger, and said carefully, "Give your solemn oath you will not interfere with Williamson, and I'll let you go this very minute."

Sutherland looked sidelong at Brodhead, seeing a good but compromised man who was in deeper than he could handle. Sutherland did not blame Brodhead, but he would not go along with what the colonel was allowing to happen.

"You'll regret this campaign, Colonel."

"By gad, Sutherland!" He whipped his tricorne to the plank floor. "By gad, don't you see that I've promised the Washington County men this campaign?"

HONOR
The Eighth Powerful Novel
in the Northwest Territory Series

BLOODY BATTLES CONTINUE TO RAGE ACROSS THE FRONTIER. CAN ONE MAN'S LOVE FOR THE LAND, HIS FAMILY AND JUSTICE STOP THE MINDLESS SLAUGHTER?

OWEN SUTHERLAND. A leader in the trading community, head of a strong frontier family, he is branded as an Indian-lover, but his first love is the land itself...

ELLA SUTHERLAND. Wife of the proud head of the frontier traders, mother of a strong-willed daughter, her enduring love binds the Sutherlands together...

SUSANNAH SUTHERLAND. Beautiful daughter of a powerful man, she must choose between passion and responsibility, or learn to balance both...

JAMES MORELY. Head of the rival trading company, threatened by the father of the woman he seeks to possess, he must decide between genuine feeling and consuming ambition...

DAVID WILLIAMSON. Ruthless commander of a hardened frontier militia, he is driven by his hatred for Indians...

ENTELLUS GREYSON. A young Maryland officer, he has serious doubts about ridding the frontier of Indians, even though he stands to profit by it...

NIKO-LOTA. Self-appointed defender of the Moravian Indians, he must cut all bonds of trust with any save his own race, even if it means fighting his friend Owen Sutherland...

EVANGELINE. A Christian Indian who gives her love to Niko-lota, her faith is tested by the ultimate sacrifice her people must make...

NOAH MAXWELL. Right hand to the scheming James Morely, he winks at the injustices he has learned to conceal under the guise of business as usual...

NORTHWEST TERRITORY · BOOK 8

HONOR

OLIVER PAYNE

Created by the producers of
Wagons West, The Australians, and
The Kent Family Chronicles.

Chairman of the Board: Lyle Kenyon Engel

BERKLEY BOOKS, NEW YORK

HONOR

A Berkley Book/published by arrangement with
Book Creations, Inc.

PRINTING HISTORY
Berkley edition/June 1987

Produced by Book Creations, Inc.
Chairman of the Board: Lyle Kenyon Engel

ISBN: 0-425-09886-9

*To the memory of all the peoples of
the Old Northwest*

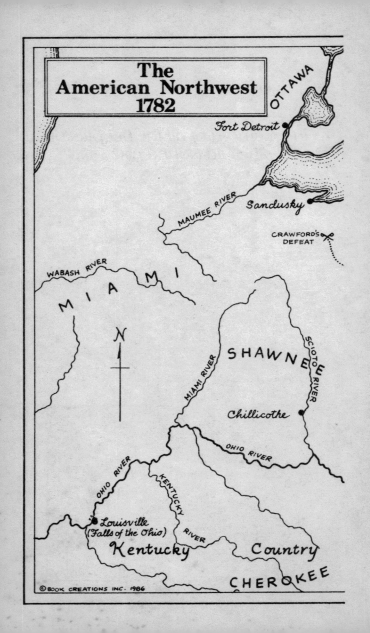

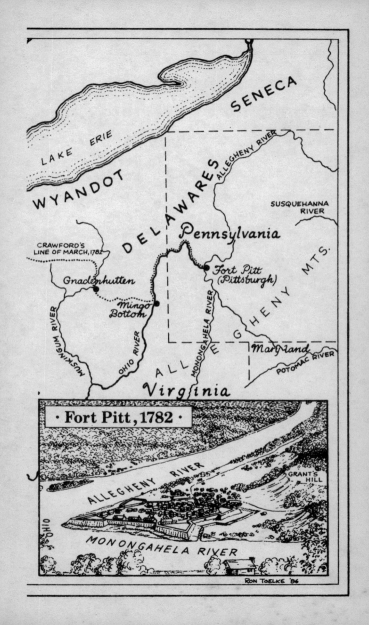

LAKE ERIE

SENECA

WYANDOT

ALLEGHENY RIVER

DELAWARES

SUSQUEHANNA RIVER

Pennsylvania

CRAWFORD'S LINE OF MARCH, 1782

Gnadenhutten

Fort Pitt (Pittsburgh)

Mingo Bottom

ALLEGHENY MTS.

MUSKINGUM RIVER

OHIO RIVER

MONONGAHELA RIVER

Maryland

ALLEGHENY

POTOMAC RIVER

Virginia

· Fort Pitt, 1782 ·

ALLEGHENY RIVER

GRANT'S HILL

OHIO

MONONGAHELA RIVER

RON TOELKE '86

Prologue

To a man, his house means rest and comfort, a place of his own taste and feeling, where he shuts out the world as it is and enjoys the world as he has made it within four walls. Valenya was like that, a place of rest.

For a woman, her house is all this and more. To Ella, Valenya is a living thing, part of the family. A poet might say the house is the body, and the people are its soul, giving life and purpose. Today Ella said, as we stood looking out at the Ohio River, that without us, the house we built on the Detroit straits must be like a corpse, without life. Valenya must be without soul.

Without soul was what I added as we stood there thinking about the old days, so long ago they seem now, before the colonies rose against the king, before the biggest war this country has ever known.

And what about us? Ella asked. We Sutherlands are like wraiths, like disembodied souls, wandering and longing to return to their home.

But a corpse cannot be reborn, I said, and she gave that knowing look, the way she can when things are hard and she is determined to push on through them, no matter what. She said the house at the straits is not a body. Valenya is only a house, of wood and stone and glass. . . .

Then she spoke of the sash windows we brought all the way from Philadelphia back in seventy-four or so. Thinking of those fine windows brought back other memories, and I saw a tear in her eye and I felt it myself and thought of the view from those windows. I could see the orchard and the cornfields, and how in spring the canoe brigades returning from the fur grounds would salute us and the house with a fire of joy. That was something! Five hundred rifles roaring all at once and for miles the shoreline filled with people waving and singing.

Valenya was alive then, indeed!

And now? There has been no news from Detroit for nearly two years, and for all we know, the loyalists may have torched the house by now. That's a troubling thought that has wakened Ella more than once, and myself as well. But if Valenya was gone, someone would have sent us word. They all know what the house means to us. Even enemies would take pleasure in telling us our home had been destroyed.

Will we ever go back? Will the house be ours again? We still have plenty of friends out there, red and white and half-breed, people who care nothing for the Revolution and want only to trade and trap and enjoy life. Ella hungers to go back, though three hundred miles of wilderness stand between Detroit and Fort Pitt, though ten thousand warriors are bitter at Owen Sutherland for having joined the rebels to fight the Indians.

Maybe they will bury the tomahawk now that the rebels are winning. The fighting has nearly stopped back east ever since Cornwallis and his army surrendered at Yorktown. Maybe the tribes will see it is no use to fight on, for the British will not back them much longer, and the Northwest eventually will fall under the control of Congress and the states. Even Canada may separate from the Crown before long.

Maybe the red men will see there is no use making war, that they have to make peace. Then the trade will open up, and we can go back to Detroit and talk about starting the trading company once again. If blood has not flowed too freely and old enemies forgive and forget, there may yet be peace.

Then we Sutherlands shall return to Valenya, our home, give it life once more, give it a soul. For the first time in too many years, we will find rest.

> Journal of Owen Sutherland, trader
> Fort Pitt settlement, February 18, 1782

PART ONE

The Moravian Trail

chapter 1

WINTER PILGRIMS

On the south trail, through deep oak forest, there was always the danger of attack, and the travelers well knew it. But they ventured forth from camp that February morning in 1782, unwilling to let fear hinder their journey.

Walking or riding in single file, elders in advance, children and women in the middle with packhorses and dog-carts, they moved through the winter forest, putting their trust in God. After an exile of nearly a year they were going home at last. Not far away, at the end of this forest trail, stood their empty cabins and their locked chapel. Their fields of ripe corn were yet unharvested, and a rich harvest it would be!

These people had been away long enough, had been poor long enough, and now were determined to get home and rebuild life in a community that had been abandoned in the face of a ruthless enemy. They were filled more with anticipation and excitement than with dread, even though the south trail was very dangerous, and they were in peril at every step.

Wind whistled through the bleak winter woods all around them. Trees creaked in their nakedness, swaying against a sky that darkened, gray and cold, promising a

3

storm. Frozen snow blanketed the forest floor, running with shadows of moving branches. Shadows of branches —that was all they were, a young woman told herself as she walked along, glancing through the trees. Those were shadows of clouds and branches, not glimpses of men stalking, spying, plotting. . . .

Beside this young woman were two children, a boy of eleven and a girl of eight, who plodded along uncomplaining at her side. Christoph and Maria were tired and hungry, and they did not speak much these days, for the journey had been long, and they instinctively saved every ounce of strength for taking the next step and the next one.

The footsteps of a hundred travelers and the hooves of horses crunched steadily on the packed snow. No one spoke, except in whispers. No one sang, though these folk loved to sing, and at hymns they were an angel chorus. They must be quiet, lest an enemy hear them pass. When they were home again, their pretty chapel would resound with their joy and the music of their faith, just as it had for two generations. The village was called Gnadenhutten, German for "blessed dwellings," and there was scarcely a community on the frontier to match it for its fine log cabins and rich, well-husbanded soil.

Every step brought them nearer, and every mile returned to them familiar sights: places where their children played in times of peace, or where lovers often wandered. Once it had not been dangerous to be here. Now few men dared walk these paths alone. Now folk seldom traveled, even in large numbers such as this group. Usually, good fighting men escorted folk who had to take to the trail, but none of these travelers were fighters, and the few men carrying firearms were inexperienced at using them. None had ever fired at a man before.

Their village would not promise them safety, either, and they knew that. But where else was it safe on the frontier anymore? And if they had to face danger, better that it be at home, by their beloved chapel, trusting the hand of God for protection, for salvation.

The cold sky deepened, and the treetops bowed and rushed in the rising wind that swept down from the northwest. Snow was on the way, but before the storm hit they would be home. The wind was harsh, but they were glad for its noise in the forest—louder than their footfalls, so that even camps of fighting men might not notice their coming. Unless enemy scouts roved the south trail, no one would detect the travelers. Maybe the scouts would have made for a warm fire by now, with bad weather at hand. Maybe these people would get through undisturbed, after all, just as they had come through nearly three hundred miles already.

Yes, they were glad for the wind and the approaching storm. It was a sign that surely they were protected by the merciful hand of their Savior, Jesus Christ. Softly, some of the women began singing a hymn, and little children joined in from where they sat bundled on horseback or crowded onto dog sleds with a family's essentials. The wind rose, and the louder it howled, the louder sang the travelers, one voice strengthening another. They thanked God with song, grateful to be coming home at last.

The young woman also sang, but her eyes roved the forest, watching those fleeting shadows, seeing movement where there was no sunlight on the snow. She saw a flash once, as of metal reflecting what little sun slipped through the gathering clouds. It gave her a start, but the song of her companions comforted her. She prayed silently, drawing her eyes from the forest edge and back to the trail.

She was not far from the front of the column, just behind the leading men. Beside her an old packhorse was blowing and stepping out gingerly on a sore foreleg. Every person and animal was sore by now, every one of them with blisters or chilblains, bruises that would not heal, and aching muscles. Soon, very soon, there would be warm rooms, beds with pillows, plank floors, hearths blazing with a homey light.

There! That time she was certain—men were standing in a thicket off to the right, staring. There were at least five of them. Her heart leaping, she called out to the man walking just in front of her.

"Behold! Brother Abraham! See there, in the trees!"

Without turning, the big man, wrapped in a muffler and greatcoat, nodded, saying, "We know, Sister Evangeline. They've been dogging us all morning, and now it seems they mean to talk, that's all. Have no fear."

She did not believe him. She gripped the hands of the children. Those five men in buckskin and fur were fighters —anyone could see that by their arms, by the glitter in their eyes as they stood and stared, some of them grinning like hungry animals. The girl found herself trembling and, like the others in her party, stopped walking. The singing had also stopped. More men came out of the woods, until there were ten of them, grim and ugly and got up with feathers for war.

They were not whites from Virginia, the Longknives, the girl could see. They wore waistcoats and woolen shirts under buckskin jackets, and flat hats unlike Longknife woolen hats, which were invariably white. Their moccasins were plain, not adorned with beads, as were those of most Virginians. These, the girl knew, were Pennsylvania backwoodsmen, hard and cruel and dreaded by her people, who were Moravian Christian Indians on their way home.

Abraham moved toward them, for he was the leader of the Moravians. As Evangeline watched the whites crowd around him and other elders in the lead, she felt her blood chill through her body. She prayed there would be no trouble. For twenty years and more Moravian Indians—con-

verts to a German Protestant sect—had suffered the hatred
of Pennsylvanians. Though Moravians practiced nonviolence, they were still Indians—mostly of Delaware blood
—and were suspected of cooperating with war parties.
There had been brutal assaults by whites on their villages,
wanton murders, and wholesale slaughter that was seldom
prevented or opposed by Pennsylvania law.

Now these armed woodsmen on a scout, obviously
looking for Indians to kill, had come upon the defenseless
Moravians, and Evangeline could imagine what they were
saying. From this distance she felt their hatred, their longing to hurt all Indians—for all Indians were their enemies,
all Indians responsible for shedding the blood of their
friends and families during thirty years of border war.

Voices rose as the whites jostled Abraham, who was
calm, stoic. He stood steady before them as they cursed
him. Women paled, fear in their eyes. Children gaped, and
men protectively moved forward toward the whites. From
here, the Moravian Indians with their short hair and linsey
shirts, their clean breeches and linen stockings, looked
more civilized than the bearded whites in their buckskin,
grime, and turkey feathers. Indeed, the Moravians probably were more civilized. No whites were better farmers, or
more skilled at crafts. Moravians were wealthy by comparison, and that was another reason the white backwoodsmen, especially the impoverished Pennsylvanians, hated
and envied them.

Terrified, Evangeline left the children with their mother
and drifted forward, listening to the angry words of the
Pennsylvanians. She knew their language, having learned
it from a young white man who had been a prisoner in her
home village of Chillicothe, many marches to the west.
Evangeline had been with these Moravians only a couple of
years. She was a full-blooded Shawnee and had broken
with her people when she joined the Moravians out of

faith. Now her parents had abandoned this land, had migrated west last year, fleeing the incessant war that brought such dangers upon them. She had stayed, however, unwilling to depart from the country she loved. She was determined to stand fast with the Moravians returning to Gnadenhutten, after having been ordered by the British to winter up at Sandusky for their own protection. They had journeyed back in the hope that the killing soon would be finished.

"Lousy red niggers!" spat a muscular young Pennsylvanian with a curly black beard and eyes that seemed dead, empty of human compassion. "You ain't going nowheres less'n you step over my corpse! By morning there won't be no Moravian town, after Colonel Williamson here gets through!"

This fearsome character turned to nod to a taller, almost distinguished-looking man of middle age, who was robust, clean-shaven, and had a cold, remorseless expression. The "colonel" listened smugly to his companion curse and taunt Abraham.

"Spies and snakes you be, every last one!" the first frontiersman said with a snarl, and suddenly struck Abraham full in the chest with the butt of his rifle.

Abraham was strong. He did not flinch, but a ripple of horror went through the Moravians, who now were bunched up on the trail. Once violence began, nothing would stop it. The Pennsylvanians were outnumbered, but they knew the Moravians had sworn never to fight. The woodsmen chuckled and mocked their companion who had struck Abraham, for clearly the man had been startled by the Indian's fortitude.

"Give 'im a real lick, Mike!"

"That the best you kin do, Grub?"

"Don't bust a good rifle butt on that heathen! He's like a tree, an' you be needin' an ax!"

The one called Mike Grub stepped back and spat on his hands, before gripping the barrel and hefting it, about to smash Abraham full force.

Abraham was calm. He turned to speak to his people, who were restless, some of the younger men itching to fight back, though they knew their faith admonished them not to.

Abraham said, "Trust in our Christ, my people, for He shall be thy protection!"

Grub screeched. "Don't use Christ's name in vain, you godless heathen!" He brandished the rifle, but paused when Abraham suddenly addressed him.

"Consider, brother, what you are about to do, and ask whether the Lord Jesus would have you do otherwise."

"What? You dirty—" Grub swung the rifle butt with all his might.

The Moravians gasped and cried out, but almost casually, Abraham caught the gun and wrenched it from Grub so hard that the Pennsylvanian was hurled to the ground.

Other frontiersmen cursed and surged forward, rifles coming up. Grub was scrambling to his feet, snatching out a skinning knife, but the rifle in Abraham's hands abruptly changed his mind, and he hesitated, knowing that if he were wrong about Moravians being sworn to nonviolence he would be the first to die.

Colonel Williamson moved forward, showing not the slightest concern about Abraham's loaded weapon. He spoke in a deep, angry voice.

"I know you'd like to shoot me . . . shoot us all, redskin! You prattle about the Lord Jesus as if he was your very own, but under that red skin of yours is a heathen's heart, and devil's blood. . . ." He brought his own rifle to bear on Abraham's chest. In the crowd of Indians a woman was sobbing and little children were beginning to whimper.

Evangeline gasped in horror and rushed forward, shouting, "No! Do not kill! Please, white man! Have mercy! We do nothing to you!"

She came between Abraham and the colonel, whose rifle was now aimed at her. Her desperation gave the colonel pause for thought, but there was no compassion in him that she could see.

Mike Grub whistled. "Don't plug her yet, Colonel Williamson." He licked his lips and moved forward, the knife still in his hands. Evangeline cringed back against Abraham's rifle, aware that these whites saw her as a long-legged beauty, though she was just seventeen summers.

"Hold off, Grub," said the colonel. "We're soldiers, not rapists."

"Aw, Colonel—"

"You heard me, man!" Williamson pointed his rifle again at Abraham, who seemed momentarily unsure whether to lay down the gun he held. The colonel was grim, and Evangeline knew he believed these Moravians were as guilty as any war party for the killing and sorrow that had fallen upon the Pennsylvania frontier during six bloody years of fighting. Ever since the Indian outbreaks in 1777—the Year of the Bloody Sevens, the settlers called it—the Moravians had been in the middle, between war parties and white raiders.

Evangeline shivered. She sensed that behind her Abraham was laying down his rifle. The whites advanced a bit, watching their colonel, who blanched as if ready to kill.

"Have mercy," Evangeline whispered, for she knew the Moravians would not even try to flee if they were attacked. "These are good, God-fearing people...not your enemies...."

Colonel Williamson's mouth turned down, his eyes narrowing. Grub was chuckling softly, peering at Evangeline. It was going to happen, she told herself. They were all going to die, and there was no way to avoid it. She mur-

mured in prayer. Abraham raised a hand and motioned for
his people to fall to their knees; then he turned to Williamson.

"What you are about to do, do quickly. But in the name
of God, let us pray first."

A bit confused, Williamson glanced at his men and back
at Abraham.

Grub cursed, saying that Abraham had no call to tell
whites how to be Christians. But Williamson wavered, as
if he did not know what to do. His men, with Grub at their
head, were all for killing, that was clear, but he himself
seemed unsure. In a battle, he would have had no com-
punction about killing them all—men, women, and children—for that was the way of frontier war, and neither
side was known for showing mercy. But these forsaken
Moravian Indians would never fight back! They might plot
and scheme against frontiersmen, but they themselves
would not fight!

"You dogs!" Williamson grumbled hoarsely. "It is my
solemn duty to clear this country of all our enemies, to
fight warriors! But you snakes only buy from Indian raiders
what they take from our dead, and you bargain for what
they have stolen on their raids, and they profit from selling
to you what they kill us to steal! I demand you stand and
fight!" The rifle quivered as he aimed it at the stolid Abraham, who slowly shook his head.

"You're cowards and dogs!" Williamson shouted, trying
to work himself into a killing frenzy. "Pick up that rifle! By
God, use whatever guns you have! Let's have it out here
and now—"

There was a loud report of a rifle, and before Evangeline's wide eyes the gun in Williamson's hands leaped
into the air, shattered by a bullet. Then there was another
shot, and another, and the forest suddenly was full of attackers. Grub leaped for his own rifle, but bullets made

him duck aside. The Pennsylvanians shrank back, seeking cover. Their enemy obviously numbered many more than they. The Moravians' packhorses bolted in fright, neighing and stamping, and whining dogs scampered away, their carts overturning and clattering behind.

Still on their knees, the Moravians began to sing, while Evangeline stood transfixed, watching the gun battle erupt all around. From behind, Abraham reached up to pull her to the ground beside him.

"No use tempting fate, sister," he said, as if the words were part of his prayer. ". . . He restoreth my soul . . ." Bullets whizzed past, and cursing, wounded Pennsylvanians were dragged by companions into the thickets. ". . . in the path of righteousness for His name's sake. Yea, though I walk through the valley of the shadow of death, I will fear no evil . . ."

Evangeline, eyes closed, and wincing as lead came buzzing by, prayed with him, and the hymn rose to fill the winter forest, punctuated by the report of rifles. Soon the firing drifted away, the attackers in pursuit of the fleeing whites.

Then it was over, only a packhorse killed, everyone amazingly unhurt. The Pennsylvanians were gone, and the forest all around was hushed once more.

The Moravians, shaken and teary-eyed, collected their possessions and sought out their panic-stricken animals. Weeping children were soothed, and a frightened woman cried aloud that she prayed the Pennsylvanians had been driven away by whoever had come to the rescue.

A moment later, out of the woods came a dozen Delawares in full war paint, all of them fierce and utterly fearless. The Moravians gazed in silence as the warriors approached Abraham and shook hands with him. Their leader was a short, swarthy man of about forty, with intelligent eyes and the grave bearing of a war chief.

"I am Niko-lota of the Delawares," he said to Abraham, and Evangeline moved closer to see him, her heart full of gratitude for his courage at attacking so many well-armed whites.

"I know of you, Niko-lota," said Abraham slowly, glancing at a belt of dried scalps that hung from the Delaware's waist. "And so do the Pennsylvanians."

The Delawares stood with arms folded behind their leader, feeling for all the world like the proud and capable warriors they were. For generations their folk had been driven steadily out of eastern Pennsylvania, and now they were making their stand, fighting to the end—at least most of them were. Other Delawares had been the forebears of most of these Moravians.

Abraham spoke. "I know of you as the brother of Sister Aleta, one who was dear to me."

Niko-lota's eyes shadowed and he became even graver, if that were possible for so sober and warlike a man.

"Yes, uncle," said Niko-lota, addressing his elder in terms of Indian respect and veneration. "My sister was one of you, a Christian."

He looked hard and long at Abraham, whose eyes, to Evangeline, seemed touched with hurt and pity.

Niko-lota said, "And she died young because she was one of you!"

Abraham spoke softly. "She died of fever."

"As a prisoner of the Philadelphians!"

"As a ward of Pennsylvania, being protected—"

"Shut up in a white man's council house, like a prisoner, unable to walk outside for fear of killers like those men who threatened you here!"

Abraham did not reply but stood with head high, not showing emotion that Evangeline knew he must feel. She had heard about the terrible years in Philadelphia after the French and Indian wars of the last generation, when Moravian Indians were driven from their homes, often butchered though they were completely innocent. Many had been forced to flee to Philadelphia, where the sympathetic Quakers and Benjamin Franklin organized to protect them against thousands of hate-filled borderers who would have killed them all outright. There had nearly been civil war, but Franklin and the Quakers withstood the peril and saved the lives of many Moravians.

Some, including this Delaware's sister, had died of smallpox while living a bleak and lonely existence in the center of Philadelphia, under guard, unable to leave.

"We must go on," Abraham said, and waved to his people to prepare to move. As they stepped into line, arranged their packs and animals of burden, he turned to Niko-lota, who was telling his men to advance on the trail and see to it the Pennsylvanians would keep on running all the way back to Fort Pitt.

Abraham said, "Niko-lota, you must not hold all whites guilty for injury that some have done to the Delawares or the Moravians."

Niko-lota seemed to Evangeline to refrain from making a scornful remark, and then he said, "I hold all whites guilty who come into my country to drive us out . . . all whites! I am sworn to stand against them until my last breath, uncle, and I will not waste words by warning that your people will never be safe until those whites are stopped. You well know it is true."

After a moment of thought, as the others listened for their chief's reply, Abraham said loudly enough for all to hear, "I answer to the will of my Lord Jesus Christ, and I know that His will, not mine, shall be done in heaven, and here, on earth!"

As Niko-lota stared blankly at him, Abraham drew a deep breath. "This land will not bear fruit by warfare, but by husbandry and by love it will be made into God's garden on earth."

Niko-lota said through his teeth, "And it will be your blood that waters it!"

Without hesitation, Abraham answered, "We do the work of the Lord, and we do not fear the consequences, whatever they may be."

Evangeline knew Niko-lota had been through this same debate before, no doubt with his sister, and obviously he chose not to pursue it now. He turned with a sign to the rest of his men and went forward on the trail.

Abraham signaled to his people, and his voice rose in a hymn, joined by the others in that high-pitched keening way of the Moravian choir, so beautiful and haunting in this deep forest. Evangeline moved on with the rest of them, taking the hands of Christoph and Maria, who tramped on, eagerly watching the proud Delawares vanish among the trees ahead.

It was Christoph who voiced what Evangeline was thinking. "He is a mighty warrior, Niko-lota, and I am glad he is helping us!"

Indeed, thought Evangeline, he was a great man, and she was comforted to have his protection. She wished such men—white or red—could always be relied upon to protect the Moravians, because she knew in her heart that there would be no security for her people until all the evil ones on both sides were stopped from killing.

"A mighty warrior," she murmured, and the image of the Delaware war chief stayed before her mind's eye all the way to Gnadenhutten, and would accompany her thoughts for many days to come.

chapter **2**

SEMPLE'S TAVERN

The snow came, and for three days it fell on the forests of the Ohio Valley, drifting the trails, making game scarce, and keeping enemies from hunting out one another.

Fort Pitt was blanketed, but not for long, as squads of garrison-weary soldiers were pressed into service shoveling and clearing streets, parade ground, and bridges. The houses of the town had steep roofs, and when the sun returned, the snow melted and slipped off the cedar shingles, leaving them glistening wet. The stone walls of the fort, kept clear of snow, looked down at rivers from the tip of the peninsula on which the town was situated. The sluggish yellow waters of the Monongahela flowed up from the south, and the broad, swift rush of the Allegheny came from the north. Together the rivers formed the mighty Ohio, which, after a great, seventy-five-mile loop, swung southwest into the depths of the wilderness, where Indian war had raged with brutal ferocity.

The five pentagonal bastions of the fort were also shoveled and cleaned, for their cannon meant the difference between life and death for the few hundred rebel soldiers and settlers who clung here, hoping the Indians would give up and withdraw into the west, leaving the Ohio Valley to the whites. The troops were poor but alert, their officers devoted to the rebellion, and so the atmosphere at Pitt was firmly military, though not spit-and-polish. There were no funds for uniforms, scarcely enough assistance coming from Congress in Philadelphia to keep the troops on starvation rations, and nothing at all in the way of pay for the past two years. But Pitt was strong, and the British and their Indian allies had never threatened it. Everyone knew that without Pitt, the frontier would have been abandoned in 1777 when the Indians began to overwhelm settlement after settlement, from the Wyoming Valley in the north down to Kentucky in the southwest.

Unlike most homespun frontier settlements, where folk scraped and fought for bare existence, Pitt almost flourished, with some signs of culture, of satin petticoats and silk hats. There were official dignitaries sent from the states, prepared to carve what tracts they could from lands that one day would be wrested from the Indians; there were prosperous merchants and clever, farsighted lawyers, many looking out for the interests of wealthy investors back east.

In the two-story tavern of Samuel Semple, one could even find a fine billiard table and rooms for private dining, while the large common room always held a mix of company, simple farmers and backwoodsmen lifting mugs in the presence of Virginia planters and New York speculators. This Friday morning, bright and sunny after the snowstorm, Pitt was alive with the bustle of people anticipating fine weather and the coming end of winter.

Semple's tavern had filled up early with red-faced, ragged soldiers stamping in after a morning of shoveling. They were joined by newly arrived settlers looking for someone to build a flatboat for the trip downriver next month. In a back room a few officers were in cheerful conversation with some merchants, waiting for dinner to be served by the gruff, florid Semple himself, who was be-

hind the counter bossing serving girls and whirling bowls
of stew to customers along the polished wood.

In one corner, a young Irish lad was playing a light tune
on his fife, and in another, where the sunlight streamed
through a window, two well-dressed men were deep in dis-
cussion as they poured from a pitcher of strong ale. One of
these was a big, blond-headed fellow with a ruddy complexion and huge hands. He was doing most of the talking,
sometimes throwing off the cape he wore on his shoulders,
and at other times, to accentuate his point, snatching it
back on again and shaking his head, as if in dismay.

The second man, dark of hair, with a fair, weathered
face, replied curtly, thoughtfully, as if he knew the blond
fellow had a good point, but a point that was just not ac-
ceptable. This man was older, in his middle fifties, but he
was muscular and powerful, like a young man in his prime.
He wore the simple buckskin shirt of a woodsman over his
flannel and linsey blouse, but his knee breeches were of the
finest material, his glistening boots of the best leather. In
one boot was a Scottish dirk, its handle protruding from the
top, and at his waist was a claymore, the heavy, basket-
hilted sword of the Highland fighting man. Long-legged
and powerfully made, this man had a face that was both
refined and strong. His eyes were a cool gray, his hair was
tied in a short queue, and although he appeared to be a
gentleman, he obviously had no pretensions to looking like
one. For one thing, he wore no powdered wig, as did the
officers and most of the merchants in the other room.

The blond man, rough and ready, with two pistols stuck
in his belt, slapped the table so that the pitcher jumped,
and declared in a voice full of passion but hushed enough
to keep the conversation private: "Owen, you know danged
well there ain't no chance of things out here ever again
being the way they was!" He grasped his mug and rapped it
on the table. "Any future for you out here is as good as

dead! By gad, laddie, you been a slick merchant and trader
all these years, but you're like to a dreamy-eyed greenhorn
settler these days, thinking you can ever go back to Valenya, or that there'll be anything to go back to, or that the
damned loyalists'll let you go back at all! Hear me, Owen!
Do you?"

Owen Sutherland drank slowly, put down his mug, and
looked across the table at Peter Defries, a good man who
had shared the worst of dangers with him, a man who was
as clever and honest as he was strong. Sutherland nodded
slightly and sat back with a sigh, his eyes taking in the
crowd in the tavern, noting the newcomers, the green-
horns, and the idealists that Peter spoke about.

Defries was off again: "I say you and Ella and your girl
come back with me to Albany!" He leaned across the table
and spoke with a half-growl: "These here ain't the same
fellers as you knew in the northwest fifteen years ago, and
there's more of 'em coming, more every day, filling up this
valley, filling up Kentucky, soon to be drifting north into
Shawnee country, and not a one of 'em gives a hoot about
traders, trappers, furs, or whatever! They be farmers! Indian trade is gone, Owen!

"These pioneers, as they like to call themselves, are folk
what drifts and drifts and don't put down roots for long,
but they dig and cut down and kill Injuns, and then they get
itchy and move on, and they're followed by the real
settlers, the ones with money to buy their claims and lay
out farms!" He swigged deeply, wiping his mouth as he
said, "And then the drifters go on west some more, fighting Injuns, killing and getting killed, but they don't know
shit about fur trading or commerce or making a living like
you used to have going!"

Sutherland had heard this all before from Defries, had
gone over it all himself in his own mind. Ten years ago he
had been the premier trader in the northwest, living at Fort

Detroit, now in the hands of rebel-hating loyalists and king's troops. The Indian country, as the northwest was now known to whites, had been his country, his home, and he had been the most important of men, respected widely, admired and influential, second only to the commander of the British fort at Detroit.

Now, as was to be expected, Peter Defries was trying to make Sutherland rethink his plans to reorganize the Frontier Company, a once-powerful trading firm that had won control of much of the trade of the northwest, the lakes, and the distant fur grounds of the Canadian forest. Sutherland wanted to go back to Detroit when the war ended, to make peace with those of his company who had stood and lost with the loyalist side. He wanted to forget the wounds and the hatreds, to forge again the old ties with Indian trappers and traders, and to reunite the Frontier Company from his base at Valenya, the house he and his wife had built on the Detroit River.

He was aware of the odds against success, the dangers, the bitter enmity and the bloodlust that many would feel for rebels, but he had a vision of much of the northwest as a place that could remain a rich wilderness, a productive source of raw materials, furs, and food, distant from the increasingly populous settlements along the Ohio and Mississippi rivers.

"Benjamin Franklin wrote me recently," he said to Peter, who was not surprised, knowing Sutherland to be a trusted confidant of the old statesman, "saying that the British will give up the northwest to the states—and that means Detroit soon will be under the rule of Congress, whether the loyalists like it or not."

Peter thought about that, and Sutherland paused, letting this remarkable news sink in. Few Americans had ever harbored hopes of dictating favorable peace terms to the British; it would be enough to have independence recog-

nized and to be allowed rights to the Atlantic fisheries. But
to have possession of the vast northwest too—that startled
Peter Defries.

He asked, "Why would they give it up?"

Sutherland looked up to see a trail-worn group of Pennsylvania woodsmen come tramping in, their obvious weari-
ness thrown off by sheer force of will and pride. As they
sauntered up to Semple's counter, pushing through a group
of settlers and demanding ale, Sutherland could see they
had a couple of bullies among them. He turned back to his
friend.

"Britain can't possibly hold on to the northwest, because France and Spain both have claims to it, and if Britain tries to keep the northwest, it won't be able to make
peace terms with either one of them."

Defries thought hard about that, muttering, "And Britain would rather see the independent states claim the
northwest than risk Spaniards or Frenchies invading it." He
nodded. "Aye, that does make sense. But why don't the
British just promise to turn it over to the states and then
just let their soldiers sit out there, holding on for as long as
they please, and sending the fur trade down through Canada? Then they'd be pretending to give it up but still be
getting the plunder from it, and it'd take another treaty and
maybe another war against France or Spain, which might
end with Britain reclaiming the northwest and thumbing
her nose at all of us."

"That could happen—"

There was a scuffle at the counter, and out of the crowd
came a tough that Sutherland knew as Mike Grub, who
raised a terrified smaller man over his head and hurled him
bodily out the tavern door. Other ruffians laughed, and
some rebel officers shook their heads at the wild ways of
the frontier. Sutherland had seen Grub often these past few
months, having lived at Fort Pitt with his wife and family

while healing from a serious gunshot wound suffered last autumn. Now he eased his shoulder loose, working the muscles, as if he were readying for a fight. Defries, too, turned to stare at Grub, who had put his hands under his armpits, and now raised one leg like a fighting cock, beginning to crow.

Sutherland said, "Here comes a gust from another backwoods blowhard, an eye-gouger and a whoremonger, a man who's scalped squaws and Indian children, a bully who takes his orders from David Williamson, another prime backwoods Indian-killer."

As Sutherland had anticipated, Grub began to crow and strut like a rooster, eyeing the men around him with a defiant challenge. He wanted a fight.

"This is me and no mistake! They call me Billy Earthquake!" He howled and crowed at the ceiling, and his friends laughed, all sure their man would in truth be cock of the walk here in Semple's.

"I'm a small specimen, as you can see, a mere chick, but cuss me if I ain't more'n my weight in wildcats, better biter'n a Spanish alligator, a purebred cyclone with an appetite for eyes! Cock-a-doodle-do! Whoop! I'll whip any man fool enough to stand! Come out an' die like a hero! I ain't had a fight in a week, an' I'm spoilin' for exercise!"

As he crowed, Mike Grub made himself a circle of open tavern floor, stamping and strutting around, as men drifted back, pretending to be amused, drinking to keep his eyes from theirs. More than once Grub looked a hard man in the eye—and hard men there were in this tavern—but none was willing to stand up to him. His kind fought until ears and noses and eyes were gone.

"Won't nobody come out an' scrap! Whoop! I'm the very child what refused the tit and called for rye whiskey! Look at me! I'll outrun a deer! Outswim a alligator! Outchaw, outspit, and outcuss any man alive! Look at me!"

Into the tavern came Colonel Williamson, grudging amusement on his face as he watched his man perform. Williamson still bore some bloodstains on his clothes from the fight with the Delawares, and like the rest of his beaten men he was bitter and looking to get drunk, maybe punch a few faces in the process.

Grub whooped and crowed to make the ears ring.

Peter Defries finished his ale and burped loudly. "I could use some exercise myself, Owen—"

Sutherland's hand went to his friend's arm. "Hold on, Peter—you've got fine clothes there, none for this business. Permit me, laddie."

Defries objected, but Sutherland was already on his feet, finishing his own ale as Grub screeched another challenge to the house. Sutherland wiped his mouth, ready now, though Grub had not yet seen him.

It was then that silence suddenly fell, as in strode a fancy-dressed young gentleman, dusty and trail-worn, but as fashionable as any dandy by the look of his fine frock coat, frilled bicorne, and excellent boots. The place was quiet, because this unsuspecting newcomer had blithely walked past Grub as if the backwoodsman were not there at all, and called loudly to the innkeeper for food and drink.

Across the room, amused but a bit worried for this gentleman, Sutherland prepared to step between him and Grub if Grub made to go for him. As it was, the backwoodsman had lost the look of proud boastfulness and was full of mischief. He half crouched and sneaked toward the gentleman, whose back was turned as he began to remove his cape.

Sutherland moved to interfere, and Defries was on his feet, ready to back him up, but both saw that Grub meant to play, not hurt as yet.

Grub leaped high and whooped an Indian war cry that startled the gentleman, who spun around, eyes wide. The

delighted crowd laughed, even the glum Williamson
chuckling at his man's wit.

"Well, welcome to the wilderness, yer high lordship!"
Grub bellowed and flourished a bow. "Ye've come at the
prime instant to witness the challenge of the Ohio Valley's
greatest Injun scalper, the frontier's foremost scrapper, the
nation's best gouger, the world's hardest biter and harder
drinker, the man that gives measure to the name Man!
Welcome, yer lord high lordship, and do Mike Grub the
honor of an audience! Mike Grub!" He rapped his chest
loudly and crowed like a bantam rooster. "A man among
men! The best man in this house! The best in any house!"

Grub started to crow, but the gentleman unexpectedly
distracted him by throwing the cape over the back of a
chair and calling loudly, "Innkeeper! Service, good sir! I'll
have your kind attention if you please! It's a long way from
Maryland, and I'll have a dram to celebrate my safe arrival!" He turned to the surprised Grub and said coolly,
"Now then, fellow, where is this grubby hero you're crow-
ing about? Are you his valet, what? His promoter? Bring
him on! What? For all the way from Maryland we've heard
the echoing noise of backcountry braggadocio, even
smelled its perpetrators, but as yet I haven't been amused
by the sight of one. What?"

The tavern was still, Grub's eyes wide, jaw hanging, for
no man expected anything like this from a greenhorn trav-
eler squarely in the path of cruel Mike Grub.

There was only one other sound, and that was the slow,
hearty chuckling of Owen Sutherland and Peter Defries,
standing watching. But for all this young fellow's reckless
spunk, Sutherland knew he was in trouble, and no amount
of noble manners would protect him against this outlaw
rowdy.

Grub sputtered and stepped back a pace, licking his
chops and trying to laugh. What came out was low and

nasty. The newcomer loudly called again for ale and began to remove his waistcoat. Sutherland noted now that a fine regular officer's sword hung at his side, and he realized that the man had fought in the rebellion. And if he were truly a Maryland regular, there surely was more to him than met Grub's ignorant eye.

"Give 'im a proper welcome, Mike!" It was Colonel Williamson, guzzling a drink, his voice hollow and echoing in his tankard. He did not even look at Grub, as if this would be a minor amusement of little interest to a man such as he.

Grub sprang. But in the next moment, he was on his very tiptoes, arms flailing helplessly, the point of the gentleman's sword inserted in one nostril, lifting him off the ground.

"Not fair!" someone shouted drunkenly.

"Bare hands!" said one of Grub's friends, who could see their man was in serious danger if this gentleman swordsman meant to stick him.

Owen Sutherland whistled low and nodded at Defries, a comment on the swift skill of the Marylander's blade.

"Fight fair!" Now Grub's men were closing in, and again Defries and Sutherland were ready to join in on the side of the gentleman.

But the gentleman, still holding Grub at his mercy with the sword tip in the man's nostril, cried out loudly for his ale. "Is the service in this tavern as poor as the company? Must a man fight first and slake his thirst after? Landlord! Be quick, or all Maryland will know of your poor hospitality!"

With a gulp, the astonished Semple, puffing and wide-eyed, scurried out from behind the bar bearing a tankard of ale, which he gave to the Marylander, who was keeping an eye on the helpless Grub. After a quick toast to the Congress, the man drank deeply, in one long swig, distracted only once, when Grub made a vain effort to get away—but the sword point held him fast.

Then, with a satisfied sigh, the swordsman tossed the mug onto his table, removed the point from Grub's nostril, and laid the weapon aside. He took the position Sutherland knew to be the trained pugilist's stance, right foot forward, left hand foremost, right fist held close to the chest. Again the crowd looked at one another, a few starting to laugh, among them Mike Grub, though his nose trickled with blood. Grub began to look about, as if to say something, and then he leaped.

The Marylander sidestepped, punching hard as he did, and taking the full force of Grub's leap, his fist crashing against the man's nose, knocking him down.

Grub had earned yet another broken nose, but he scrambled to his feet, scarcely hurt, and kicked aside a chair. Lowering into a crouch, he came in more cautiously.

To everyone's surprise, the bold gentleman said lightly, "Give us more speech there, fellow! I missed the start of your boast! I'll bet it was a colorful—"

Grub dived, and though a punch caught him squarely again, then another and another, he took the punishment and wrapped his powerful arms around the Marylander's waist, and they went down hard, Grub cursing and screeching like an Indian. There were the sharp sounds of fist against bone, and in a twinkling the gentleman was on his feet, clothes torn, and Sutherland could see that his right hand was hurt, maybe cracked.

Though stunned, Grub scrambled across the floor. The gentleman tried to move aside, but Grub had him again, and tripped him against a table that crashed to the floor, drinks and all. The crowd was shouting, most now for the Marylander, and the gentlemen from the back room had come out to look on. Someone had been sent to call the watch, but before the soldiers on duty arrived, Sutherland thought, there might be a killing.

Again the Marylander managed to get free, though his left hand was all he had to use, and its effect on Grub was not enough. Grub was bloodied and bruised, but seeing the injured hand of his opponent, he knew the game was up, and he paused to drain a flagon of ale that Williamson passed to him.

Sutherland stepped forward then and handed the Marylander a mug, saying quietly, "Best to submit, sir, or you will meet death."

Seen from closer, the fellow was much younger than Sutherland had realized. Despite the weathered features of the face, he was a man of less than thirty—yet one who obviously had seen war, a man both fiercely proud and willing to die. Sutherland had heard about the Marylanders and how they had saved Washington's army on Long Island with a suicidal counterattack. He saw that in this man's eyes and knew this gentleman would die rather than surrender.

The man finished his drink and with a polite nod returned the mug to Sutherland. He had taken a few blows, and his injured hand must have been agony, but he merely said, "Please, good sir, do step aside. You do me honor, sir. Thank you."

Sutherland was slow to move. From behind him came the grunt of Mike Grub. "I ain't got no quarrel with you, Sutherland. Step aside!"

Sutherland turned square to him, seeing the sweat and blood covering Grub's savage face. For the rest, the fighter was unimpaired, well able to tear the Marylander apart if he got to him.

"Leave off, Grub, or maybe you will have quarrel with me."

Grub's teeth gnashed, but he got no encouragement from his men—they all knew Owen Sutherland only too well. Had Grub himself seen the Scotsman in the tavern at the start, he would never have dared to fling out a challenge.

"This ain't your fight, Sutherland," called Williamson, who was ignored.

Grub wanted the Marylander's blood, but he was undecided now, glaring past Sutherland. To everyone's surprise, however, it was the Marylander who made the first move, going after Grub, who swung and kicked wildly. The lightning left hand stung and cut, keeping him off balance.

Defries came to Sutherland's side, big fists clenched. "He can't keep that up, Owen! That gent's done for if the watch don't show up and jump in swinging clubs!"

But the watch would not be in time. Grub got through the savage punches and viciously bore the Marylander down, pummeling and scratching.

Defries hissed, "He'll bite off his nose!"

Sutherland knew the Marylander would be killed or disfigured, an eye or his nose ruined in the next moment. Williamson's frontiersmen were shouting in glee, eager to see a dandy from back east put down. Sutherland noticed Williamson's cruel expression as the colonel gazed placidly back across the room at him.

It was now or it would be too late. Sutherland leaped into the scramble and yanked Grub off his victim, rolling over with the woodsman, who was caught in a bear hug. With a tremendous effort, Sutherland spun the man away and sprang to his feet. Grub bellowed, even Sutherland's fearsome reputation as a fighter forgotten, and he charged wildly, head down. Sutherland's fury, too, was up, and he took the full power of the charge into his gut, force against force, muscle against muscle. He lifted the bigger Grub off the ground. Grub's hands clawed at Sutherland's face, scratching for an eye, but Sutherland was too quick and hurled Grub with a bone-jarring crash to the floor. Snatching the man up again even before he had bounced, Sutherland heaved him over his head and ran to the door. The watch was coming in just then, and they scattered at the sight, muskets and hats flying, Mike Grub thrashing through the air, letting out a terrified scream as he crashed headfirst against a post supporting the porch roof.

By the time the watch had reorganized and made their way into the hushed tavern, all there was to see were men ordering drinks, Owen Sutherland showing a sweating young gentleman to a seat, and the landlord, Semple, righting an overturned table.

One of the officers who had stepped out of the back room called to the officer of the watch. "No need for your presence, Captain—all's well that ends well!"

Sutherland looked over to see this was the tall, rangy Colonel William Crawford, a key man at Pitt and a Virginia-born frontiersman of good breeding who had been fighting Indians and exploring hereabouts for twenty years. Dark-eyed and sharp-featured, Crawford grinned and nodded to Sutherland before turning back into the dining room, chuckling and slapping backs of friends and fellow officers. Sutherland noticed that with Crawford was James Morely, a young merchant who was the richest and most influential civilian on the frontier. The dark-eyed Morely, one of the few merchants not wearing a wig, looked back at Sutherland, but neither man said anything. Sutherland could not help but think how James Morely had always been jealous of fighting men, wishing he could be as good a fighter as he was a trader and manipulator of men and commerce.

Peter Defries was passing a handkerchief dipped in brandy to the young Marylander, whose handsome features were drawn and weary from travel and from the peril he had just faced. His eyes were clawed, having come close to being torn from their sockets in the time-worn tradition of the frontier.

Defries chuckled, "You did well, young sir, but when

you pugilize a customer like that, you best use a cannon-ball."

Sutherland added, "Or Roman cesti," referring to the iron knuckles used by classical boxers.

The young man felt at his swollen right hand, then straightened his blouse. Seeing it was torn, he pulled his coat over it, too proud to be seen in rags. His straw-blond hair—he, too, wore no wig—was cut short in the new style, his body well made but not very powerful in the way of the woodsman.

"Thank you, sir. I am Entellus Rogers Greyson—"

"Entellus!" Sutherland remarked with a smile, making it apparent to the embarrassed Marylander that he understood the meaning of that ancient name.

Defries muttered, "Southern folk use the uncommonest call-names I ever heard! Entellus! Tell us, what in hell sort of name for an American is that, then?"

The man flushed more deeply, then half smiled at Sutherland, who was looking away, drinking. Sutherland looked back as Defries repeated his question.

"A name," said Greyson, "that I have yet to earn, I must confess."

"You did well enough, sir," Sutherland said. "Entellus, Peter, was the Sicilian champion of pugilism, who, according to Virgil, defeated the great Trojan champion, even though Entellus was already of a very old age."

Peter considered that, nodding slowly. "You Marylanders sure get names that are hard to live up to, I'm thinking."

Touching a burst lip, Greyson nodded and tried to drink, though it hurt. "I've never broken my hand on a skull before. . . . Ye gods! What a brute he was!" He looked at Sutherland. "But you handled him easily enough."

"You'd already stunned the rogue—and anyway, I didn't want to let Peter here get at him, or there'd have been naught left of him at all."

Defries shrugged. "Mike Grub's a man, though a bad one." He eyed Williamson and the other toughs, who were just then filing sullenly out of the tavern. "And I'm thinking you ain't seen the last of him, Entellus Greyson."

Defries sighed and called for more ale, then looked at Sutherland and shook his head. "Now I do recall what fun this misforgotten wilderness had to offer a man. Always was something with a little spice to it."

Sutherland grinned. "Aye, Peter, stay here for a few months and work off that civilized gut you've grown! I won't go back to Albany with you, even though you may be right that a fortune's there to be made."

"Fortune *there?*" put in Greyson, his eyes shining with enthusiasm. "Why, it's out *here* real fortunes are to be made! This is the land of tomorrow, the destiny of the free states! This is the country of fortune, man!"

Peter grumbled that this country had made plenty of dead heroes, but as yet few fortunes. Sutherland sat back, assessing this fellow Greyson, wondering what had brought him here.

Greyson's voice was loud, excited, as he said, "There's a new day coming to the frontier! The northwest soon will be ours, and our children's, and the independent states will unite under one congress, making the United States of America the most powerful nation in the world . . . someday!"

"Hear, hear!" called a voice from the back room. It was James Morely, not much older than this Maryland dreamer. "To the United States of America!" Men rose and lifted their glasses and mugs as the slender, well-dressed Morely came to the door, his own mug high. "To our destiny, manifest in the northwest, and to the riches our victory has laid at our feet!"

Everyone drank except Sutherland, and that James noticed.

"Do you not favor a united states, Mr. Sutherland?"

After a moment, Sutherland replied slowly, everyone listening to his answer, for he was one of the most important and respected men in this country.

"Aye, Mr. Morely, I'll drink to union, but I'm not sure I can toast to your vision of the future in this country . . . a future that may not include me or my kind!"

It was a well-worn argument: fur traders wanting the wilderness kept free of settlement—an "Indian park," some derisively called it—and merchants like Morely eager for a flood of settlers to invade, uproot, and drive out the Indians, in turn buying his goods, renting his land, and doing his bidding, as he held mortgages and controlled goods for a thousand miles westward.

There was no need for James Morely to reply. Most men in the tavern knew his position opposed Sutherland's, and they also knew that James was in love with Sutherland's only daughter, Susannah.

Uncomfortable, James was at a loss for words, but immediately he was supported by the voice of another man from the back room. This was the lean Noah Maxwell, a crafty Philadelphia lawyer, middle-aged and in his intellectual prime, a man Sutherland did not trust at all.

"The future of our country, Mr. Sutherland, can embrace men of all kinds, if only they learn to cooperate with others and support a republican form of government, bent on promoting progress and prosperity!" Maxwell, whose cigar smoke could be smelled even where Sutherland sat, did not come to the door, perhaps better able to find words without the burning eyes of Owen Sutherland on him.

Morely called out, "A toast to those with the foresight to accept change, and make the most of it! True Americans who know how to profit from fortune's favor and heaven-sent opportunity. . . ." As if realizing that his words might be slightly too obscure for all the crowd to follow, James first called for a free round of drinks, to which everyone cheered, and then he got his toast—from all but Owen Sutherland. With a snort of annoyance, the young merchant went back to his meeting, closing the door.

chapter 3

SUTHERLAND AND MORELY

After taking Greyson to the surgeon, where the injured—but unbroken—hand was wrapped, Sutherland and Defries returned to Semple's, at their new friend's offer of dinner.

The tavern was still full, men chattering about the fight, nodding and smiling as the three came in. By now Sutherland had learned enough about Entellus Greyson to know he was at Pitt on a mission for Maryland land speculators, a combination of rich men who had old colonial claims to the country across the Monongahela from Pitt.

Sutherland liked the young man, though he was never sure about land speculators and their representatives. Greyson was out here to study the possibilities, to scout out what could be done with the hundred thousand acres of hills and riverbank if Congress recognized the Maryland claim—a claim granted by the Crown years back, but never taken up because of Indian troubles.

Greyson said, "Once the peace treaty is signed with Britain, my company will petition Congress for full settlement rights, and we'll proceed to send out pioneers to occupy the land...once we survey it, that is. Can you recommend any surveyors, Mr. Sutherland?"

At that, Peter Defries chuckled heartily and shook his head. "Only thing Owen mislikes more than surveyors who parcel up his forest, Enty, are land speculators from back east who send 'em out!"

The Marylander made no response to that. Defries went on, Sutherland accepting that someone had to make it plain to Greyson that not everyone on the frontier was eager for hordes of settlers and for profits from the acquisition and resale of Indian lands.

Defries said, "You be looking at the leading Injun traders in the northwest, Enty, and we be looking at our doom when we look at the likes of you!"

Greyson flushed, and Sutherland realized the fellow had much to learn before he went home to report.

He said, "Mr. Greyson, if you want to know what most folks think the future holds for settlers and land speculation, you had best meet Mr. Morely in there, the man who intends to govern this country one day, a man who is more powerful than any other out here. . . ."

Defries said, in his rasping, ale-enriched voice, "The very man who succeeded Bradford Cullen as master of Cullen and Company!"

Greyson gave a start. "*The* James Morely! Why, I thought he was a much older man, a man who seemed more . . . more . . . well, more substantial."

Through the back room door, which had just opened, Sutherland watched Morely, relaxed and confident, talking cheerfully with Noah Maxwell and Colonel Crawford. Indeed, James looked even younger than Greyson, and Sutherland felt suddenly old in comparison. Time was passing ever more swiftly, and before much longer, the way things were going, fellows like Entellus Greyson would be the competition for Cullen and Company, the huge trading and transportation firm James commanded.

Sutherland heard Defries talking quietly: "But now,

Enty, should you be a prudent man, and want to know what it'll cost in blood and money to get that fine future into harness, then I recommend you chat with Mr. Sutherland here, a man who's been in the thick of the bloodletting and the spending these past twenty-five years!"

Defries told Greyson that Owen Sutherland was a founder of the once-powerful Frontier Company, which fifteen years ago had fought and won against Cullen and Company for control of the northwest Indian trade. Now, however, the rebellion had split the company, rebel and loyalist, and it had little substance left, unlike Cullen's firm, which thrived with the war. Entellus had never heard of the Frontier Company, and that gave Sutherland an unmistakable twinge.

Defries chewed the inside of one cheek and said with a grumble, "You heard about Cullen and Company, but not the Frontier Company? Well, that beats me!"

Sutherland said it was understandable. "There's a whole new leadership back in the states and in Congress now, and they know Cullen and Company's influence, not ours, Peter. We're from before the war, before Congress."

Defries sat back with a sigh. "If Congress asks the Injuns who they know, who they'll talk to when the need for parley comes, it won't be Cullen and Company, and it won't be James Morely! There be only one man they'll listen to when Congress wants to talk peace—"

Young Greyson brightened, thinking he was on familiar ground. "Simon Girty? Yes! I've heard the Indians trust that renegade, and my company believes that if we could get him in our pay, we'd have the Indians eating out of our hands!"

The impetuous good feeling that had lifted Greyson dissipated when he saw that Sutherland was looking at him as a man might look at a child, and Peter Defries was clucking and shaking his head.

Defries said, "There's only one white man the Injuns respect without question, even though they been fighting him for the past few years, and that's—"

"Don't tell us, Peter!" It was James Morely, standing a few feet from the table, an insolent look on his face. "Let us guess who is the woodland ambassador who will rescue us all from the flash and fall of the Indian ax!" Behind James stood Noah Maxwell, smirking, eyes half closed in the smoke of his Spanish cigar. The other men from the back room were making their way out of the tavern, the meeting over. James obviously had drunk too much; his eyes were watery, his mouth loose and clumsy at forming words: "Let me guess . . ."

Defries said, "James, my boy, you shouldn't drink—it don't become a nabob to drool. Now, move along."

Morely's face hardened, the mouth turning down. James had known Peter since childhood, for like Peter and Owen Sutherland, James's father had been a founder of the Frontier Company at Detroit. By assuming leadership of Cullen and Company, however, James had aligned himself directly against these men, formerly close friends, who had once had a hand in raising him.

James moved closer, for he was plucky, if not a fighting man like Sutherland or Defries. He looked down at Greyson and spoke thickly.

"There are all manner of opinions in this country, my good sir. One you'll hear is that your host, Mr. Sutherland, is the grand wizard who can pacify the Indians if only the settlers will stop making war on them, and if only Congress promises to leave them their land as a trapper's and trader's personal preserve, and if only the traders are left to treat with Indians as of old, to bow to them as to foreign princes, to buy their loyalty with trinkets and firewater, sell them rusty birding guns for rich peltry . . ."

Sutherland was more sorry for James than angry. He

might have shut the fellow up easily, and Noah Maxwell thrown in, but he had always expected his uneasy relationship with James to take this turn. He had tried to keep the peace, for old time's sake, but it was expected that James would do his utmost to hold Sutherland's influence at a minimum.

". . . and to keep land speculators off Indian lands, lands sacred and pure, given by the great manitou, traversed by the spirits of the winds and the bears—"

Defries said, "The spirits of wind are hot and gusty in here, ain't they, Enty?"

James chuckled. "Yes, Mr. Marylander, you are in the company of the great Owen Sutherland, who will claim to know the secret of eternal bliss in the northwest!" He chuckled again, obviously not caring that Peter Defries had less patience than did Owen Sutherland, and that Defries might punch anyone, even the richest merchant prince on the continent. His expression darkened. "But there are others, modern men, who will tell you that there will never be peace, never be prosperity in this country until every last redskin is pacified!"

Someone shouted, "Deadified!"

"Drink to that!" another voice shouted. "Kill the bastards and make tobacco pouches out of 'em!"

Sutherland was used to this. Here at Fort Pitt, white men were archenemies of Indians and always had been. At Valenya, however, white men had lived for a century in harmony and cooperation with the Indians. On Sutherland's own breast was tattooed a green turtle, showing he had been adopted by the Ottawas, was a son of the mighty Pontiac himself, the chief who had led an unsuccessful uprising almost twenty years earlier. Sutherland let the curses and cries for death to the Indians die down. He remained outwardly impassive. It would always be this way on the eastern frontier, unless Congress established an effective, fair Indian policy.

"Have you not heard of Owen Sutherland?" James Morely asked Greyson as he took a cigar from Maxwell and lit it on a candle. "Well, sir, the legend is true."

For just a moment, James and Sutherland stared at each other, and James seemed to lose composure, his lips working, eyes blinking, as if he wanted to rid himself of whatever he was thinking. "All true . . . and all of it long past!"

Maxwell was there, a hand on his companion's elbow, to move him on. Sutherland looked away. James Morely had never been so pathetic, and it hurt to see a man who once had been so good, so idealistic, corrupted by the power he had won and by the men who now advised and supported him.

When Morely and his friend had departed, Sutherland said he would be happy to help Greyson get accommodations at Fort Pitt. "I'll wait until you have found your way around before I offer you the hospitality of my house, sir, lest I be accused of attempting to win your allegiance to me."

At that Greyson held out his uninjured left hand and said sincerely, "Whatever you and I believe should come to pass out here, you have my allegiance, sir! At your service!"

Defries chuckled again. "Them southerly planters got the manners, ain't they, Owen!"

He, too, shook hands with Greyson and said word would get around that they would help him in a pinch, and so Mike Grub would likely leave him alone as long as he was in the fort.

"In the woods, however," Sutherland said, "keep a look-out over your shoulder. Grub's a killer, and Williamson is tight with the fort commander, so together they may make trouble for you."

Greyson gave that confident smile again. "I'm a colonel in the Continentals, Mr. Sutherland, and the commander of Fort Pitt will be the one in trouble if I choose to make it for him . . . for him or for militia colonel Williamson."

They parted, Greyson taking a room in Semple's Tavern, Sutherland and Defries making their way toward the outskirts of town, where the Sutherlands had recently bought a cabin from an old trader friend. They were staying here until spring, when they would set out by flatboat for the settlement at the Falls of the Ohio, where they had taken up residence over the past two years. Peace with Britain was on the way, and the Sutherlands meant to be in the vanguard when settlers traveled into the Illinois country and then to Fort Detroit, which surely would be in the hands of the states before long.

As they walked, Defries tried again to persuade Sutherland to take his family back to New York, where the most well-off vestiges of the Frontier Company, led by Peter, were still operating a shipping company.

Sutherland said flatly, "The choice has been made, laddie. When the time comes, we go northwest, to Detroit, to Valenya." He looked at Defries as if to tell him there was no point saying another word about it. "Listen, Peter, there's even talk that Canada will go independent too, and that'll mean the British'll have no control at all of the trade, and I'll start again, at home, where I'm meant to be!"

They walked through the milling, bustling crowd, along rutted, muddy streets, past soldiers returning from patrol, and alongside the boatyard where handsome vessels were being built and reconditioned to serve Cullen and Company.

Defries took a while to find the words, but at last he said, almost carefully, "Owen, what if the loyalists and Injuns don't want you back? What if they've already burned Valenya? What if the traders and trappers don't give a damn about the Frontier Company and what it was? What if there ain't nothing out there for you—no Valenya, no trade, no nothing?"

Sutherland kept walking. They were leaving the town, and the air was better, a breeze whipping in, hinting at spring. In his mind appeared the faces of friends and companions who were still at Detroit, and he saw the house, imagined sunset shining across the straits on its white walls. Then he saw the holy place where seven huge monoliths stood, near the shoreline not far from the house. Those were the Singing Stones, sacred to the Indians, where the north wind howled eerily when it whipped through them.

The Singing Stones. His past, now his dream...but tomorrow, someday, they would again be near him. There, too, was the grave of his Indian wife and unborn child. There was his beginning in America, after coming from his native Scotland as an adventurer and fur trader. Valenya was his only home, and he would return there, though Peter's doubting questions rang in his mind.

Up ahead was his cabin, and out the door came Ella, a tall and striking woman, her blond hair caught by the wind, her body as lithe and strong as when he had first met her twenty years ago at Detroit. She waved, and he felt a rush of pride to be her man.

"Peter, my Ella wants to go back to Valenya as much as I do—and somehow, before long, we're going back!"

Defries was muttering with a laugh to himself: "No wonder them Injuns love you, Owen...." Sutherland glanced at his friend. "You don't know when you're beat! And you don't know what white men got in store for you!"

Sutherland grunted and stepped out more quickly toward his wife, who had been joined by their grown daughter, Susannah, seventeen and as beautiful and blond as her mother.

He called back to Peter, "I know what they have in store for this country, laddie! I know, and I mean to keep 'em honest! Once I'm back at Detroit I'll get the Indians together and put their words on paper and send it right to

Franklin and Washington, and I'll get them off the warpath one way or the other before they get rubbed out by the likes of Williamson and Morely."

"All on your own, Owen? Will Franklin or Washington back you?"

Sutherland made no reply. He did not know the answer.

Ella Sutherland watched her husband approach, her hands holding a yellow brocade gown she was altering for Susannah, who was already running to her father and breaking exciting news: there would be a ball tomorrow night, given by James Morely for all the officers and notables of Fort Pitt, and the Sutherlands were invited.

Ella saw Susannah, flushed with exuberance, hanging on her father's arm, and Owen smiling at her, though not especially enthusiastic. Ella wished her man would be friendlier to James Morely, for James had been close to the family all his life. After all, James had proved himself last fall by attempting to rescue Susannah and herself from a band of renegade loyalists who had captured them. Although it was Owen who had succeeded in the rescue, and had been wounded for it, James had risked his life. . . .

Yet Ella was certain Owen would never be fond of the man who ran Cullen and Company, with its pervasive corruption and shady dealings. He would go to James's ball for Susannah's sake, but he would not be enthusiastic. Still, he would shine, the handsomest man there, even though he did not dress like the popinjays and blades who thought themselves Paris fashionable. How she loved Owen! Her heart skipped a little as he looked at her and smiled, approaching and taking her hand to enter the cabin. Susannah was on the arm of jovial Peter Defries, whose own wife and a daughter of Susannah's age were back in Albany, managing company affairs.

Inside, Susannah grasped the gown and held it before

herself so her father could admire it, and he complimented her, saying she would be the belle tomorrow night. Ella was satisfied with their lives these days, though this rude cabin had been impossible to spruce up, impossible to make into a fine home, for all her cleaning and scouring, sewing and painting. The rough timber walls were white-washed, and there were powder-blue curtains and a Persian table-covering, and the chairs were good. Still, it was not Valenya, and nothing else ever would be.

Nor were the Sutherlands wealthy, as when they had built Valenya. Ella poured the men coffee and thought about how Owen had spent so much to support the rebel-lion, had financed the little army of George Rogers Clark in the taking of the Illinois country a few years back, and how not one cent had been repaid by either Congress or Virginia, which had authorized Clark's campaign. When that vast sum was repaid, the Sutherlands could live as befitted the leaders of a once-great trading company. But Ella had no expectations of repayment soon, not with the states so gutted by war, and Congress so divided in its policy-making.

Again she thought of Valenya, the finest house in all the northwest, where her lovely spinet stood in one corner, and her grand kitchen had a brick oven and pipes that drained outside from a stone sink. . . .

She regarded her hands, rough and sore from hard work, like those of any settler's wife. Yes, that was what she was now—a settler's wife, almost poor, struggling for daily bread. Owen was trading with friendly Indians and building up business slowly, competing with Cullen and Company and James Morely, who controlled so much, from boats to packtrains to warehouses. It was a long haul, however, with trade goods scarce and credit scarcer.

Yet little by little the Frontier Company was righting itself, and Owen poured every cent of profit back into the firm, acquiring goods, hiring agents, and sending presents to the Indians who so desperately wanted to trade for white goods, Indians who trusted and respected him. The war had hurt everyone out here, white and red—everyone but Cullen and Company. Somehow they prospered, finding ways to get paid for what they sold, and profiting from the war.

Ella put the coffeepot back on the iron stove and thought that there might, like her, be other daughters of British gentry struggling for a living out in the northwest —but she had not met any. Her youth in an English mansion, and even her life back in Massachusetts with her first husband, who had died long ago, had not prepared her for this. Yet she would not change places with anyone. Owen was all she could ever want in a man, and Susannah was a daughter to be proud of.

The others were talking about the ball, Defries teasing, Owen laughing as his daughter gave as well as she took. How good it would have been if Benjamin were still here. Her son by Owen had been killed by Indians two years ago, and she would never get over that loss. Another son, Jeremy, by her first husband, was a doctor in the Illinois country, where he and his wife served Indians and French and a handful of Virginia soldiers under the command of George Rogers Clark. The Virginians were holding the Illinois Indians to the rebel cause—to Virginia, actually— and so closing off the Illinois against the loyalists and British troops at Detroit. Ella wished she could see Jeremy and his family again soon.

"And what will you wear, lass?" Owen was speaking to her, holding out a hand for her to sit and have coffee with them. "You'll have to go some to match your fair daughter here!"

Ella brushed back her hair and sat down, smiling. "I'll find something, but I doubt anyone will outdo Susannah. Who will escort her, then?"

It was Susannah who sprang at Defries and asked if he would be at her side, and he cheerfully agreed, saying he wanted to see all the top dogs of the Ohio Valley barking in one room. "I don't ever expect to come back to this country, and it'll give me something to remember—and something to tell young Jeanette when she asks about you, Susie."

"And will she ask about James Morely, too?" Susannah prodded, and Ella knew her daughter was wondering whether Jeanette Defries still held some hope of marrying James Morely, as once she had.

Defries laughed, but without humor. "No, dear one, my Jeanette has more sense than that, now that she knows how James has turned out." He lifted his cup, as if not noticing that Susannah's face fell at his words. "She has every rich Dutchman in Albany pursuing her, so she don't need no lickspittle of Bradford Cullen's, no matter how rich—"

Susannah turned away, and Defries noticed then that the Sutherlands were staring at him, Owen pointedly clearing his throat. Defries looked from one to the other, then at Susannah, who had taken her dress to sit sewing before the window, her face red.

Ella did not know what to say. It was apparent Defries was unaware of the difficulty here—that Susannah still held a spark of feeling for James Morely, a man who once had been decent and kind, and who still longed to charm Susannah, for whatever reasons were behind it.

Still, Defries was clever, for all his bullishness, and winking at Owen's glance of warning, he slurped some coffee and said loudly, "Well, every man to his own poison, I say, and I suppose there's those who'd fault me for being loyal to the Frontier Company when others've made their fortune selling to the rebels and the British both, like Cullen and Company. . . ."

No, that would not do either, and a look of pained exasperation came over Defries. Ella knew he was trying to say something to change the mood, to lift Susannah's spirits, for the young woman hated to hear bad things said about James Morely. As it was, Owen would refuse to give his daughter's hand in marriage to anyone who represented Cullen and Company. Along with Noah Maxwell, James Morely was the most powerful man in that company, and that cut him out as a possible suitor as far as Owen was concerned.

The uneasiness in the room was lifted when Sutherland said, "There's a new young man in the fort—a regular colonel from Maryland, a good fellow and a likely chap, well spoken and brave. He stood up to Mike Grub this morning, though he's a gentleman and not a brawler." He observed Susannah's interest out of the corner of his eye.

With a smile, Ella asked, "And is he handsome?"

Defries slapped the table and declared, "He was till Mike Grub laid into him!"

Ella gasped, thinking that a nose or an eye might have been lost, or at least an ear, but Defries waved her fears aside, saying, "Thanks to Owen here he's still got all his parts and he'll be pretty as ever afore long, but he's made enemies in Grub and Williamson." Turning to Susannah, Defries said cheerfully, "Next to me, this fellow would be the best one to escort you, girl, and lucky you'd be for it!"

Susannah tried to smile, but it was evident she was still stung by the criticism of James Morely. She was sewing furiously, determined to make the dress fit perfectly. Ella hoped this new young gentleman would be at the ball, to take Susannah's mind off James. As it was, Ella suspected James had arranged the event in order to be in Susannah's company. Ella could see it all leading to more trouble between Owen and James, and she prayed that Susannah would not be hurt further.

Once more her mind drifted to Valenya, their home at far-off Detroit. Once they were back there, away from the

Ohio Valley and James Morely, Susannah would find other interests, other men. Detroit soon would be greater than ever, a center for growing commerce, and on occasion Susannah could travel down to Montreal, to Albany, even to Philadelphia. One day she would find a good man, a man Owen could respect without reservation.

Once, years ago, Ella had wished James could be that man, as once it seemed he would be; but absolute power, the lust for wealth, and daily contamination by the foul affairs of Cullen and Company had changed him for the worse. For a time he had even been married to Cullen's daughter, who, with her baby, had died in childbirth, last year just before her tyrannical father had passed away and left his empire to James. Ella had thought that James's marriage to Linda Cullen would put Susannah off for good, but there was something more, something deeper between James and Susannah. They had known each other all their lives, had forgiven faults, had fought danger side by side, had laughed and hurt together. There was a bond between them that did not easily dissolve.

Even now, Susannah held out hope that James would change for the better. Ella wished she could hope the same, but she did not. Instead, she hoped for Susannah to escape this country. Valenya—that was their future! Valenya's magnificence and the goodness of their former life was their hope. They would return one day soon, and then Susannah would see how wonderful life could be. Then they would once more be the Sutherlands, with the Frontier Company reborn at last.

chapter **4**

PLANS AND GAMES

"He's the sort of fighting man we can count on! He's a true-born backwoods killer, as slick as they come, and with every pretense to gentility that's sure to make him a governor one day!"

It was next morning, and listening to Noah Maxwell speak, James Morely paced the Persian rug on the floor of the cabin of his luxurious keelboat, which stood in drydock near the Allegheny River. Maxwell sat behind a polished cherrywood desk, his feet up, the ever-present thin cigar between his yellow teeth. Sunlight fell through the glazed windows, glittering on a jeweled pin in Maxwell's purple cravat. To James, Maxwell was the slyest, most devious man he had ever met—after Bradford Cullen himself, devil take the old man's soul! Furthermore, Maxwell was the stoutest, most dependable partner James could want. A man born for greed, grasping at wealth, Maxwell was ever anticipating James's own plans for the company—plans that were keen and far-thinking, and instantly understood by Maxwell. James's words were often just a sentence ahead of the attorney's own spoken thoughts, sometimes even behind and not so well schemed through.

"Williamson's a man we can use," Maxwell declared, waving the cigar. "And a man who particularly needs us right now, and would owe us a debt that will be repaid manyfold before we're through with him. I say deal, and give him what he wants."

As Maxwell puffed, and a discreet steward prepared food in the well-appointed galley adjoining the cabin, James stopped to stare at the open coal stove burning in one corner. He looked down at the rich carpet and the gleaming oak floor and pondered the proposal of Colonel David Williamson, a proposal that Maxwell backed fully. In a few minutes Williamson would arrive for a meeting, seeking financial support to raise a small army to attack the Delawares. The regular rebel troops at Pitt were too few to do it or even to join in, and the fort's commander was too poor to supply the fighting men Williamson was raising from miles around. James Morely was the only man wealthy enough, well-supplied enough, to outfit the force Williamson said soon would be ready to ride out and destroy unharvested cornfields and villages before Indian raiders could use them as supply bases for their springtime raids.

Maxwell voiced what James was thinking. "Congress will be more than generous to those who clear the Indian country of savages! The company that can back Williamson will be first on the list for land grants, and any lands said company claims will be cheerfully authorized by act of Congress."

James nodded slowly. He was not a man for wanton slaughter of Indians, having been brought up among them out at Fort Detroit. He did not despise all Indians as did men like Williamson, nor did he view them as creatures to be exterminated, like snakes or wolves. Yet he was not averse to financing white fighting men on a campaign, and he had intended doing just that when Fort Pitt's commander was ready to march into Indian country with a regular military force.

Williamson's raiders, however, were another matter. They would shoot first, capture later, if at all. They might not follow the rules of war, but they would certainly be effective in clearing out areas where Indians had settled, and might even reduce the effectiveness of the tribes' warm-weather raids.

James turned to Maxwell. "Will the man be loyal to us afterward? These frontier woodsmen can be like Indians themselves, changing sides according to whoever gives them the most presents or most honors."

"Bless me!" Maxwell declared, rising and tossing the half-smoked cigar through the cabin door and onto the shoreline of the ice-choked river. "Dave Williamson's an ambitious man, a hard man, one who'll stand by us! One whose personal interest lines up with our own, James."

Maxwell grinned and moved to touch James on the shoulder in reassurance. "I guarantee that if we cooperate with him in his moment of personal glory, Colonel Williamson will be at our beck and call, he and all his fighting men, for many years to come . . . at least for as long as need be, as long as they will be useful to us."

There came a knock at the door, and at James's call a sentry led David Williamson into the room. Williamson was well-off as backwoodsmen go, and like them he was proud, so he did not show his astonishment at seeing the leather chairs, the silken pillows, and a china setting on the table. He was rough but educated, dignified in his raw way, and every bit a militia colonel.

After they had drunk and eaten, speaking of plans for Cullen and Company and expectations for the coming Indian outbreak, James asked Maxwell to elaborate on the proposal Williamson had made that morning.

"Bless me," Maxwell smirked, "but I'm no fighting man to fathom such matters, Mr. Morely." He nodded at Williamson, who lifted his chin, his beefy face flushed from brandy and food and the overwarm room. "If you would, Colonel."

Clearing his throat, Williamson began in a determined, booming voice, cursing all Indians, especially Delawares, and promising that he would wipe them off the face of the earth for all the wrongs they had done him and his people. The brandy, James noticed, had coarsened the man's speech considerably.

"Men such as I have good cause to risk this, Mr. Morely, because in the end it's either us or the Injuns will come out alive! I aim to see it's us! And furthermore, I aim that it be Pennsylvanians what clears the forest of redskin ratholes, and not them lousy Virginians, who'll make to claim the entire northwest when the war's done!"

James was well aware of the rivalry between Pennsylvania and Virginia, both of which states aggressively claimed Fort Pitt and the surrounding district, the gateway to the west. He also understood that he would likely have to choose a side before long and stand with it when the moment came for deciding who would rule the northwestern lands. It had not escaped his notice that there were plenty of Pennsylvania fighting men hereabouts these days but not many Virginians, except in the garrison. Most of the other Virginians had gone downriver to Kentucky with George Rogers Clark.

Maxwell said, "But, sir, Mr. Morely is concerned that friendly Indians might suffer from a wanton assault." He glanced at James with a nod. "How do you propose to assure him—us—that your men will be under control, and will not cause more trouble than ever amongst the savages?"

Colonel Williamson cleared his throat, as if preparing a memorized speech. "Upon my honor, gentlemen, I bear no enmity to Indians of proven loyalty to the rebel cause! Upon my honor and the honor of my men, we'll punish only Indians who are proven enemies, Indians who have fought alongside raiders, have abetted raiders, and who have profited from trading with raiders!" He looked at Maxwell, as if awaiting approval.

After a moment, Maxwell caught himself and smiled. "There! Mr. Morely, you have heard it all. This will be a well-organized, disciplined campaign of the first order, one that will turn the tide of the Indian war, and save thousands of white lives."

"Right you are, sir!" Williamson beamed, and they toasted as James made it clear he would go along with the plan to finance the campaign.

Williamson drank a few more brandies, twice pouring his own first, and said, in a jovial voice, "We'll take 'em by complete surprise, on an unparalleled lightning march! My men are the best shots, hardest riders, and coolest under fire of any in the world!"

"The world?" James asked, glancing at Maxwell and smiling behind his drink. He was thinking of George Clark's fighters, who had taken the vast Illinois by sheer bravado and guts.

"The world, sir!" Williamson clearly was feeling his liquor more than James and Maxwell, who were more practiced indulgers in brandy. "Why, just yesterday we was ambushed by Moravians and their allies and fought our way through, even though there must've been two hundred of 'em—"

"Moravians?" James could not believe the docile Christian Indians would make war, ambushing Pennsylvanian fighting men. "Come now, sir—"

Williamson slammed the table with his fist. "Ambushed, I tell you! No! Maybe them heathen snakes didn't shoot at us theirselves, but their red brothers did, Delawares, at least two hundred, catching us from behind while we was parleying with the Moravians, who decoyed us!"

Maxwell obviously did not want Williamson any drunker or talking much more, and he laughed lightly, making to rise. "It's well known the Christian Indians often traffic in stolen goods—"

"Stolen women and children too, I'll warrant!" Williamson blustered, not taking the hint to rise until Maxwell offered to shake hands and motioned for the steward to fetch Williamson's hat and cape and open the cabin door.

"I'll warrant!" Maxwell declared, slapping the departing militiaman on his broad back. "But all that'll soon change, eh?"

"I'll warrant it will, sir! They's a standing passel of corn up there in them Moravian towns, rich fodder for war parties, and we'll—"

Maxwell hurried him out the door, winking back at James, who thought how unfortunate it was that so many settlers despised the peaceable Christian Indians. James could scarcely understand how anyone could take seriously tales that the Moravians were in league with raiding parties, and he said so after Maxwell closed the door.

"James, my good friend," Maxwell answered, hands on hips, "don't worry yourself over the well-being of a few churchgoing savages—"

"Not worry, Noah! But I won't finance hurt for them if it can be avoided!" James, too, had drunk too much, and he wanted to take a nap, but the possibility of Williamson's manhandling the peaceful Moravians troubled him. "I want orders sent with Williamson that only proven enemies are to be attacked. . . ."

Maxwell was waving his thin hands, throwing on his own hat and cape, about to leave. "As you wish, James. But just think of the greater consequences of a successful campaign. There hasn't been a triumph on the white side for two years, and the Indians are getting bolder, despite the fact that Britain's losing the war. Why, bless me,

James, if we don't teach the redskins a lesson soon, there'll be so much white blood spilled that the settlers will all turn tail and run back over the mountains, as they've done before. And you know what that will mean to our plans."

James knew, indeed, what such a setback would mean. Over the past forty years, generation after generation of settlers had tried to penetrate this country, only to be driven back by Indian raiders. If the Indians were to win again, especially without British and loyalist allies, then his and Maxwell's plans to profit from the anticipated flood of settlers would be ruined. A barrier would fall over the northwest for many years to come and the future of Cullen and Company out here would be lost, to old-fashioned traders trusted by the Indians. Men such as Owen Sutherland.

James nodded as his friend departed. Although he had much to think about, much to plan, he went groggily into his sleeping cabin and lay down, fully clothed. He stared up at the colorful ceiling painting, a scene of rural bliss, with a river winding lazily through a wilderness pacified, cultivated, and made bountiful . . . and afloat in the midst of it was this very keelboat, the *Linda*, named after his late wife. Yes, that picture was the future, and James Morely was determined to sail through it as a ruler, as potentate.

As he dozed off, another scene came to mind, unbidden. It was the Sutherland house at Valenya, and remembering it gave him a start. In the doorway was Susannah, smiling and waving, love and admiration in her beautiful eyes. James was suddenly fully awake, but the effect of the liquor was strong still as he stared again at the painted scene on the ceiling. The painting was fine, but not fine enough. It bore no image of Susannah Sutherland, and so it was lacking. A hunger rose in him, a need, an aching that was more than lust, fiercer than love. He closed his eyes once more as he willed the scene of Valenya and Susannah, but he could not bring it back. Instead, he saw only the image of Owen Sutherland in buckskins, hard and lean, stubborn and immovable. Sutherland, with nothing caring in his expression, only dislike—not even hatred, as if dislike were quite enough, all that was worth feeling for such as James Morely.

That afternoon the wind picked up and the weather turned sharply colder, with clouds gathering and more snow in store. The sudden cold made a fine glaze on the ice of riverside ponds, and in the late afternoon young men and boys appeared with sticks and skates for a fast game of shinty before dark.

A game brought across from Scotland, where it was played on fields with crooked sticks and a ball, shinty had become popular with traders, soldiers, and Indians throughout the northwest. This gray winter's afternoon, one pond in particular was crowded with skaters whooping and shouting, sweating and straining to shoot a wooden ball into the opponent's goal. Just below the fort, this rink was the most popular, looked down upon by spectators who cheered and shouted and bet for their favorites while tippling hard cider or rum.

Torches were lit against the approaching dark, for it was Saturday and the soldiers would stay late, having time off tomorrow. Men played hard, anticipating a night of drinking or carousing in the many lower taverns for which Pitt was well known—for numbers and for lowness. Shinty was a favorite winter pastime on the frontier, though those who had come down here from farther northwest called the play a poor imitation of the real thing at places like Detroit and Sandusky, where the fastest skaters were the Chippewas, and the toughest players were the Detroit traders—especially one in particular who had come to Pitt, but seldom played anymore, if ever. That player was James Morely.

As Jake Smith sped along the ice, reaching for the ball,

missing, and falling hard on his chest, he cursed and wished he could get the knack of this frustrating game. Jake liked shinty and was strong and quick enough, but at eleven he was as yet too young, and too small—as his friend Benjamin Sutherland once had been.

Little Jake—that was what his friends called him—got to his feet, the ball momentarily lost in a snowbank. He skated slowly back toward his goal, his head down, regret filling him to think of Benjamin, who had been like a brother to him. Benjamin had taught him about the forest and the trail, had treated him as an equal despite Jake's shortcomings and youth. Benjamin had given his life to fight off Indians who were attacking a convoy of boats on the Ohio River. He had given his life so that Jake could escape, live—and now play shinty like a fool, not good enough at all!

Jake was short and wiry, strong for his years, and forever impatient with himself for not being stronger and older and better. He drew a deep breath of cold air and looked up at the deepening blue sky. He played on a good team, but today they were up against the best. His team was losing, and he had scored only twice. By now Benjamin would have scored ten times, would have stopped a hundred attacks, would have—

There came a shout from the shoreline, and he saw Susannah waving and calling that it was suppertime and he had better come. Although Jake was no Sutherland, he had been living with the family for two years since his natural parents had been killed by Indians in eastern Pennsylvania. A prisoner of Senecas, he had been taken to Detroit, there to be rescued by Owen Sutherland. He had remained with the family as a younger brother to Benjamin, in all but name. The Sutherlands had never formally adopted him, and though Jake knew they loved him, he would never mean as much to them as Benjamin had.

He waved and called to Susannah that he would take one more turn, and would she stay and watch? She nodded and drew her cape about her, patiently looking on, almost like a real sister. The game began again, and the score drew even. Since sundown was near and some of the players had to leave, it was agreed on that the first team to score three more goals would have the victory. That stirred the blood, and the fray became hot and rough. At last an opportunity presented itself, and Jake, digging into a crowd, sprang the ball free, leaped over outstretched legs and sticks, and broke for the goal. He was on his own, only the keeper to beat, and he heard Susannah's cries of encouragement. He rammed the ball ahead and skated, cut across the face of the goal ten yards out, feinted a shot and—his skate caught a rough spot, and he went down heavily, the ball bounding harmlessly away, the crowd groaning in disappointment.

One of the opposition kindly helped him to his feet, but words of encouragement were lost. Angry with himself, Jake had worse to think about, for his ankle was badly twisted. He could play no more. Susannah hurried out to the ice to give him her shoulder. She was thoughtful enough not to joke or tease, and he was glad for that. Although the Sutherlands were good sports, Jake had yet to learn to accept defeat or failure, and he could in no way understand how anyone else could.

"I'll help you get your skates off," Susannah said cheerfully, kneeling at his side. "Let me see that ankle . . . not too bad, eh, but a sore sprain just the same."

Jake hardly spoke, wanting to say something right but not knowing what. He watched his shorthanded team struggle on, scored against once, clearly doomed to lose without him.

Susannah said, "Why, you're almost as good as the men, Little Jake! You do us northwesters proud!" She smiled as she helped tie the boy's leggins.

He shrugged, hoping she meant what she was saying. "You're kind," he managed to reply. "Too kind, Susannah."

"I'm just saying what's true, Jakie, and don't be so glum about whatever you're glum about!" Her lovely smile lit up the gathering twilight. "There's a ball tonight, and everybody's merry!" Jake had to smile back at her, but there came another goal against his team, and he knew they would lose.

"You're good to me, Susannah, just like Benjamin was." He eyed her sidelong and noticed that her face fell; it had been but a year and a half since her brother's death, and the hurt of mentioning his name made Jake sorry he had. "But I wish you could teach me some shinty like Ben did! Now, that would be fine!"

Susannah recovered her smile, and just then there came a whir of small wings, and a blue jay landed on Jake's shoulder. It was Punch, tame and faithful, always appearing when Jake wanted company. Punch had been Ben's pet, and now he had come to stay with Jake, and the boy was glad for that.

Susannah said, "Ben learned from the best shinty player who ever skated, up at Detroit." She became thoughtful and sat down on the log next to Jake. The hood fell from her head, releasing long fair hair over her shoulders as she spoke softly, half watching the one-sided contest on the ice. "Even Pa agreed James was the best at shinty—a magician, unbeatable!"

The sound of a horse and sleigh passed and stopped behind, and Jake turned around, seeing it was none other than James Morely himself.

The boy said, "Speak of the devil—"

Susannah turned, surprised, and they observed James intently watching the game, his driver bored and chilled.

By the look of the young merchant's shining eyes, Jake could see how James loved this game, although he was apparently far too busy to play these days. Jake was surprised when Susannah abruptly got up and busied herself with her cape, attracting James's attention—or trying to. James still did not see her, and that was all right with Jake, because he shared Owen Sutherland's distrust of James Morely, though he had no good reason to do so.

Susannah turned sharply and exclaimed, pretending she was startled by the sleigh and James Morely. Jake watched, a bit annoyed, as Susannah was greeted enthusiastically and James jumped down from the sleigh to kiss her hand. In the failing light, James seemed a decent enough character, and anyone who knew nothing about him and only heard his friendly voice would think him a fine fellow. Jake had heard otherwise, however.

Next thing Jake knew, James was at his side, talking comfortingly about the injury and saying things like "Get better soon, for it'll be spring before long and shinty'll be gone with the ice," and "Soak it in salts, and ease into playing again, but don't ever wrap that ankle too tight. . . ."

The man crouched by the ice, almost forgetful of both Susannah and Jake, and gazed at the game, his body moving side to side as if he were playing. Nearby were someone's extra skates and several sticks, and Jake saw James gazing at them for a long moment.

"Why don't you play?" It was Susannah who asked, her voice soft, and Jake was unable to tell whether it was a question or a suggestion or encouragement or all of that at once. James looked around at her and shrugged, speaking to Jake again.

"Your team's losing without you, eh?"

Jake let his eyes drop. "I ain't much to be without."

By now, some of the players had taken note of James and called friendly greetings—some overly friendly, others making a point to get his attention. James meant much to nearly all of them. His money, his company, his whim could one day make or break all of them. With him watching they played harder, but no one could score and there were just about ten minutes of daylight left. The crowd on the battlements above was thick, and James glanced up at them, a certain good-natured gleam in his eye that Jake had never expected to see in a man with such a reputation for hardness and ruthlessness.

Susannah startled Jake by touching James's shoulder and saying, "Show them how a man of the northwest can play, James. Let me see the man I used to know . . . before . . ."

There was a silence, long and heavy, and Jake was uncomfortable. He shifted and mumbled, "You as good as Susannah says?"

He caught and held the man's eyes, and again saw that certain light, a mixture of pride and confidence. In the next moment, James had called out to the players that he would join the shorthanded team if they allowed, and he strapped on the skates with much cheering and solicitation and warnings to take care.

As James hefted a stick, tossed it down for another, then turned to skate, he winked at Susannah, saying, "For the Frontier Company that used to be, Susannah! And for you!"

He was smooth and free, with wings on the ice. Jake watched with wonder as James skated once or twice around, gathered in the ball, and felt at its weight and liveliness with his stick. He flicked the ball back and forth with some players, and every man on the ice, everyone watching from above knew they were seeing a talent of James Morely's that none had ever guessed possible. He was better than skillful—he was a master!

The game began again, and Jake felt a thrill to watch

James, seeing the familiar, astonishing moves and magic of Benjamin—once James's best pupil, Jake understood. He had also heard that Benjamin was said to have been better than James, but Jake would never have guessed it, as James skated and handled the ball with ease, with speed, with brilliance.

Brilliance that scored a rocket of a goal within two minutes of the restart, and two more to win soon thereafter. The crowd applauded and whistled in admiration. Laughing with delight and pure enjoyment, James excused the others by saying that they were tired, and asked that they play again, just for fun, whoever gets two goals first being winners.

There was talk among the players, and some suggested that a man from James's team join the other side. They wanted to see just how good he really was, for he was better than anyone they had ever seen. Jake was enthralled to watch James dart through a crowd, pass and get the return, use his body to much better effect than bigger or stronger men, and score two magnificent goals just as the light faded.

There were congratulations from all around, the men clapping James on the back as he skated from the ice. Jake was enthralled—but not so much as to miss Susannah's excitement as James came back to them, breathing hard, and happy.

James spoke first to Jake. "Now, get that leg better, lad! Ice's soon to be gone."

Jake asked quickly, before Susannah could take the man's full attention: "Mr. Morely, sir, will you teach me shinty?"

"What?" James seemed truly surprised. "But I don't teach . . . shinty anymore." He tried to smile and glanced at Susannah. "You all must know that. . . . Why, I hardly play anymore, and in an hour I'll be laid down with body ache, scarce able to welcome my guests at the ball!"

Suddenly he was cheerful again, smiling warmly at Susannah, who was looking intently at him, saying enthusiastic things about the northwest folk, about tonight's ball, and agreeing to save for him this waltz and that minuet. Jake watched, not sure what to think, but knowing now that there was a lot more to Mr. Morely than he had imagined.

James and Susannah drifted into conversation, and soon the driver came down to help Jake into the sleigh, and they were carried off in style. Jake did not speak much, for he did not like the warmth in Susannah's eyes and the answer in James's.

Nor did he know what to think when Susannah said softly, "I saw the man I've always known tonight . . . the man I have missed of late, James."

The sleigh pitched and jarred over a hump, and man and woman wound up in each other's arms for a moment—an uncomfortable moment for Jake, who cleared his throat loudly to make them stop staring that way at each other.

James smiled and looked away at the lights of windows and lanterns passing the moving sleigh. "I'm who I always was, Susannah," he said, "but we all change, and we all have to decide what is important in this world, and what will bring us success."

Susannah kept gazing straight ahead as James turned back to her. She said, "Success . . . for its own sake? I believe, James, that there's more to life than that." She looked him full in the face, and Jake stared at them both, understanding now the depth of feeling between them. "And I pray, dear James, that one day you will remember that you once believed the same, and one day you will again be the man I know your heart wants you to be."

The sleigh drew to a stop with a lurch, and Jake moved to get down. James hardly noticed him, did not acknowledge his good-night, did not even reply to Susannah as she left the vehicle and helped the boy to the cabin, not looking back, as though she could not.

chapter 5

THE BALL

Owen Sutherland had no inclination to attend a ball given by James Morely, but for the sake of the women, who so desperately needed relief from winter's long boredom and drudgery, he would go. But not without complaint.

"They don't really know how to make a dance out here!" he declared as Ella sewed up a small tear in the back of the best frock coat they had managed to acquire during the past years of leanness. It was deep blue, of Canadian French cut, and he wore it while she finished the last stitches. "What's a dance without French fiddles and *metis* singing and a few howling Chippewas to liven things up? These backcountry nabobs are Calvinist prudes and—"

Ella gave him a shove with the side of her hip and then worked again on the back of the coat. They were before the hearth in the main room of the cabin, and she was already dressed in a pretty blue gown, frilled with white lace that Susannah had crocheted that winter. The lamplight lent a wash of warm colors to the scene, and as Owen playfully teased his wife, he thought of how indeed they had enjoyed some wild celebrations up at Valenya, especially in the autumn when the fur brigades went out eager, and again

64

when they returned in spring, laden with peltry.

Here, most people were so used to dancing in little cabins that the best they could do—even when they got outside—was to stand shoulder to shoulder, hands clasped and held high, and kick their feet back and forth while one couple hopped about in the middle. Out at Detroit, where a white family seldom had to fear that Indians might be creeping in the nearby woods, people danced in the great fur warehouses or in open-sided pavilions. When they celebrated they demanded room and got it. There had always been plenty of single men and women around to liven things, and there was always excitement about who would win whom. At Detroit folk were untamed, free, inheritors of a mighty sky and endless waters. Here, on the frontier, young people were married in their early teens, or were so firmly betrothed they might as well have been married. Sons were born destined to farm patches near their elders' cabins, and daughters were brought up to give birth to more farmers, and grandchildren did the same.

It was a different country, and different people, but Sutherland admitted there was much to be said for it. Yet Pennsylvania—or Virginia, as the point of view may be— was not his kind of country, not fur country, not the reaches of the free and happy northwest.

Even as he stood there before the fire, Ella fussing with the back of his coat, Sutherland was thinking of wind rushing down from Lake Superior, and of the wide lands and wider water where a man had room to feel the wind, the freedom, and never have to think much about tomorrow. He began to hum a *voyageur* song about men of the north.

"There!" Ella stepped back, taking the needle and thread from her lips and giving the coat a last brush. "It'll have to do!" She looked at him and smiled admiringly, saying, "There won't be many from the far northwest here, but any who are will recognize you by your *bourgeois* coat!"

Outside there rose the harsh, rough laughter of a group of men passing, and the sound of curses, shouts of defiance, and boasting. Sutherland opened the cabin door and looked out, seeing in the dimness at least forty men on horseback, all carrying rifles and outfitted as though about to make a long march.

"Hail, there!" Sutherland called out. "Where are you lads bound, so ready for the trail?"

A hoarse Pennsylvania drawl returned, "Hail yourself, mister, and doff your hat to Washington County militia, off to kill redskins where we find 'em!"

Sutherland presumed they were mustering here at Pitt before departing, and he called out, "Who's to lead you?"

"Colonel David Williamson!" came back a loud reply, with all the militiamen cheering the name.

"What Indians you going against?"

"Red ones!" Laughter followed, accompanied by shouts for a gathering at certain taverns that were favorites of men from Pennsylvania's Washington County, a region that had suffered terrible losses from Indian raids.

Sutherland understood too well the meaning of the reply to his question. He stood in the doorway, Ella coming to his side, as the men rode past and into the settlement. He would have to find out more about this campaign and where it was aimed so unusually early in the year. It surely could not go very far into the wild, with the weather and forage being so undependable. Yet there were not many hostile villages close enough to Fort Pitt. . . .

Ella took his arm. "The ball, dearest."

He turned, not yet able to shake off his uneasiness, but smiling just the same and glad to see the happy anticipation in his wife's expression. From the back room in swept Susannah, fully gowned and powdered, hair done up in the latest style of Philadelphia—according to what the women had heard, at least. She looked absolutely enchanting, her yellow gown radiant, her eyes shining with excitement. She spun lightly, holding the gown wide, and asked her proud father for his opinion.

"Good you never got to Philadelphia last year," he said, referring to a planned journey that had not come to pass.

"What do you mean?" Ella demanded. "She would have been the queen of them all!"

"Aye, that's my meaning. The British would've come right back to capture the city, Susannah with it!"

His daughter liked that, and she asked if it was time to go. Soon, she was told, after Peter Defries came to escort her; Peter was off with Little Jake, hiring a sleigh and driver for the occasion, for the style of it.

It was not of sleighs and style that Owen Sutherland was thinking, however, as he and his wife and his daughter shortly joined Peter to attend James Morely's grand winter ball. It was of the Pennsylvania militiamen and their coming campaign.

Indeed, it had been far too long since the whites had won a battle on the frontier, although brave George Rogers Clark was able now and again to lead a raid in strength into Indian country. As it was, the white settlers shuddered at the thought of another brutal year of Indian attacks. Already some were talking about giving up, making the long journey back over the mountains, and others wished they could afford the trip. It was like last year all over again, when people had said that the settlers down in Kentucky all would have fled, if only the Ohio flowed the other way.

Sutherland knew that if the frontier was to be held and another disastrous year avoided, there was desperate need for a swift, deep thrust against the Indian population centers at Sandusky and Chillicothe. It would, however, take more than a few eager companies of Washington County militia to do that, and it would take a small fortune to supply a large enough army in the field—a fortune that Fort Pitt's commander did not have.

Well, Sutherland thought as he escorted Ella along the gravel path toward Morely's lit-up house in the center of the fort, even a small raid would have its effect on white morale and would give the Indians a shock. If it worked. It must be well led and carried out. David Williamson was a hard man and brave, but Sutherland had serious doubts about his strategic ability. Not even the best backwoods fighters would find it easy to surprise hostile villages along the Allegheny, where the toughest bands of Delawares still lived despite several incursions by rebel armies. Surely it was against the Allegheny villages he would be going, not too far north and east of Pitt.

As he was thinking this, Ella jarred him from his reverie and said he must be a gracious guest and avoid making trouble with James Morely. He promised to do his best and winked—yet her expression showed she was not certain about how well he would keep the peace.

She said, "I'll keep you dancing all night until your feet ache, if I even suspect you of exchanging hard words with James!" She softened. "Please, Owen, for Susannah's sake, just let it be tonight!"

For Susannah's sake . . . Yes, she deserved some fun, but Sutherland had no wish to make it any easier for his daughter to be courted by James Morely. He would be polite to James for as long as appropriate, but he would never accept the ruler of Cullen and Company as a son.

The inside of the Morely house was more magnificent than ever, the whole place having been done over after the death of Cullen. James, who had inherited the house, had spared no cost, ordering the best furnishings and having them shipped west in a score of packtrains. Music was playing, and every large downstairs room was crowded with richly dressed dignitaries, who flourished and bowed, smiled and kissed hands, laughed and whispered and laughed again. There were a good many powdered wigs and more satin than Sutherland had seen since his last visit to Philadelphia years ago. Even men who had been born and raised in buckskin and linsey now wore borrowed coats, with lace and hose and buckled shoes. Food and drink that few people on the frontier could ever imagine overflowed in every room, with tables bountiful and splendid, candles and whale-oil lamps, bright fires crackling, the air warm, heady, and aromatic.

Over the fireplace in the ballroom was an oil portrait of old Cullen himself, standing with his silver-knobbed cane. Big-headed like a gnome, like an ogre, the old Puritan was got up in the best but plainest broadcloth and looking down on the living revelers with a sneer, as if saying, "Laugh and be merry tonight, but you won't last, not the way I lasted, more than eighty years, and *I* never wasted anything on a laugh or merriment. Yet I was prince, and no one could match my wealth and power . . . no one!"

Ella stood quietly at Sutherland's side, while across the room Noah Maxwell was calling for a minuet. As the Sutherlands let pass the answering cry and surge of happy people, Ella looked long at Cullen's portrait, a shadow over her eyes.

"He still haunts this place, haunts us all, Owen."

Sutherland understood. As long as Cullen and Company thrived, the ghost of Bradford Cullen would be with it. As long as evil was done by Cullen's followers, as long as someone like James Morely could be corrupted and dragged down, the triumph of Bradford Cullen would linger on, even in death.

They went to another room, where they saw a painting of Cullen's wife, Helen, as thin and angular as her husband had been squat and fat. Helen faced across the room to an oil of Linda, stout and melancholy, an unhappy soul whom James had married because he wanted the Cullen empire.

In so doing, he had spurned the love of Susannah Sutherland and had hurt her very soul. For that Owen would never forgive him.

"Poor Linda . . ."

It was Susannah's voice, and Owen looked around to see his daughter's face, upturned, sympathetic. She glanced at her parents, while at her side Peter Defries gave her a nudge, offering to take her to watch the dancing.

"I can clog and birl, but please don't ask me to minuet, Susie!"

She smiled and turned away with him, moving through the throng that was clapping and laughing at Noah Maxwell's loud, charming inanities. The orchestra, bewigged and silk-dressed, began an elegant Handel piece, and Sutherland saw Ella soften to the sheer pleasure of music to which she had been born. For her sake he was determined to make the best of it, but in the back of his mind was the question about the new soldiers coming into Pitt. Other than David Williamson, one man could tell him what was afoot, and that was Pitt's commander, Colonel Daniel Brodhead, who was somewhere in the crowd.

A moment later James Morely himself appeared, dressed more rakishly than Sutherland had ever seen him, to gallantly ask Ella whether her husband had the next dance. Like Defries, Sutherland had no love for the minuet, but his wife did, and he bowed in cordial agreement as James led her away. Sutherland took the opportunity to find Colonel Brodhead, a solid, big-chested Pennsylvanian, decent and honest, but for too long forced to suffer under a hopeless military situation at Pitt. Forgotten by the states and Congress, with no supplies, no pay for his troops, no hope of sallying against the Indians and loyalists who had struck again and again on the frontier, Brodhead was forever somber. Even tonight his face was deeply lined with worry, and he evidently had come here not for enjoyment's sake but out of good manners and duty to James. Still, he seemed pleased to greet Sutherland.

"A fair revelry, is it not, Mr. Sutherland?" he remarked congenially, though a bit stiffly, clearly himself not one to minuet. Ella and Susannah were enjoying the dancing, and Sutherland was surprised to see that the young Marylander, Entellus Greyson, had become his daughter's partner—and a skilled dancer he was. They were an attractive couple.

Brodhead was speaking. "Our better sort of people need this, and thanks be to Mr. Morely and Mr. Maxwell for their generosity." Sutherland noticed Brodhead was fingering the cloth of his uniform coat—obviously a new one. It must have cost far more than a colonel's pay for two months. A gift?

Sutherland said, "Yes, Cullen and Company is making a show of it for Pitt." He saw Williamson, also well dressed but in civilian garb, for he was not a regular like Brodhead. "Is this affair for the occasion of Colonel Williamson's departure against the Delawares?"

Brodhead looked around sharply, his face coloring. "What do you know about the colonel's plans?"

"Little—but there's no secret now that his men are coming in, whooping and hollering about attacking . . . the Delaware Allegheny towns, was it?"

Brodhead looked away, lower lip and chin jutting. "Let it rest at that, then, if you would, Mr. Sutherland. It's confidential."

The music went on, and neither man spoke until Brodhead nodded toward Susannah, who was laughing at something Greyson had said.

"Your lovely daughter has made acquaintance with one of the most influential gentlemen in Maryland—perhaps in all the southern states." Again surprised, Sutherland asked about Greyson and was told he was the son of a congressional delegate, from a family with vast landholdings and equally vast claims to the country west of Fort Pitt.

"He has letters of introduction from men whose very whim can change affairs in America," Brodhead said, clearly impressed. "And he has orders for me that give him almost a free hand to go whither he pleases, with whom he pleases, and my blessing to be given!"

Sutherland listened as Brodhead tried not to sound too envious of so fortunate a fellow. The poor Pennsylvanian had been cooped up in Pitt for two years, unable to attack, scarce able to defend, and now a young, clear-browed hero had appeared, a man whose reports back home might very well influence those who would judge Brodhead's performance as commander of the most strategic rebel post in the northwest.

Sutherland said, "Greyson knows how to fight . . . did Williamson tell you?"

"Others told," Brodhead chuckled. "Williamson dislikes the lad quite thoroughly, and I can't say I blame him much. I wouldn't care for a young man of rank telling me I had to take him on a campaign, like it or not!" Having seemingly forgotten his earlier effort at secrecy, Brodhead was almost grinning as he watched the bulky Williamson attempting the minuet and becoming tangled with his partner while trying to go under the arching arms of James and Ella. "Yes, Colonel Williamson is a good fighting man, and he knows how to teach the redskins a lesson. He's a daring one, and I venture to say that young Marylander'll quail in his Continental shoes afore this campaign is over!"

"He's game to want to go, though," Sutherland pressed, "with all the risk, and his inexperience fighting Indians." After a moment he added, "He means to look over his land claims, I gather."

Nodding, Brodhead applauded with the rest as the music stopped and the dancers parted, laughing, for the punch bowls. As he smiled at passersby, Brodhead said, "He'll find his land claims out here a deal more troublesome than cultivating his holdings back in the tidewater. I'll warrant he'll turn tail for home as soon as he realizes the impossibility of taking control of his claims." He licked his lips, eyeing the punch being poured, then parted with Sutherland, saying, "This godforsaken country'll yet cost us a deal in blood—Maryland blood, too—if they try to settle it too soon."

He vanished into the crowd, leaving Sutherland thinking hard. Greyson's land claims were well west of Fort Pitt, not northward in the Allegheny Valley, where the Delawares had their villages. West of Pitt the war-ravaged country was almost vacant for a hundred miles or more, the hostile Indians having withdrawn. Even the peaceful Moravians had been forced to leave by the British at Detroit, who had been right to remove them for their own good. If Williamson was marching two hundred men westward, looking for a fight at this time of year, he would have to go a long way, and it was certain he would never return once the Indians knew he was there.

Still, Williamson was a true wilderness leader, smart and tough, a man who would not go off on a march without a definite purpose in mind. Perhaps Entellus Greyson already knew and would tell something, if asked correctly.

The celebration went on, a welcome interlude to winter's hardships, and a needed relief in the long, weary wait for spring—a spring that would bring death and terror once again. Before long, Colonel Williamson got good and drunk and had to be led away by a couple of Brodhead's junior officers. Noah Maxwell made speeches that most of the merrymakers applauded—speeches about the northwest becoming a settler's paradise, a land of promise and riches, and so on.

Susannah was not to be seen for a time, having gone for

a stroll with Entellus Greyson, according to Ella. It was clear Ella liked the Marylander, and she was well pleased when Sutherland told her that he did, too. When they later caught sight of their daughter, she was standing between Greyson and James at the drawing-room hearth, watching a servant ply the fire with wood and laughing gaily at some remark James had made. There was still something deep between James and the girl, and Sutherland clenched his teeth to have to admit it.

Indeed, Susannah enjoyed the attention of the two young men, both of them cheerful and strong, each vying with the other to seem brighter in her eyes. It was amusing to watch them, she thought, although the aching intensity in James did not become him at all. More than once he rudely interrupted Greyson or simply ignored him. Greyson, for his part, seemed not to notice or care, apparently confident in his ability to charm a young woman. Truly, Susannah had never known anyone quite like him, and she thought she had never seen a handsomer man. And to think of how her father had praised him! Owen Sutherland praised few men like that.

Susannah was enjoying herself so much that, before she realized it, the evening had flitted away. Most of the company had left, including all the junior officers from Pitt and most of the notable settlers. All that remained were a few principals from James's company—two of them trying gamely to outdrink Peter Defries at a table over in one corner—and her own family, who were talking with Colonel Brodhead again. No doubt military matters, as ever! Forever war, but at least James and Entellus knew how to talk of things that interested her: of theater and polite society in Philadelphia, of good wines from Spain and Portugal, of Paris fashions, and of Boston ladies who were beginning to make an impression on the flowering culture of a free America.

They talked of the arts and culture, of what Pittsburgh
—as some called this place—would be like in a hundred
years. They talked of idealistic groups coming overland
determined to found cities, to conquer the wilderness, to
build utopias and Gardens of Eden, each group with its
own particular religious beliefs, some communal, others
staunchly individualistic. It was exciting talk, and informa-
tive, and Susannah thoroughly enjoyed it, so much so that
it pained her deeply when the evening was over, clocks of
all sizes chiming twelve at the same instant.

Owen and Ella were watching her, while Brodhead held
forth on some subject or another. Susannah could see they
were ready to leave. In a few months they all would be
back at the squalid, smelly, uncultured settlement at the
Falls of the Ohio, back in the direct path of the largest
marauding war parties.

Susannah saw her mother discreetly incline her head as
a signal, but she did not want to go as yet. To her surprise,
it was Greyson who said, "It appears your parents wish to
depart, Mistress Sutherland—more's the pity." He bowed
over her hand and kissed it. "It has been an honor." Susannah sensed James stiffen; he had kept his back pointedly
toward her mother and father.

"It has been my pleasure to make your acquaintance,
Mr. Greyson," she replied. "I hope you will call from time
to time, as long as you are at Pittsburgh."

"That," said James clumsily, before Greyson could answer her, "will be difficult for our mutual friend, for he'll
be off in the wild, scouting prospective land claims, and
won't be back for many weeks." James was smiling, his
satisfaction hardly concealed.

Susannah was disappointed to hear that, and she said so.
"Your presence has so brightened up our little company,
hasn't it, James?"

"Quite." James also kissed Susannah's hand, as Owen

approached. "And your presence, Susannah, is a beacon in the wilderness, a restorer of our souls! We hope you'll remain here with us for a long time to come."

Sutherland was there, offering Susannah his arm and cordially thanking his host. Susannah wished she did not have to leave. She looked from Greyson to James and was a bit startled at how closely both regarded her in return. James she had half-expected it from, but Greyson's interest was another matter.

James shook hands with Sutherland. "We had no opportunity to converse, Owen."

"Perhaps next time." Sutherland nodded, then shook hands with Greyson. "We're at home tomorrow afternoon, sir, if you would do us the honor of your company . . . say one of the clock?"

Greyson beamed, and James turned sour. Susannah felt a pang for James just then, but at the same time she would be delighted to see Greyson again. James would always be here, no doubt, but she might never have another chance to become better acquainted with the young man from Maryland.

Still, she felt sorry for James, and as they got into the sleigh she told her father not to be so bluntly unkind to him.

"He's trying, Pa! Why, you should have seen how good he was to Little Jake today . . . he might even teach him shinty." She glanced at her mother on the seat beside her but got no encouragement. They simply refused to understand.

Sutherland reached down from his seat in the sleigh to haul a staggering, humming Peter Defries inside, the Dutchman's bulk making the vehicle rock. Defries was drunk, happily so, and he lolled against Sutherland; two Cullen and Company officers were vomiting in agony at Morely's backhouse. Ella threw a blanket over her own and Susannah's legs.

As the sleigh moved off, it was Ella who said what Susannah knew her father also was thinking. "We wish James would change and be as he was, dearest, but if you pin your hopes, your future, on that, I fear you'll be sore hurt someday."

From his half-slumber, Defries grumbled, "Susie girl, don't waste your pretty charms on that turncoat snail." He gave a soft snort. "Think about Enty, now! There's a good man for you, for all that he's got a funny name and comes from a place that makes you sweat just to think about summer there!"

Susannah blushed as Defries sluggishly went on. "Enty's a good duck, tough as nails, and you can trust him. He just wants to own half the damned country, not all of it, like James boy does!" He mumbled, yawned, and began to slumber. "Tell your girl, Owen—James don't give . . . a hang . . . for anybody but . . . himself. And he'd play sly with himself . . . if it . . . meant . . . profit. . . ."

His words deeply hurt Susannah, and she resented that her parents made no attempt to defend James, or to excuse him at least a little. Especially when it was obvious she still cared for him. She was sure James still had good in him, and one day it would come out. He was not bad, for all that he had made mistakes of judgment.

Saying nothing, she stared out from the covered sleigh as a group of rowdy drunks stumbled past, startling the horse and getting curses from the driver. They returned better than they got, then broke out into a song about killing Indians.

Susannah was lost in her own thoughts and did not notice how quiet her father was as he gazed at the drunken men, his face intent, as if he knew something was very wrong but could not quite figure what.

Early the next afternoon a letter arrived for the Sutherlands by way of an itinerant trader who had been to the outlying farms west of Pitt. Having heard of the return of the Moravian Indians to their villages, he had stopped in Gnadenhutten, where he had been given a letter by the Shawnee girl Evangeline.

Some years ago, before she had gone to live with the Moravians, Evangeline had helped Benjamin Sutherland escape captivity with the Shawnees, and back then the youngsters had fallen in what they took for love. Since that time the girl had learned English well from the Moravian missionaries, and she had been waiting for an opportunity to write to Sutherland, to tell him what was in her heart.

Sutherland read the letter aloud, while Ella and Susannah paused in their preparations for afternoon tea with Entellus Greyson, who was expected to arrive soon. Little Jake sat in a corner, listening. He had been working hard at his hornbook letters and was glad enough to stop.

"'. . . I have lately heard the sorrowful news that Benjamin has fallen victim to the violence which has our country in its grip . . .'"

Evangeline was also acquainted with Jeremy Bently, Ella's first son, and sent word that she had heard he and his family were well and doing much good for the whites and Indians of the Illinois country. The last bit of news in the letter, however, was totally unexpected, and it jarred Sutherland.

"'Now that my people have been permitted, thanks to God, to return to Gnadenhutten and to the villages of Salem and Schoenbrunn, we are near enough to you at Pitt to meet you and to visit. It would do my heart good to see you all, as it does my heart good to be here again, home at last, where the will of our heavenly Father has led us.'"

Sutherland leaped from his chair, and Ella and Susannah were startled, at first not understanding what he said.

"They're after blood! That's it, the dogs! Blood and plunder! Williamson's hungry to kill Indians and rob the villages. And there's none easier to get at now than the Moravians!"

"No!" Ella was staggered. "But they're harmless! They've helped whites——" She had to sit down at the table, the horror of understanding overcoming her. "Dear God, no! Owen, it mustn't happen!"

Susannah stood there helpless, her eyes wide, as they all realized the terrible danger in which the Moravians and Evangeline would be if Williamson's force went against them.

Sutherland was throwing on his hat and greatcoat, crying, "I've got to stop Brodhead! He can't authorize it! Damn Williamson! Damn any man that's involved in this!"

He yanked open the door, and there, pleasantly smiling, was Entellus Greyson, who lifted his hat and bid Sutherland good day.

"Damn!" Sutherland shouted, pushing past. "Damn my eyes if it's a good day, land speculator!"

He stamped away, leaving the dismayed Greyson at the door, until Ella and Susannah, both pale and trembling, came to let him in, and to explain to him why Owen was in a fury—a fury that would not be quelled until he had his way. That, or he had been stopped by main force.

chapter 6

ARREST

James Morely stood in the sunlit parlor of his house, looking out the window as Owen Sutherland strode swiftly past, Little Jake hurrying behind. Noah Maxwell, too, was in the room, and he observed that Sutherland was headed toward the headquarters of Colonel Brodhead, a few buildings away.

"Sutherland's out for business," Maxwell remarked, pursing his lips. "Likely sticking his nose in somewhere it doesn't belong, telling Brodhead how to manage the war."

James stared at Sutherland, who entered the headquarters brusquely, obviously ignoring the challenge of a sentry, who followed him inside.

James said, "Be glad Sutherland is not managing the rebel side of this war out here, or your loyalist agents would have been caught and cleaned out by now, Noah."

Maxwell snorted, "Bless me, James, but you do show admiration for that Indian-lover! And what do you mean, *my* loyalist agents?" He stepped away from the window and shrugged in his coat, straightening it. "They are Cullen and Company agents, just as we have agents on the rebel side, and all are working for the greater good of our company and our country."

"Yes, yes," James said, exasperated by another of Maxwell's self-righteous speeches. "I'm just tired of playing both sides—a game I inherited from old Cullen, and one I want to wash my hands of as soon as possible."

Throughout the course of the war, cunning Bradford Cullen had maintained a network of spies and agents on both sides of the fighting, profiting from intrigues and espionage, and selling supplies to both sides. Ever since learning about the secretive system last year, James had been compelled to perpetuate it, mainly because it meant such great profit to Cullen and Company. Its success also meant riches for a score of smaller, subordinate companies operating in the British Empire, Canada, and in the British-controlled part of the northwest.

Noah took a pinch of snuff from a silver box, and his eyes watered as he said, "War's about done anyway. And you'll soon be grateful for old Cullen's foxiness, James, for no one will have the international connections we will, all over British and independent America. All over the world! While rebel merchants will be shunned by the British, we'll be darlings. Why, we'll have a hand in every major commercial enterprise from Detroit to New York before long, and people on both sides will forget the war soon enough."

James stepped away from the window and went to sit behind his polished desk—also inherited from Cullen. He leaned back in his cushioned chair and tented his fingers to his lips. He sincerely believed that, given time, he could reorganize Cullen and Company, discarding the most corrupt, changing the complexion of the firm so that no one could accuse him—as they had Cullen—of ruling over an evil, bloodstained commercial empire.

But now, as ever, Maxwell had an argument for postponing any change. "Think on this, James: in a few months the treaty will be signed, and my loyalist agents say the

British will give up the northwest on paper only, meaning they will continue to hold the forts and to control the trade for many years to come. No power in America will be able to stop them, not for a long time. Stick with our allies, James, and they'll lay the trade of the northwest at our feet!"

Yes, Maxwell was always practical. James would go on financing rebel soldiers, like David Williamson, while at the same time dealing secretly with spies, traders, and war profiteers on the loyalist side, from the northwest lakes to Quebec City and across the sea to England and France. It was too soon to cut off the secret loyalist agents, especially since there was the added danger that they might expose the illegal dealings of Cullen and Company if they were betrayed.

James sighed, feeling the weight of responsibility, and yet he was well satisfied with his immense power, and knew even greater things were to come for him. Soon the entire northwest would be thrown open to settlement, and the Indians would be ousted. There were unmatched profits to be made, new states to be established and governed, and perhaps even independent nations to be born, ruled over by men such as he. There was no limit to what was possible for someone with intelligence, foresight, and the financial resources. The northwest would be bountiful, strong . . . one day a country of its own, if he had his way.

A sudden commotion erupted outside in the hall, and James could hear the voice of Owen Sutherland telling off the butler. The door to the room was suddenly thrown open, and in strode Sutherland, anger and determination in his face. James stood up. Maxwell shrank back, as if afraid.

"Don't let it happen, James!" Sutherland demanded fervently. "Don't let Williamson go against the Moravians!"

"What?" James did not understand and glanced in question at Maxwell, who just stared back, his left eye nervously twitching. "Who said anything about Moravians being in danger? What is the meaning of this, Owen?"

Sutherland steadied himself, fists clenched, fury barely controlled as he leaned forward on the table. "You're financing a massacre, James, because Williamson is heading for Gnadenhutten! He means to plunder and kill them all! Don't finance the raid, James!"

James had thought the raiders were marching against Shawnee or Delaware villages to prevent them from being used as bases for warm-weather attacks. He said, "You'd better talk to Brodhead about this, Owen. And what makes you think I'm putting up the money for Williamson?"

Exasperated, Sutherland straightened, saying, "No one else has the resources to finance Williamson. Already Brodhead has refused to listen to me—" He looked out the window, where the fort's watch were collecting, an angry Daniel Brodhead preparing them to come after Sutherland.

James saw this, and remarked, "You must have said the wrong thing to him, Owen."

Maxwell, also seeing the troops, gained some spunk. "Perhaps Brodhead fears for your safety in the face of Mr. Sutherland's wrath, James . . . and I confess, so do I."

Sutherland ignored Maxwell. "Will you withdraw your funds from this campaign?"

Maxwell interrupted, stepping forth. "Surely you must know our company's word is its bond—"

Sutherland lifted him by the shirt and hissed, "What're you getting out of this, you swine?"

Afraid for Maxwell, who was stammering helplessly, James quickly came around the table. "Owen! Leave off!"

The troops were almost at the house. The butler was on the walk, gesticulating and pointing at the front door. Maxwell squirmed like a hooked fish, eyes bulging, as Sutherland tightened his grip and demanded again to know what the man was getting from backing Williamson.

James reached for Sutherland's arm but was cuffed stingingly aside. Then Sutherland tossed Maxwell to the floor and turned again to James, who sprang to his feet, ready to go at it, though he knew he would be beaten. Sutherland shook a fist. "I've tried, man! I've tried to keep out of your way! I don't want to fight you the way I had to fight Cullen!"

"Then leave off, I say!" James cried, blood at the corner of his mouth. "Don't try to order me, Sutherland! I've paid for no massacre, but my business affairs are my own!"

Before Sutherland could speak, Brodhead stormed in, calling James's name, and followed by soldiers with bayonets. Maxwell began to kick from where he lay on the floor, raising a fuss as if Sutherland had half killed him. James was livid at Sutherland but said nothing, for Maxwell was making enough commotion. The chatter of the frightened butler behind the troops added to the confusion, and people were running to the house to gawk. Outside, Ella and Susannah, joined by Little Jake, Defries, and Greyson, were hurrying to help prevent trouble. They were already too late.

Sutherland stood squarely in Brodhead's path, between the colonel and James. For an instant, Brodhead seemed uncertain of what to do.

"He attacked me!" Maxwell squawked as a soldier went to see how he was. "Arrest him, Colonel! Arrest him for attempted murder!"

Brodhead calmed himself, staring hard at Sutherland, whose anger had subsided to a smoldering rage.

"I told you the campaign is aimed at hostiles only, and that Colonel Williamson has no quarrel with any peaceful Indians—unless, that is, he finds proof of collaboration—"

"Don't act the fool, Brodhead," Sutherland said casually; he saw that Ella and Susannah were pushing through the crowd.

Brodhead turned red in the face, shaking with anger. Sutherland had a reputation for facing down senior officers and coming out on top. James wondered whether the colonel knew that.

James stepped forward, before Brodhead had Sutherland arrested on the spot. "Colonel, there's been a misunderstanding, and I'm sure Mr. Maxwell will not charge Mr. Sutherland with anything."

"Call off the campaign," Sutherland said flatly to Brodhead.

"Mind your own damned business," Maxwell screeched, holding his throat as if it had been brutalized. "Indian-lover!"

"Call off the campaign, Brodhead, or Congress will immediately know what you've allowed to happen."

Brodhead exploded. "You'll not tell me my duty, Sutherland, and won't threaten me, either!"

"Call off the campaign or I'll march after Williamson myself and stop him!"

Sure of himself now, Brodhead motioned with one hand. "Arrest him, men. We'll give Mr. Sutherland some time and a place to cool down."

"No!" Ella gasped and rushed to her husband's side. A soldier shoved her roughly away, and Sutherland grabbed the man, lifted him, and threw him into the crowd, knocking other soldiers down, including the astonished Brodhead. Bayonets were leveled, and James saw Owen's hand go to his claymore.

"Hold!" James cried and leaped between Sutherland and the others. "Owen! Not like this, man! There's nothing you can do now! It's been decided! Don't!"

It was James's intervention that stopped real bloodshed, and Sutherland was led away to prison, Ella and his family following dejectedly. As they went, James tried to catch Susannah's eye, but she did not look at him, even though it was he who had saved her father from serious injury, perhaps from death.

As the room emptied, Maxwell called for a drink, and the distressed butler brought him brandy on a silver tray. James did not feel like joining in, for he was sorry to see a man of Sutherland's stature arrested like this. How the world had changed. . . . He looked at the smug Maxwell staring out the window at a group of David Williamson's soldiers, who were pleased to see Sutherland under arrest. Among them was Mike Grub, a grin on his ugly face.

"That'll teach him," Maxwell was muttering. "A little dishonor for the great Sutherland. A few weeks in jail will soften him up."

"You talk like an ass!"

Maxwell turned, surprised. "What's that? You still have feeling for that rogue? Hah! Bless me, James, if your affection for Susannah hasn't fuddled your thinking. Bless me!"

James was slow to reply, his thoughts filled with self-accusation. Was he backing men like Mike Grub at the cost of a deeper rift with Sutherland? What kind of policy was that?

Almost languidly, he asked, "Will we ever benefit from aiding David Williamson?"

Maxwell was confident, smooth, as he replied brusquely, "Men such as he are the future of this country. Men such as he and his followers know how to fight Indians, but Sutherland . . . well, bless me, James, but you know he'd rather trade with them and coddle them than persuade them to sell their lands to us."

James thought about that. There were other sorts of men than Williamson and Grub settling out here. And those others all were far more pliable than Owen Sutherland, who wanted things to turn out only his way.

"There's a war here," Maxwell said, voicing thoughts in James's own mind, "and wars hurt many people. But if it's them or me, then I know my choice, and I'd rather have Williamson get this war over by winning quickly than let idealists like Owen Sutherland perpetuate the misery by keeping the conflict from ending."

James had no delusions about how Maxwell expected the fighting to end: the Indians would be obliterated forever, and in their stead would be farms and villages, one day great cities and highways . . . and over it all would be Cullen and Company. But at what cost? And would James emerge unstained when it was over? Would he stand on Owen Sutherland's forgotten grave?

"Men such as Sutherland want only . . ." he began. Maxwell listened, but James could not finish, for he did not have the proper words.

Owen Sutherland stood at the barred window of the cell, looking out at the crowded parade ground, where nearly two hundred well-mounted, spirited Pennsylvanians were readying to ride out. Facing them, drawn up in companies, with faded flags unfurled and slack-eyed drummers beating a slow march, were the three hundred weary Virginians and Pennsylvanians of the Continental regiments stationed at Pitt. It was a sharp contrast: the garrison's Continentals were hollow-faced and ragged, their morale as poor as their physical condition; but the militiamen were strong, dressed for winter traveling, and obviously well fed over the winter at their own cabins.

Sutherland watched as Colonel Brodhead shook hands with Williamson, whose beefy face glowed with confidence. Near Williamson was Mike Grub, who grinned and spat tobacco juice as he nodded toward Sutherland's barred window. Sutherland did not react. His mind worked on how to get out and warn the Moravians. Though Brodhead had flatly denied any intention to attack Moravians, Sutherland did not believe the man was facing up to the truth. No one was paying the personal expenses of the raiders—militia here never were paid—so they must have been promised an equal share of any booty taken. There would be no richer booty on the frontier than the Moravian villages. Sutherland trembled to think of what might happen in a few days.

The troops began to ride out in double file. Near Williamson was Entellus Greyson, who also saw Sutherland at the window and gave a discreet nod. What did he know of Indian fighting, of the bitter blood-hatred, and of what these men were capable of once their anger was up? For all Sutherland knew, Greyson might meet his own fate at the hands of Mike Grub before the campaign was over. A disaster loomed, and it had to be prevented!

Soon there came a rattle at the door, which opened to let in Colonel Brodhead, looking determined and angry. He ordered the guards to wait outside in the corridor. Facing Sutherland, he sighed in obvious disappointment and exasperation. "You gave me no choice, sir, and it is only at the intercession of Mr. Morely that Noah Maxwell has not pressed serious charges—"

"The hell with Maxwell, Colonel! He's as guilty as you are for what will happen."

"Damn my eyes, but you're a stubborn Scotch ba—" Brodhead caught himself at the last moment, shook off anger, and said carefully, "Give me your solemn oath you will not interfere with Williamson, and I'll let you go this very minute."

Sutherland looked sidelong at Brodhead, seeing a good but compromised man who was in deeper than he could handle. Sutherland did not blame Brodhead, but he would not go along with what the colonel was allowing to happen.

"You'll regret this campaign, Colonel."

"By gad, Sutherland!" He whipped his tricorne to the plank floor. "By gad, don't you see that I've promised the Washington County men this campaign? Don't you see that if I call them off now, if I bow to your fears, I'll lose their allegiance forever? Don't you understand that there are other campaigns to come, and if I let them down there won't be a militiaman for hundreds of miles who'll muster when I call? Surely you cannot deny what I am telling you?"

Sutherland sat down heavily on the straw-filled mattress of his cot. Gloomy, he said slowly that Brodhead's career would be ruined by Williamson's campaign. "You've picked the wrong man to lead it—"

"He's the best leader I could ask from this country! His men follow him unswervingly, and he was able to persuade James Morely to supply him! Williamson's the man all right, and this summer I'll be the man who'll wield an army of his and my own at Detroit, sweeping back to take Niagara if Congress lets me!"

Brodhead's eyes were alight, but his voice was weakened from fatigue and poor rations. After years of frustrating inactivity, he meant to have his moment in the sun, and was obviously expecting to win accolades in one final great campaign. Williamson's raid was only the first part of that strategy, and Brodhead was committed to it. Sutherland knew it was true that if the colonel did not let Williamson go now, all attempts to raise a full-scale army in the summer might go for nothing.

"At least," Sutherland said, "send junior officers with him to make certain he commits no atrocities."

Brodhead nodded, saying, "Although I have no men to spare, young Colonel Greyson will be at Colonel Williamson's side throughout."

"That's not enough," Sutherland replied, his anger rising, the urgency to escape suddenly rising, too.

"It will have to do, sir! Now, I ask you again for your promise not to interfere, and you may go free."

Sutherland sat back on the cot, looking away. "Thank you, Colonel, but I'll not give that promise."

"Very well—you leave me no choice." Brodhead picked up his hat and thrust it under his arm. "You'll languish here until Williamson's long gone, and in the meantime I'll think up some charges—" He spun abruptly and left, stamping down the corridor and calling for the guards to lock the cell door.

Sutherland sat, thinking, wondering how he could get word to the Moravians in time. There was too little time, and Williamson's men would travel fast, surprise and speed being their advantages in Indian country.

He went again to the window and stared out, seeing Peter Defries and young Jake standing near a wagon, looking back. Not even Peter could help, because it would take a woodsman to make the grueling journey over the fifty miles of wilderness to the Moravian village on the Tuscarawas River. Sutherland knew no one but himself who could make it faster than the raiders.

But if he did not get out soon, it would be too late even for him to try.

After the show of parading on horseback out of the fort, Williamson's little army soon boarded flatboats to travel two days down the Ohio to flats called Mingo Bottom, after the Mingo Indians who once had cornfields there. From there, plans were to remount and dash across country toward Upper Sandusky, a stronghold two hundred miles from Pitt, and a major staging area for loyalist and Indian raiders. At least this was what Entellus Greyson was told by Williamson.

The weather was cold but clear, the river rough with ice floes, wind strong in the faces of the militiamen as their boats floated downstream. Men worked great sweeps at the stern of each of the twenty craft, all of them ponderously laden. Horses were packed tightly in half the square-prowed vessels, other boats were full with supplies and tents, and the rest held fighting men, eager and confident in their strength.

Greyson had been in plenty of battles and skirmishes, with huge armies in open fields and with handfuls of soldiers in forests. He was not afraid of flying lead, and he knew dependable men when he met them. These Pennsylvanians were solid, just like the hundreds who had formed hard-fighting Continental regiments under Anthony Wayne. Many of the best riflemen in the rebel army had come from this country, commanded by Daniel Morgan, a Virginian who was part Pennsylvania German.

Greyson felt as if he already knew these men well, having fought alongside many like them. He trusted their courage and staying power. Even though two hundred seemed few in the face of thousands of Indians who might rally to snare them, he believed their fast-moving raid would encounter little organized opposition. Williamson had said the warriors would still be painting their faces and doing their medicine dances when they heard the raiders had struck Sandusky.

"We'll hit Upper Sandusky like a hammer!" Williamson boasted as he stood next to Greyson on the leading flatboat, which leaped and thudded through the ice floes and waves. "What Injuns are there we'll kill or run off, and then we'll burn everything—corn, orchards, hovels—and be back in Pitt within three weeks!" He clapped Greyson hard on the back. "You're a seasoned fighting man, sir, but we'll give you a taste of frontier fighting—no quarter asked or given, and every lurking heathen man or boy or squaw an enemy who'll slit your throat and worse if you sleep with only one eye open!"

Greyson ignored the jovial taunts of the men around him, who egged Williamson on to tell the story of the Marylander who came out and tried to learn frontier fighting ways but who got lost in Fort Pitt's orchard and had not been seen since. Or the tale about the greenhorn who tried to journey down the Ohio during the time of melting ice, and when the ice suddenly jammed in a dam a distance below his moored boat, he was washed so far inland by the flood that he woke up in a Delaware village. They burned him alive, Greyson was told.

The teasing went on until a dark-eyed, bearded settler with the rough and gnarled hands of a born farmer came to stand next to Greyson. The others grew quiet, including Williamson, and drew off. The man introduced himself as Captain Charles Bilderback, from near Fort Pitt.

"I know," he began, in a hoarse, low voice, "that you gents from back east don't understand what we're about out here, and wouldn't rightly care much about us if'n it wasn't that you want a share—a big share—of this country all fer yerself."

There was a pause, but Greyson had not much to say in reply, instead watching the snow-covered hillsides drift by, thinking how glorious this country would be when trees were in leaf and winds were less bitter.

Bilderback went on. "You don't know about us, and we don't know you, and who cares? But it's folk back east as has some say in what goes on out here, and I want you to know that what we do to Injuns is fer everybody's good, and there ain't no other way fer it!"

Again the man paused, as if Greyson should have something to say, but the Marylander just waited to hear what he was getting at.

"If'n ye're out here long enough . . . and if ye're man enough to fight Injuns, ye'll be seeing things that yer courteous reg'lar armies back east'll never know, never stomach."

The too-familiar vision of men bloodied by grapeshot, decapitated by cannon, and slashed by saber suddenly came to Greyson. He knew something of death, but he willed the vision away and listened.

"Well, sir, we were born to kill Injuns, and they born to kill us, and it'll go round like that until there ain't nobody left to kill on one side or t'other."

Something fierce and sorrowful seemed to well up in Bilderback then, and he could not restrain a sob. He appeared to want to say more, but could not, and turned away without another word.

Then Greyson was joined by Colonel Williamson, who said quietly, "Mr. Bilderback's entire family was massacred a little while back—wife, children brutally murdered." He was cold in his words, but his eyes burned with hatred. "We aim to avenge them, Mr. Greyson, to avenge many lost loved ones, before this raid is done."

Night drew on, but in his cell, Owen Sutherland could not sleep. He lay on his cot, having paced for hours, listening to the slow, bored conversation of the two guards in their room at the end of the narrow corridor. The light of their lamp shone faintly, and the smell of tobacco was strong in Sutherland's cell. He was thinking that with every passing hour the raiders were that much closer to the Moravians, that much more difficult to prevent from doing their worst.

Were this a military campaign, designed to meet and defeat hostile Indians, to destroy crops and resources, Sutherland would have been with them. For all that he had close ties to Indians of nearly every northwestern nation, he had chosen his side in this war, and he knew the fighting would not end until the Indians were shown decisively that they could not win. The sooner the better.

Now that the British would in all likelihood be withdrawing from the frontier war, forced by treaty to stop supplying the Indians with guns and ammunition, the Indians would have to rethink their strategy. For generations the red man had been a brilliant forest politician, playing the French against the British and vice versa, lately playing the British against the colonists—all the while, against enormous odds, managing to keep their country free of white settlements.

Those days were over, however, with the final defeat of British power in America at hand. Soon it would be Indians alone against American whites. And when Congress finally resolved to invade Indian country in force, the way of the red man would be gone in a few years. For now, though, Congress was still laboring under tremendous war debt, wrestling with problems of unity and financing, and struggling to keep a half-starved army in the field.

Sutherland believed the destiny of America lay in the settlement and development of the northwest, but he hoped it would be done hand in hand with Indians, knowing they must change their way of life whether they wanted to or not. Change or be destroyed forever.

Just then the acrid scent of smoke came to him—the smoke of wood burning, of tar and pitch. Even before he could sit up there was a shout, "Fire! Get out! Fire!" and the lamp in the guardroom was snuffed, followed by a crash of tables and chairs, loud cursing, and a thick billow of smoke suddenly filling the cell.

"Fire! Everybody out! Get them out! Open the cells!"

Sutherland knew that voice. He dropped to his knees, the smoke so thick he could scarcely breathe. There was nothing to see but black night, and it was impossible to take a breath without coughing.

Then the door was unlocked and swung open, followed by a guard's shout of surprise and the sound of fist against flesh. Sutherland heard Peter Defries gasp, "Out the door, Owen! Out and look for Jakie! Go now!"

In a flash Sutherland realized Defries was dragging the slumped, unconscious form of a guard down the corridor. The other guard, also unconscious, Sutherland stumbled over as he went through the guardroom. The next moment he was outside, his eyes bleary and tearing from the smoke. As they cleared he saw a flaring, smoking smudge-pot just inside the doorway. Defries was dragging the two unconscious guards over the threshold.

"Here, Owen!" It was Jake, grabbing his hand and leading him into the clear air of night, hurrying him away as he coughed and tried to recover. "There's a canoe waiting, and your claymore, and all you'll need. Come quick!"

By the time Sutherland's head had cleared, he was at the riverside, and someone was throwing traveling clothes over his shoulder. It was Peter Defries, who spoke quickly:

"Neat and slick, Owen! Them guards's snoozing, and we made little enough noise, so that the rest of the fort won't know you're gone till the watch changes!" He let out a high-pitched giggle of glee. "You still do have some fun out here in the middle of nowheres! Now let's go!"

"Not you," Sutherland said.

Defries and Jake hesitated, but they would not be put off. "Three paddles's better'n one, Owen," Jake said stubbornly. "We'll let you run cross country yourself if you've a mind to, but let us go downriver with you."

Sutherland said, "Go back to Ella, both of you, before Brodhead finds out and you're hunted, too!"

"We're going," Defries said, and stood like a tree in Sutherland's path. "Let's not waste time jawing, or we'll all be jailed!"

As if that decided it, Sutherland slapped Defries on the shoulder. As Sutherland got into the canoe, he rubbed Jake's head. Then, at the last moment, he pointed to the fort. "They're coming!"

Both Defries and Jake turned, but no one was coming.

Sutherland shot the canoe swiftly into the black water, leaving the others on shore. Defries cursed and Jake cried out in dismay, but to no avail.

"I don't know what will come of this, men"—Sutherland used the word "men" as a compliment to Little Jake—"but watch over Ella, and don't let on you were involved in my escape. Farewell, and don't fear."

Jake yelled, "There's a letter from Ma in your pack . . . Pa!"

Sutherland grinned, aware now of how blind he had been to what a fine lad Jake was, how much like a son he was.

"Take care of . . . your ma, Jakie, son, and keep her from worrying!"

Then Sutherland was far from shore, out into the surge of swift waters. Soon he would be in the Ohio, rushing along in the canoe like a twig in a torrent. It would take skillful paddling and vigilance to get downriver, and there was no time to lose.

His thoughts went to Evangeline, and then back to the many Moravian Indians brutally killed by borderers near Philadelphia years ago. He could not have prevented that, but he would not be stopped until he prevented this one massacre, at least.

chapter **7**

GNADENHUTTEN

As she turned from washing the wooden steps of the chapel, Evangeline looked across the central yard and saw the Delawares who some days ago had rescued them, returning with the handsome Niko-lota in the lead.

All morning Evangeline had been cleaning the interior of the chapel, moving outside later as the weather turned warm and sunny, a perfect day. In the little while they had been back, the Moravian Indians had done much to set to rights the neglect the village had suffered in the past months, and there was much left to do.

The row of log cabins past which Niko-lota's proud warriors strode had been cobwebbed and musty, some overrun by mice and squirrels, others damaged by the harsh winter weather. In each, women and children were sweeping, washing, and scouring in the hope that by springtime all the other inhabitants would return from their exile at Sandusky. Perhaps even their four missionaries, ordered away to Detroit by the British, would also come home again.

Home, Evangeline thought with satisfaction. This was a good place, and it would prosper in the times of peace to come. She wiped her brow and smiled as Niko-lota approached, rifle in hand, a cloth bag slung over his shoulder. The others in his party divided up to visit with the Moravians, some of them going to the fields to watch the standing corn being gathered, others about to enter the squared-log chapel, wanting to climb up to the white belfry and play there like children. Evangeline firmly stopped them, saying to their confusion that the chapel must remain clean. Disappointed, they grumbled and left.

Niko-lota, however, was pleased to stay with Evangeline, and she guessed it was not simply because she reminded him of his dead sister. She welcomed him and said he might have a meal with them that evening, and that he would also be welcome to attend their meeting in the chapel afterward.

Niko-lota smiled and said, in Shawnee, "Do not be offended if I gladly accept your food, but not your faith . . . yet it would please me to listen from outside as you sing the magic chants that you praying Indians are so famous for."

She, too, smiled, saying, "Magic, indeed—the holy magic of our Savior, who has blessed His praying Indians with sacred music of the soul."

Niko-lota took something from the bag on his shoulder, and to Evangeline's surprise it was a pretty purple velvet dress.

"I traded with some warriors going north—they were passing through and needed some tobacco for the trail." He must have seen the questioning doubt in her eyes as she wondered whose dress this had been. But he said no more, holding it out for her to take as gift.

Evangeline's heart raced, and she wiped her hands on her apron, carefully taking the beautiful dress, holding it against her and seeing how much Niko-lota, too, admired it. She wanted to ask what was the truth of how he had acquired it, and please, God, let him not have murdered for it. But before she could voice the question, he anticipated it.

"This Indian does not kill women—but I did not ask the warrior where it came from."

She did not know what to say, but had to admit to herself that it was probably taken in an attack somewhere on the frontier. Her hands shook a little as she held it out, wanting so much to accept it, but afraid of the truth. Did a woman lie dead somewhere? Or perhaps it *had* been traded for, or—

"Oh, Niko-lota!" She released a sigh and smiled at him. "You do me honor with this gift. . . ." That was all she had to say, and he nodded slowly.

"You are a fine woman, Evangeline, and one day you should be a mother."

Just then, the two children she had been caring for, Christoph and Maria, came running up, babbling that the Delawares had brought maple sugar and toys. The boy showed off a blue spinning top and a handful of marbles, and the girl had a dirty doll with yellow hair that she already loved dearly. Evangeline managed to smile, but again she wondered where these had come from. Although she would not say anything to spoil the children's fun— they deserved it after such a hard and lonely winter at Sandusky—she could not express happiness that she did not feel in her troubled heart. How these were trying times, when even a child's toy spoke of death!

Niko-lota again guessed her mind. "There can be no evil in their joy with those things, woman. Do not trouble your soul with dark thoughts."

He had seen much of war and killing. He was hardened, practical; he knew how to take pleasure in the moment, before it was gone. As she bade farewell to Niko-lota, who went off to join the men working in the fields, Evangeline knew she loved him, for the good and the courage that was in him. The two children were scampering along after the war chief, and he laughed and cavorted with them as though he were totally innocent, and not a man alone in the world, whose own family had died of fever and left him with only the company of the fighting men at his back.

Evangeline looked at the purple dress and then let her eyes rove over the tranquil scene of Gnadenhutten. She loved this place with all her heart . . . the chapel, so fine with its fresh-painted belfry aglow in the sunlight, and the mission house beside it. Both were stoutly made and larger than any village house or church on the white man's frontier. Whites built blockhouses, and the Moravians built chapels.

She saw the youngest Indian children playing with hoops and balls while older ones, dressed in white man's shirts, skirts, and breeches, carried water, chased stock, fed pigs, and cut firewood. A blacksmith's hammer rang out as he repaired a grate for someone's stove, and an old man was sharpening scythes for tomorrow's cutting of the standing wheat. At the far end of the village a man and some boys were making barrels, their wooden mallets thudding rapidly. It would be good when the white missionaries returned to read sermons and to lead them in prayer, but for now Abraham could give the readings from the pulpit, and the choir would restore their weary spirits in the evenings.

Once she learned the German well enough, Evangeline would also join the choir and sing those lovely hymns that Indians thought so magical. She recalled the story about Indians on the warpath years ago, about to attack a town of Moravian Germans, when the singing of the choir enthralled and frightened them all at once, and the raiders slipped off into the night, awestruck, sure the village was protected by powerful spirits.

Evangeline sighed and put the dress on the iron railing

of the chapel steps. She resumed her washing and thought that Gnadenhutten was indeed protected by good spirits. Here in the wilderness, between white and red warriors, feared and misunderstood by both, mistrusted and suspected by both, often abused and robbed by both, the Moravians had yet renewed themselves in their promised land.

They were at last home again, the war was almost over, and their missionaries soon would return to shepherd them. In her mind she heard the lovely singing of the choir, and she eagerly anticipated the evening in the chapel. Before long it would be Easter, the time of resurrection! And how they would sing!

She knew the meaning but could not pronounce the words of a German hymn sung by the flock back in January, when they were in exile. It was Epiphany, the celebration of the coming of the three wise men to Baby Jesus, and the choir had sung so beautifully, "Jesu, rufe mich."

Jesus, call me! Evangeline worked as she whispered, "Jesus, call me to do Thy work. Thy will be done, Lord."

Her thoughts were in Shawnee, and they gave her strength. She thought of Jesus in the stable, and hummed the hymn that she loved so well:

> Not Jerusalem,
> Rather Bethlehem
> Gave us that
> which enriches us;
> Not Jerusalem.

> Honored Bethlehem,
> Pleasant I esteem;
> From thee springeth
> What gain bringeth;
> Honored Bethlehem.

She started to sing softly, trying to approximate the German words, thinking of the holy birth, of the rebirth and the resurrection, and it gave her hope, gave her strength.

> *Jesu, rufe mich!*
> *Jesus, call me!*

•   •   •

Entellus Greyson felt as though he had truly penetrated the great northwestern wilderness. It had been two hard days riding along the Mingo Trail, through the hilly forest of giant oak and hemlock, surrounded by shadow, without even a bird's song in the brooding, dark forest. Indian country. Dangerous, silent, and every step deeper and deeper, approaching the enemy.

He was excited, but he trusted in his brave companions, for they were generous with food and equipment, courteous to a fault, and pleased enough at how he took to their ways. They were tough, and poked fun at outsiders in the reckless, carefree manner of such men, yet they came to respect him, especially after someone told around a campfire of how well the Marylanders had fought against the British. It had been Captain Charles Bilderback, to Greyson's surprise, who spoke so warmly of the Maryland regiments. Bilderback had heard it all from a brother with General Wayne, and there was no man like his brother for understanding the truth. The brother had called the Marylanders "men," good to have at one's shoulder. Bilderback's apparent wanting to like Greyson because his brother favored Marylanders brought Greyson into close company with many others.

Night camps were cold, without fires, lest they be detected. Food, too, was cold, except when they stopped for a quick fire near a stream now and again. No one complained. Every man pushed himself to the limit through hard country, overly rich in rock and cliffs, it seemed. The only man Entellus Greyson mistrusted was Mike Grub, but even he seemed willing to keep out of the way, although it was obviously expected that Greyson would do the same. Apparently Colonel Williamson had warned Grub off, knowing that abuse of a Continental colonel could not go unpunished by the militia's commanding officer. So there was an uneasy truce between Greyson and Grub. As for Williamson, he was accommodating enough, and even took the trouble to explain the ways of Indian fighting as he and Greyson rode side by side.

"We don't aim to let 'em surround us by surprise, so we'll hit hard, run right through 'em, and out the other side. While they're looking for us here, we'll be there, and when they come after us, we'll ride back through 'em going the other way!

"We'll move too fast for 'em to muster enough riders to run us down, and we'll stay only long enough in a Injun town to loot it and burn it down. Last thing you want is to let 'em start chasing you home, picking at your flanks, biting like wolves until they've bled you and forced you off of your trail. If they do get enough men to cut us off, then we split up into small parties and scatter, everybody knowing which way to go, everybody with a captain who has a map of the trails back to Pitt. . . ."

But the raiders really did not expect trouble from any large bands of Indians, for it was too early in the year, and the Indians were not ready to fight.

"First off, we got to destroy their forage, got to ruin any feed they can get at, and stop 'em establishing supply bases for raids into our country." Williamson gave that a moment to sink in, then added, "Every hut we come across, every patch of corn, every head of Injun stock has got to go down. It's been a mean winter for 'em, and they'll suffer more if we can make it that much meaner."

A little while passed, leather saddles creaking, horses

blowing, the trail rising and falling, and the wind soft for
early March. Greyson began to think how rich and fine this
unspoiled country was, how well it would serve his superiors. He had taken calculations with surveying equipment
to mark the latitude, and he knew this land was all well
within his company's claims.

"First business is to look in on them praying Injuns at
the Moravian town on the Tuscarawas." Williamson
glanced to see whether Greyson had any reply.

He did. "They're peaceful, of course." No answer.
"Have you ever heard a Moravian choir, Colonel? No?
Well, it's as if angels had come down from on high, and
their very music could lift one to the heavens. I heard them
at Bethlehem, near Philadelphia, in company with General
Washington. . . ." He enjoyed the memory, the glory of that
brief interlude to war. "Ah, Colonel, that was music! Just
like angels!"

"No doubt," Williamson said dryly. "Moravians'd make
better angels than people."

"All our officers loved their music."

"And horses love their corn . . . white horses and Injun
horses, both."

Greyson understood, more or less, and knew it was no
use to talk to Williamson about a stranger's religion, especially a religion that preached nonresistance. Unlike Williamson's Calvinist deity, a god of revenge and crusaders,
the Moravian god was gentle, merciful, all-loving. Still,
Greyson wondered whether Williamson had ever heard a
Moravian choir, and what it would do to him if he did.

A Moravian choir sang that evening in the chapel at
Gnadenhutten, and outside, sitting at a campfire with his
war party, Niko-lota remembered.

He remembered his sister, Aleta, and how she had sung
with her choir of whites and reds, and how the music had

made him flutter inside and tingle, soothing him, like a balm for the soul. He remembered the high-pitched voices that called to the spirit world, and he knew there was a mighty power in them, a power for good—perhaps too much good for this world. He remembered the organ music, the choir of trombones in the great belfry at Bethlehem, and the procession of singers as they went to and from the buildings of the Moravian town.

Through it all he saw his sister's face, heard her speaking to him, pleading with him to forgive her, to understand her, pleading with him not to go on the warpath. Aleta, so young and so good. She had died young, of white man's disease, a prisoner of stupid whites who had meant to help her. Even in helping Indians, whites did wrong, most of them. Now there was nothing else for it but for whites and Indians to kill each other, and there was no hope. Niko-lota of the Delawares well knew his people would lose and lose and keep on losing until the Indian spirits abandoned this country and the manitous lost their power.

There was only one white man he really trusted, and that was Owen Sutherland—the one the Ottawas named Donoway, meaning "fearless in the flames," honoring his courage when they tortured him as a prisoner. It was said that when he was adopted by the Ottawas, Donoway's white blood had been washed away in the ceremony. Perhaps. Donoway had spared Niko-lota's life in battle many years ago, and in turn Niko-lota had saved Sutherland's. Neither owed the other anything—nothing but trust, one fighting man to another. Donoway loved the Indians, but he had chosen his side in this war, and now was an enemy, like all the rest of the whites. Except the white Moravians. They were deluders, but they meant well.

The singing rose to a crescendo, lofty and beautiful and as enthralling as any Delaware sacred song to the manitous. Niko-lota closed his eyes, the fire hot and bright in his face. He forgot his men, forgot his memories, and drifted away on that haunting, enchanting song. He did not understand, never would understand, but he believed the medicine of the praying Indians was strong, and that though they were surrounded by enemies, white and red, they would come through somehow, and they would thrive.

At that moment, Niko-lota of the Lenni Lenape, war chief and leader of the best men his nation had yet to offer, knew what tranquillity was, knew what love was, and prayed to his own Great Spirit that one day the lovely Evangeline might share his lodge and bring forth his sons, in a world without war.

At that moment, Owen Sutherland was moving in the dark, past the white men's camp, slipping through the forest close enough to see the men around the fires, sleeping by their rifles.

He had expected they would take this, the Mingo Trail, the easiest and safest route to the Moravian towns. It was high ground most of the way, with many a view over the surrounding countryside. Once he was ahead of them they would never catch him, but the toll on his body had been heavy. He was utterly exhausted, bruised and cut by the rigors of his dash. Yet he had finally caught them, and they had been mounted and moving fast. He had taken short-cuts, rocky and difficult. He had run for twenty hours straight, and now he was passing them. By morning he would be another few miles down the trail, and he would reach Gnadenhutten first.

He moved past, not worried about being detected, for these men were at best good hunters, not Indian scouts or rangers.

They did not hear him, and he ran back onto the trail. His chest ached, every breath an agony. His legs were numb, and his heart pounded sorely. He longed to rest, but the moon was half full, and that was enough light for him. He would go on. He had been over this ground many times through the years, and he knew there were no lodges or villages between here and Gnadenhutten. He would get through, but with no time to spare.

When the singing ended, Niko-lota's men went to sleep in a nearby barn, and he watched alone as the Moravians filed off to their own quarters.

In the dimness, carrying a lantern, Evangeline saw him and stopped, letting the others pass. Standing ten feet apart, they gazed at each other, she so young but already so full of life's experience, he nearly forty, with the loss of a family in his heart.

To her surprise and embarrassment, Evangeline was joined by Abraham, the kind and wise elder, who had just come out of the chapel. He, too, stared at Niko-lota, as if wondering what would come of this growing bond between Evangeline and the Delaware.

The other Moravians were gone, the last lights in the chapel snuffed, when Abraham spoke quietly. "My nephew of the Delawares, this child-woman is a Christian. She cannot live the life of a warrior's squaw; she cannot and still be a Christian."

Neither Evangeline nor Niko-lota answered, though their eyes told of their love. A moment passed, then the voices of young women singing wafted over from Evangeline's house, stirring her, breaking the spell.

She glanced at the kind face, lined and wrinkled, of Abraham, and then at Niko-lota's face, angular and full of inner strength. Both men were Delawares by blood, both great leaders, both fearlessly committed to what they believed. And she was almost a full-grown woman . . . a Christian woman, and Niko-lota did not believe, never would believe.

Abraham touched her shoulder, and she turned her eyes from Niko-lota, who drew back, bidding her good night. She looked at Niko-lota then and saw him smile, man to woman, and she knew, at that moment, that she no longer was a child. With a thrill of understanding, she smiled back at him, a tear coming to her eye as the magic singing of her people called her away.

"God be with you," she said to him. "And may you, by His will, see the light of truth."

She began to depart with Abraham when Niko-lota said, "May the Great Spirit show you the right path, Shawnee woman, and may you walk it as a true Indian."

Evangeline moved quickly away, her breath short in the chilly air as she whispered a prayer for strength, saying again and again, "Jesus, call me . . . Jesus, call me! Please, Jesus, call me!" And the words were in her Shawnee language.

When the others were asleep, Evangeline slipped downstairs into the common room and there lit a lamp from a taper ignited in the fire. In her hand was a package, which she carefully opened: the velvet dress, radiantly purple in the lamplight.

She moved toward a window, where the light splashed and wobbled and gave back her image. She let the dress hang in front of her. It was so fine, so rich. Few Indians could ever hope to have one like it, and no Moravian Indian would ever be willing to wear it, for the vanity and pride it revealed.

For just a moment, though, in secret, Evangeline saw her beauty, let her vanity go free, and in the glimmer of reflected lamplight was the woman that Niko-lota had called forth.

Then the spell broke as someone upstairs called to her. It was a beautiful dress, but soon she would make better use of the material, perhaps for some baby quilts or for a nice bonnet or two. For tonight, though, it was a gorgeous velvet dress, and it made her a startlingly beautiful woman —if only for tonight.

Before dawn, Evangeline was the first one up, carrying milking pails on a yoke over her shoulders, making for the barn where the cows were, and where the Delawares had slept. She was tense, excited, having scarcely slept the night before, thinking about Niko-lota and how he stirred her within. She wanted to see him, though she did not know why.

She carried a lantern, and her shawl was wrapped close against the night air. She expected the Delawares to hear her coming; alert as ever, they would meet her at the door with jokes and friendly words. Niko-lota and his men would be the first to partake of the warm milk—she would see to that. Men of war though they might be, she respected them, and she prayed for their mortal souls.

When she got to the barn door and drew it open, she was surprised at how still it was within. The milk cow mooed in greeting, but the barn was unusually quiet, as if—

Her heart thudded as she realized the truth. They were gone! Niko-lota and his men had left in the night. Had they sensed danger?

Evangeline suddenly felt afraid and vulnerable. Her people were alone now, unprotected. Even loyalist Indians could be a danger to them, for many hated them as Christians and turncoats. It would have been good to have these friendly Delawares here, at least until the white missionaries were allowed to return.

That was not the only reason she wanted Niko-lota here, of course, and Evangeline knew it. She loved him, but she did not understand that love. She wanted him near, but now he was gone back to war, back to the terror that destroys a man's mortal soul. And when he returned from the killing trail, she feared she would not know him. Shuddering, she moved in a daze toward the waiting, chewing cow.

"Pray God," she whispered, "that he does not return with another gift for me, for never will I be sure what he did to get it."

Owen Sutherland was running down the trail, the very last of his strength driving him on, keeping him going. His legs were knotted into iron, his stomach taut and retching with exhaustion. He hardly sweated, because his body fluids were used up, and he was overheated even though winter was yet on the land.

He drove on, knowing that in just a few miles now, down a long, rugged slope, he would be in the village of Gnadenhutten. He would warn Abraham, and the old man would believe him. There were still some hours left before the raiders arrived, and the Moravians would need every minute to make good their escape. He was worried that the whites would keep going after them, not being satisfied to burn the houses and destroy the crops, but wanting scalps as trophies. They had to get away! Had to run! He had to run! Hard snow pounded his moccasins, branches tore at his skin and clothes. His rifle weighed him down, his claymore weighed him down, his very body weighed him down. Yet he must run, and they must run, and there was no time.

It may be that the whites had found his trail, knew they were discovered, and even now were pushing their mounts to a gallop to catch him. At any moment they might come thundering behind, bearing down on him from the last turn in the trail. Then he would have to fight them, maybe kill them.

On he ran, the blood pounding in his head, his lungs aching as if they would burst, his heart deathly sore from exertion. He was no longer a young man, but he had made this brutal run as if he were. Few could have matched his stamina; none but an Indian could have found the way through the forest at night. Two days and two nights of wilderness running—and how many miles?

On and on, and soon he would be there, though it almost killed him. For the first time ever, Owen Sutherland knew he had pushed himself too hard, knew this run might indeed bring him to the brink of death, a place he knew only too well—

Suddenly there was movement. His heart leapt, senses saying there were others in the trees, many others, and he sprinted, legs somehow lifting, arms pumping. There were others, and they were coming after him. They were close. He ran even harder, leaping over fallen logs, stretching his legs, lifting, stumbling, hearing grunts and rapid footfalls behind. They were very fast, and he was not fast enough. They would catch him. He had to fight. Now he had to turn and fight!

Around a bend he skidded to a stop, yanked off his rifle, and readied it like a club. Instantly the first pursuer was there, rounding the corner. Sutherland could hardly see through the panting rush of exhaustion that gripped him, but he raised the rifle, unloaded as it was, and timed his swing. The first one would go down hard.

The man was upon him, war club upraised. The rifle came in, butt first— And then Sutherland held off, astonished at what he saw.

"Niko-lota!"

"Donoway!" The war club chopped down. Sutherland could not block it.

"Ah!" A terrible agony coursed through him, his heart tearing and thundering, and he fell to his knees, half seeing other warriors coming up, their eyes wild, tomahawks raised . . . and the rest he did not know.

chapter **8**

VENGEANCE

The white raiders took a different trail, a round-about approach that brought them in north of Gnadenhutten. When less than a mile off they divided into two groups, one of fewer than twenty men, led by Williamson and Greyson, intending to confront the laborers in the fields, the remainder proceeding directly into the village.

Greyson was relieved when, ten minutes later, Williamson dismounted and stepped casually into the open fields, where some forty Indian men and boys were working happily at the corn. They were dressed much the same as any white settlers. Williamson raised his hand in the sign of peace, and the Moravian elders smiled politely and came to greet him and the other whites. In the late winter sunlight, the setting was tranquil and correct, thought Greyson, as he listened to Williamson speak.

"It has been too long since the white chieftain at Fort Pitt has welcomed Moravian Indians into his house, and in these times it is good that our Christian brothers parley with us."

The Indians glanced around at one another, some grinning, some uncertain, but Williamson's words were smooth and fair, and when he promised rich bounties of presents and food for these people if they came with him to Pitt, it was obvious he made an impression.

"Come with us now to your village, and we will talk more of it. The commander at Fort Pitt has sent me as his emissary, and my words are his, his promises my command." He gestured in the direction of the village, half a mile through the trees, saying, "Leave your tools here, for it will take but a little time to tell of my superior's promises, and you may come back to finish cutting your corn."

Greyson thought he had never seen Williamson look so benevolent, so kind. The Marylander wondered what was the actual plan. Would the Indians be forced to destroy their own corn in return for food from Pitt? Would the harvested corn be stashed secretly? Would there be trouble when Williamson said the corn must be ruined to prevent Indian raiding parties from using it?

These things went through his mind as they set off together toward the village, the whites grim but calm, the Indians—or at least some of them—in high spirits to think they were again in the good graces of Fort Pitt's commander. A few years back a delegation of their people had been welcomed at Pitt, treated very generously, and sent home with many presents of good will. Some in the group evidently remembered that occasion and anticipated its being repeated.

Greyson rode at the head of the party, beside Williamson, and he thought that this enterprise would surely be a success. Once these unarmed Indians saw the strength of the rest of the force at their village, they would not dare to protest when terms for destroying the corn harvest were explained. By the next day, the whites surely would be dashing westward, on the way to attack hostile villages, while these innocent Moravians were sent back east to Pitt for temporary safekeeping.

Again he thought of how good this land was, and of

how well the Moravians had nurtured and cultivated it. All around were prodigious fields of corn, newly turned vegetable patches awaiting the spring seed, firewood standing in neat cords along the way. There was even a sizable industry in timber and sawn lumber being conducted here. Greyson recalled having heard that the first water-pipe system in America had been made by Moravians farther east, using hemlock cut right here and shipped down to them. He was sure that when his company's claims were recognized by Congress, these enterprising Moravians would be made welcome to stay and develop the land.

Greyson was in good spirits as he rode into the village, marking how clean and orderly and well made everything was. Like the men in the fields, the women and children in the crowd up ahead were dressed like whites, their hair combed and clean, their gowns as crisp, bonnets as white as any settlement's women could make them.

But in the next moment, Greyson saw that something was very wrong. Glancing to one side, he saw two bodies lying near one of the cabins—an Indian man and a woman. Apparently they were unseen by the laughing, joking Moravians coming in. Greyson's heart raced. He saw that Williamson, too, was aware of the corpses, for the man observed them and simply looked away without remark or emotion. In the next instant, the women and children saw their men approach, and they gave a great howl, a wail of chilling fear, and tried to push out through a ring of frontiersmen, who brought rifles to bear and forced them to stay huddled together.

Abraham's alarmed voice was louder than the cries of his followers: "In the name of the Lord, what is this, Colonel Williamson?" His hands were held out, and he hurried to catch up with the white commander, who did not look back, but instead spurred his horse toward the main body of his men at the center of the village.

"Colonel!" Abraham shouted, and began to run for-

ward, young men and boys overtaking him as they sprinted
into the midst of their women, embracing, asking questions, protesting uselessly. Fear gripped them all.

Greyson's horse was acting up, aware of the tension and
danger. Greyson disliked this show of force, so obviously
unnecessary with these people. He trotted after Williamson, who, still mounted, was ordering Mike Grub and
Charles Bilderback to organize the imprisonment of the
Moravians in their chapel and in the mission house that
stood next door.

Greyson said loudly, "Colonel, is there need for this,
and why in God's name were those people killed back
there?"

Williamson glanced at him, looked away, and continued
telling Grub and Bilderback what to do. Then he casually
replied to the Marylander, "These are Injuns, Colonel, and
they are all dangerous."

"But they are Christians, sir!"

"Damn it, sir! So, too, are the loyalists Christians! And
the British army's Christian, and the French Canadian
scouts are Christians, and they are our worst enemies!"

Just then, the furious shout of a white man rose over the
clamor of the Moravians, and everyone turned to see one
of the raiders come striding out of Evangeline's house, her
velvet dress raised high.

"Bilderback!" he yelled. "This was your woman's
dress!"

Charles Bilderback let out a shriek of horror and ran to
the dress, snatching it away, trembling with sorrow and
horror as he crushed it to himself. Abraham stepped forward to Williamson and firmly said the dress had been a
gift, given after having been traded for, and that they had
no idea how it had been come by.

"Colonel Williamson, surely you know we would
never—"

Bilderback shrieked again and raced across the courtyard, right through the Indians, pummeling and kicking in his madness, and went for old Abraham's throat, throwing the Indian to the ground and leaping on him while not a white man moved, and not an Indian dared protest in the face of those rifle muzzles.

Only Greyson reacted, leaping from his horse and dragging the powerful frontiersman off.

"No! Don't do this, Captain! Don't! Surely they're innocent!"

Bilderback was frothing with insane hatred, and he fought back Greyson, breaking away and attacking the stunned Abraham again.

"Call him off!" Greyson yelled at Williamson. "This is a crime! This is murder! Call him off!"

The angry voices of the frontiersmen sounded in objection, and Williamson obviously knew their desires. He would not stop Bilderback, who was bent on avenging the destruction of his family.

Greyson cried out in his own fury and again threw himself at the frontiersman, again wrenching him off, and this time getting up quickly enough to draw his sword when the man made to renew the attack. Without hesitation, Bilderback yanked out his tomahawk.

Greyson yelled, "By the authority of Congress, I command you to stand fast, Captain! Replace your tomahawk, or you'll be court-martialed!"

"And you," said the voice of Mike Grub, "will be dead!"

Wary of the sword point, but heedless of any consequences, Bilderback began to circle, and the place fell hushed. The frontiersman wanted blood.

"No man stands between me and revenge! God-given duty! No man stands between—"

The arc of the sword was like a glimmer of light, and as if by magic the tomahawk fell to the ground, cut in half.

Bilderback's eyes widened. Greyson knew that even this would not stop him. He would attack until he was dead, as soon he must be.

Perhaps Williamson knew the same, for in a sudden movement he drove his horse between the combatants. "Captain! Stand fast!" Bilderback seemed still ready to strike, but he wavered. "Hold, Charles! Hear me! You'll have your chance!"

Bilderback stood shaking with venomous hatred, and Williamson said angrily, "Colonel Greyson, you have no authority here but are under my command, and should you dare disobey me, you will be charged with mutiny and, if need be, punished on the spot!"

Greyson was willing to risk it. "Keep your men from harming anyone, and you'll have no trouble with me, sir!"

"No trouble?" The horse neighed and reared as Williamson sprang down to tower over the Marylander. "I'll have no trouble from you, one way or the other!"

Surprising Greyson, Mike Grub came in from behind, as if anticipating his commander's wishes, and threw his arms about him. Williamson snatched away the sword and hurled it to the ground, where the distressed Abraham was sitting up, recovering, hands on his injured throat. His people rushed to his side, women weeping, men pale with worry.

Williamson bellowed: "Do not force me to place you under arrest, Colonel Greyson, and do not force me to court-martial *you*!"

As Grub held Greyson, Williamson turned and ordered his men to herd the Indian men into the chapel, women into the mission house. Greyson could do nothing, and he realized he would be of no use to anyone if he were tied up. He ceased to struggle against the huge Mike Grub and, at Williamson's command, finally was released.

Williamson said savagely, "Keep your eastern nose out

of this, Colonel, and all will be well."

Greyson made no reply, but felt anger and fear all at once, knowing these Indians were in mortal danger.

A half hour later, after the Indians were locked up, he was allowed to stay and watch while Williamson mustered his men, on foot, in three ranks. Williamson sat on his horse and addressed the militia.

"We have two possibilities, gentlemen, and as there are supporters of both amongst you, I do not wish to go against the general opinion!" He looked smug, but also cruel as he stood in his stirrups and went on. "Death, or deportation en masse back to Fort Pitt, where they will likely be imprisoned as conspirators, the evidence of collaboration in raids being profuse in every household here. Make your decision, gentlemen! All in favor of sparing their lives and taking them back to Pitt—and as a result aborting our campaign to strike westward, of course—all in favor, step forward one pace!"

Greyson prayed the men would be merciful. There were a hundred and twenty of them here now, the rest off on forays or guarding the base camp back at the Ohio. He knew they would be divided, but how deeply he could not guess. There was a long pause, as men looked at one another, few certain what to do. Then a young fellow stepped boldly forward, and there was a grumble of anger, mutterings that he was a coward, Indian-lover, or worse. But then another stepped forward, and another, and then in groups of three and four they stepped forward, and Greyson's hope suddenly rose.

Some men were courageous enough, humane enough. . . .

Then Mike Grub's voice was heard. "Well, Captain Bilderback, I guess these red murderers'll be let off, and your poor wife and children don't matter!"

Bilderback was at the front of the ranks and turned to

face the men, his face livid, his eyes black with fury.

Although a few more stepped forward anyway, there were not many. When Williamson made the count of those for mercy, there were only eighteen, including Greyson, who called out that he be included, although he stood off to the side.

Eighteen for mercy, the rest for killing. Greyson felt as if he were in some mad dream. They could not murder harmless women and children! They must not!

"So be it!" Williamson cried out, a scowl on his face, and he dismissed the men to have dinner while he dismounted and advanced with Grub and Bilderback to the chapel, to tell Abraham about the impending doom.

No matter what the risk, Greyson would not let this happen. He ran forward, though unarmed, and blocked the way. No words were spoken at first, until Williamson said, "We're a free country now, Colonel, and nobody'll tell us how to fight our wars! This is our war, not yours, so go back to the tidewater, and keep away from us, for to me you're no better than a Britisher, trying to rule us from afar!"

"It's murder, that's all it is, and you'll be punished for it! Think again, Colonel, in the name of God, man! Think again!"

Bilderback said with a low hiss, "The men've voted, and there's no going back now!"

"You can't—" Greyson began, but Williamson made a motion, and Grub and Bilderback grabbed at him. He fought back, fists flying, but he had no chance.

When it was over, Greyson was battered and bloodied and hauled off to the encampment, which was already knee-deep in plunder from the cabins. Men cursed and jeered at him as he was thrown down by his captors near a well at the edge of the village. Alone, beaten, and helpless, he lay there, watching Williamson enter the chapel, the door closing with finality behind him. Greyson knew that even if he gave his life in the attempt, there was nothing he could do to change what was about to happen.

Niko-lota knelt at the side of Owen Sutherland, the mighty Donoway, once thought invincible, and now pale and unconscious upon a bed of balsam branches next to the campfire.

Donoway, lying near death, on a lonely trail. This, Niko-lota well knew, was how many a giant, white and red, met his end in frontier warfare. Many a solitary hero was shot from ambush, many a forest warrior died alone, often of wounds suffered in single combat with another fighter, far from any lodge, unseen. Men disappeared in the wilderness, and it was not unusual. At least, should Donoway die, someone would be here with him to tell of his fate, and to send news to his lodge and his squaw.

Sutherland lay ashen-faced, breathing fast and shallow, and he was very cold. His eyes were partly open, but there was no sight, no understanding in them. If he were not yet gone, his spirit was surely wandering in the borderlands of death. Niko-lota was deeply sorry, for he loved Donoway, a man he might have fought to the death in pitched battle, but a man he would not have wanted to kill.

One of the younger warriors, an aggressive and hard youth, came alongside Niko-lota and looked down, eyes glittering. "So this is he of whom I have heard? The one my father spoke of, the hero of the whites, and the greatest trader of them all—Donoway!" He laughed softly. "It seems you scared him to death, Niko-lota. . . ."

His laugh was cut short as Niko-lota sprang to his feet. "You speak like a boy, and not a man! Do not mock him, for you and your playmates will never again see his like!" He turned away from the surprised and confused young warrior and looked down at Sutherland. "All the greatest are dying, ours and theirs. A day is passing, and the world will never be the same when the last of them are gone."

He knelt at Sutherland's side. "Donoway, I would that one last time I might have spoken with you, have told my stories and heard yours." He touched the man's hand, feeling how icy it was. "A great heart! And a great heart, too, must stop its beating."

"Just the same," said the now less-intrusive voice of the warrior behind him, "you may claim the scalp, for it is your right! You would have killed him, and so the trophy is yours!"

Niko-lota did not turn, but felt the sad burden weigh him down. "Why are you here, Donoway? Why have you come here, running like a man pursued by devils? What has driven you to run until your heart might burst?"

Niko-lota did not know the answer, but should Donoway die here, he would go to his Maker a whole man, and no one would dare take his scalp.

Near evening, Entellus Greyson withdrew to the nearby well and pulled up a bucket of water to slake his thirst and wash his own blood from his buff uniform. The Moravians, he knew, had been left to pray and ready themselves for death. They would be killed in the morning—each one beaten to death with clubs and hammers. They would die in their chapel and mission house.

As he drank from a dipper, Greyson could not forget the strange look in Williamson's eyes when the man had addressed his troops, saying that the Moravians would be allowed the night to pray. There had been something there that Greyson had not expected would ever show through . . . something human. Perhaps even moved, Williamson apparently had been shaken by his meeting with Abraham and the Indian elders.

While men like Grub were laughing and drinking, dividing the booty from the emptied houses, others, including Williamson, were somber and sat quietly, as if they, too, felt this was a strange dream. Greyson put down the dipper, rinsing his mouth and spitting out blood from his cracked lip. He looked across the campground at Charles Bilderback. The man was hunched over, sitting on the ground, his wife's dress beside him. In one hand was a barrel-maker's mallet, and he kept slowly striking it again and again into the earth.

Greyson did not like the looks of this unhappy creature, and decided to take a little walk, passing a sentry at the entrance of a path to the forest. The early evening was soft, the sky deep blue, the first stars twinkling on. It did not feel cold. It did not feel like anything. Perhaps if it had been bitter cold, Greyson still would not have felt it. He wondered whether he should get his horse and simply ride out. But that would not do. If nothing else, he was determined to be a witness for Congress, a representative of the Continental Army, and he would report all that had occurred when the time came for an inquiry.

He walked a short distance along the trail, head bowed, heart heavy. He thought of Susannah Sutherland, and of how lovely she was. It was no wonder she was so fine, however, for her father was Owen Sutherland, who had been right all along. He had known what would happen, but Greyson had not believed it possible. Greyson had thought Sutherland too jaded by years of frontier war.

After all, this had not been in the plan, and surely Colonel Brodhead had not wanted this. This was unthinkable— a nightmare, but it was real. And no one who could—

Someone was coming down the path! He heard the light sound of laughter, and children's voices. People were approaching, surely Indians who did not suspect the peril.

He hurried forward, glancing back through the dusk to make sure the nearest guard was not yet alerted. A woman's pretty voice began to sing, answered by the voices of children chiming in:

Nicht Jerusalem,
Sondern Bethlehem
Hat bescheret
Was uns naehret;
Nicht Jerusalem.

"Stop!" he said, as loud as he dared. "Stop, there!
Please!" He ran forward, along the deepening dark of the
trail.

Werthes Bethlehem,
Du bist angenehm;
Aus dir kommet
Was mir frommet,
Werthes Bethlehem!

Greyson scrambled ahead, pushing aside branches, trip-
ping on rocks, slipping, all the while hearing that beautiful
hymn. He begged they would not be heard by the sentry.

Then he was upon them—a young Indian woman and
two children, carrying beeswax and honey in pails, and
all frightened by him, confused by his battered appearance. As the children cowered against the woman, who
stood her ground despite her fear, Greyson held out his
hands, imploring them to listen.

"Go no farther, please! Do you understand? Stay back!"

Evangeline spoke in English, her voice trembling. "I
know your words, but . . . but I do not understand, sir!"
The children huddled close to her, their eyes bright like
those of fawns, and she the doe protecting them.

His own voice hard to control, Greyson said, "There
are enemies, white enemies, and they have taken your
people—"

Evangeline gasped, hand to her mouth, dropping the

honey. In the next instant she made to run, but Greyson caught her by the arm.

"No! You must not!" He looked quickly at the children. "Send them back! They will be killed! Stay, children!"

"They speak no English. What are you saying? My people? Let me go!"

"No!" He held her arms painfully tight, and his throat was parched as he tried to tell her the horrible truth. "They are all to be killed!"

"No!" she almost screamed, and he feared the guard had heard it.

The children began edging away, ready to flee. Evangeline looked at them, and Greyson knew she must not let them go.

"Keep them here, I beg of you, woman! Keep them safe!"

Evangeline was quivering from head to foot. Now she grasped the truth only too well. The boy and girl were watching her, looking at the white man, glancing anxiously at the trail leading to the village.

"Hold them!" Greyson begged, himself shaking with fear. "They must not die! Trust me, please! You must not go!"

Evangeline said with great self-control, "We must go and look."

Greyson nodded. "From somewhere safe . . . the whites are everywhere around the village. Please do not let yourself be caught, too! I have tried, but I cannot stop what they mean to do."

Evangeline almost swooned, and Greyson held her up. With effort, she weakly told the children to take her hand, not to go to the village.

Within an hour they were on a rocky outcrop, looking down at the village from a distance, seeing the campfires of the white army on the common. The Moravians were singing—men in the chapel, women in the mission house —and they sang gloriously, as if they all were together in the same house of God, and they were worshiping as one. And from her hiding place, Evangeline sang, too, as if she were with them, as always she would be with them, forevermore.

Owen Sutherland was on a trail, running. It was a trail that never ended, a trail that led to doom, and on he ran, for he must reach the end, no matter if it meant his own death.

He ran, and could not feel his legs. He ran as if he were flying. He ran and ran, though there was no trail any longer, and the land was far below. Indian country, wintry and gray and still, as if dead. He ran, his breath easy, heart strong, and he knew where this race would end, where he had wanted it to end for a long time. He crossed the lake and rushed on, seeing the ice-choked straits of Detroit drift by, and on he went, past *habitant* cottages along the shore, past Indian lodges, poor and old, emptied now of their strong young men, visited instead with poverty and starvation.

The straits narrowed and turned northeast, and there was Fort Detroit, palisaded, proud, a British Union Jack flapping in the breeze. Now winter was over and the straits were busy with bateaux and canoes, rowboats and skiffs, and there were two warships at anchor, and when their cannon spoke, Indians broke from the fields around the fort. They attacked, were beaten back, and retreated until the fields were quiet again. Pontiac had been driven off, his attacks failing as ever they must, but there was blood, white man's and red man's blood, and war was going on as ever.

There, across from the fort and upstream, stood the seven great stones, black against the pebbled beach.

Among them were dancers, dancers feathered and painted, strange and ancient, and Sutherland did not know them, but he understood them.

The Singing Stones came to life as the wind changed and blew from the north, bringing weather and clouds and making a whistling sound through those great and sacred stones.

Valenya. The holy place of the Singing Stones. Valenya, Owen Sutherland's house . . . but there was no house, only his old lodge, of rude bark and hide, his home of twenty-five years ago. The lodge of his manhood's prime, the lodge where Mayla lay, waiting for his return. Mayla, daughter of the Ottawa, the people who had initiated him as a son. Mayla, dark and beautiful and full of love, and full of life—full with his unborn child. This was Valenya of his younger days, different days, if not better days. A time when a man knew his enemy, when war was between nations, the French and the British, and not a revolution, not a civil war of rebel American against loyalist American. Detroit, the straits, Valenya, the stones and the lodge, there on the shoreline, awaiting his return . . .

But he could not return to the old lodge, for it had vanished, and in its stead was the great house he and Ella had built. In the midst of the standing stones now was a smaller stone of granite, brought over from his native Scotland to mark the resting place of Mayla and his unborn child, killed by an enemy.

The great house stood as if it belonged there, like the stones, like the straits themselves. It was on a knoll, backed by bountiful fields and a rising hill that was Ella's orchard. There was the barn, filled with the harvest of a good year, so long ago.

Valenya, white and happy in the sunlight, filled with the cheerful music of Ella's spinet and the singing voices of the children—Jeremy, Benjamin, Susannah. A home, and a dream.

He was dreaming, remembering what was no more, hoping one day to bring it back and give it his life again. A dream of a home. Of Valenya. So far away . . . so far that a man would die trying to get there in time, before it was too late.

And Owen Sutherland was running, and running, until his mighty heart would break, but it was still too far, too far. . . .

Sutherland knew he was on his back, in the forest, and that dawn was breaking, but he did not at first know why he was here or why he felt so hopelessly weak.

He gazed up at the last of the stars, smelled the smoke as a morning breeze scuffed the embers of the campfire nearby. Where was he, and why? He tried to move, and his hand came to his face, and his fingers opened and closed, seemingly without his willing it. He felt drained, as if there were no blood, no vitality left in him. Had he fallen? Had he been shot? Who had brought him here?

He made an effort to roll onto his side and look at the camp, and his vision blurred. He remembered the dream, Valenya in the sunlight, the standing stones, and he remembered running and running on a trail that seemed never to end, a trail that would kill him. But he was yet alive.

Then it came back, with a shock that hurt physically, and he sat up, dizzy and angry and frightened for the endangered Moravians. Weakly, he tried to rise, but it was so difficult, and before he got far, someone was at his side, and he knew he had been captured.

He slumped to his knees, looking up at a silhouette, a familiar image against the lightening sky.

"Donoway, you yet live, my brother."

"Niko-lota! It is you!"

As Sutherland tried to keep from falling, the Delaware eased him back onto his bed. Sutherland could tell there were several others there, but how many?

After a moment, he said, in Delaware, "It seems you were quicker than I when we met, and that your war club found its mark." He felt at his head, which had been bruised when Niko-lota instinctively had swung at him.

The Delaware grinned, his teeth white in the dimness. "Indeed, Donoway, unlike you I had not the ability to stay my hand, though I slowed the blow as best I could." He chuckled softly. "You, brother, could have sent my head rolling down the trail had you not held back as you did. Do I once again owe you my life?"

Sutherland made no reply, his mind working, trying to think what he should do next. He presumed he had lost a day and a night, and the fear that thought gave him worked like some beast in the pit of his stomach. How could he tell Niko-lota about the whites advancing through this country? If he gave the whites away, then he would have betrayed them to the Indians, and their massacre would be on his head. For all that they were hard men, they were not evil, for the most part, and he would not give them away unless there were no other choice.

Niko-lota was speaking while he passed a bitter drink to Sutherland in a pewter cup. "But it was not my hand alone that felled you, Donoway."

Sutherland downed the stuff, wondering what Niko-lota meant. Then the Indian said, "I believe your heart has taken a blow, my brother, and that you have lain near death."

"How long?" The dismay of what he knew must have happened to him was overridden by his need to find out how much time had been lost. When Niko-lota told him he had been there since yesterday morning, a thousand questions stormed him, but how to ask them he did not know.

"Niko-lota, has there been fighting near here?"

The Delaware shook his head. "Where I and my men travel there will be fighting—but not here."

"Tell me . . ." He found it hard to breathe, but he forced the words out. "What do your scouts say about the trails hereabouts? Are they. . ."

He hesitated, for he simply could not reveal any hint that a white army was near. Yet if he did not, he would be deceiving Niko-lota, who perhaps had saved his life, perhaps stood between him and those young bucks at the Delaware's back. The light was better now, and Sutherland could see the surly, hateful faces of the younger warriors. No doubt they all would like to lift his hair.

Niko-lota said, with some mounting suspicion, that there was no trouble here. "But you have come, and perhaps you have brought trouble—or perhaps it is pursuing you, eh?"

"Perhaps." He thought, drinking the invigorating concoction. He was terribly weak, but he could travel some. He was just hours from Gnadenhutten, and he prayed there was yet time.

He made a bold attempt. "I am not a spy, and I did not come into this country looking to fight Indians, my brother."

A moment later, the reply came. "I trust your word."

"But I have come on an urgent mission, and I ask that you permit me to pass, immediately."

That was another matter. Niko-lota shook his head. "I have sworn an oath to the king, and therefore you are my prisoner, Donoway, and you will be brought to Detroit to await the end of the war."

Sutherland was desperate to tell the truth about the white army. He fought with the right and wrong of it. For a moment he even considered joining forces with these Delawares to attack and drive off the raiders, but there were too few Indians. Further, there was the slight chance that Williamson's troops might not attack the Moravians at all, and if he revealed their presence to these Delawares, then he would be responsible for the consequences.

Another thought came to him. "Take me to Gnadenhutten now. Accept it that I cannot betray my cause by telling
you why I am here, and I will face whatever the result. But
in the name of our friendship, take me there now, Niko-
lota, and do not waste a moment!"

"I will do so."

They mounted horses and hurried along the trail, seeing
not a sign of Williamson's passing. Barely able to stay
aboard his animal, Sutherland yet had hope, though he
knew there were approaches to the village other than this
trail, others more secret and better for attackers.

It was not long, however, before Sutherland's fears took
real form. From the descending ridge line, they could see
billowing smoke trailing from the distant forest. The fire
was in Gnadenhutten!

Niko-lota cried out in alarm and sped his horse along.
Sutherland, giving his animal free rein, followed hard behind, and the other Delawares came after.

The closer they got, down the steep, sliding trail, the
worse it looked. The village was hidden by trees, but there
was so much smoke that Sutherland knew many buildings
must be burning. He urged his mount on, along a winding
trail, past cornfields that were blackened—burned yesterday, apparently, the entire crop destroyed so that the Moravians would be without food this spring.

Then, as his horse rounded a curve and the village was
directly ahead, Sutherland saw that every building was in
flames. There was no one in sight, however, which gave
him hope that the Moravians had fled. His spirits lifted, but
his heart and chest ached. There was no sign of a fight, of
slaughter, of sudden attack in the night.

Niko-lota was riding ahead, into the center of the village, where discarded goods, smashed furniture, and other
ruined plunder had been left by the raiders. The flames

were loud, crackling and roaring, and it was hard to hear voices as the Delawares called to one another, dismounted, and shouted the names of friends.

There, in the midst of the destruction, before the flaming chapel and mission house, were two children, who came running and screaming toward Niko-lota. They saw Sutherland was white and spun away, terrified, throwing themselves at Niko-lota. Sutherland dismounted and hurried as best he could toward the chapel. Then he saw Evangeline, sitting on the ground, her head in her hands. Niko-lota was first at her side, the children with him, and he embraced her as she shook and wept.

Sutherland was downcast, his head hanging, and he walked toward the steps of the chapel. The roar of flame was loud, the heat oppressive. Everything these people had built, all they had labored so hard to make, was lost. What a waste! Whites could not have had a more faithful friend in this country than the Moravian Indians, but now the village was gone, and perhaps the Moravians, too, would soon depart.

It was then, while his thoughts were drifting, that he heard Niko-lota shriek in fury, and he turned to see the war chief come dashing by, wild desperation on his face as he ran to the edge of the blaze consuming the chapel. The other Delawares also began to howl and ran forward, past Sutherland, who looked to Evangeline as she stood there, her face sallow, streaked with tears.

She spoke in Shawnee, through her sobs. "They are all gone, Mr. Sutherland." He looked closer at her, then at the fires, before which the Delawares were tearing their clothes and leaping about in despair and anguish.

With shock, Sutherland understood, and he groaned in sorrow. Evangeline spoke his thoughts, burying her hands in her face. "They were all killed, all of them, and they are all in there, burning."

• • •

The Delaware warriors wanted to kill, but they were restrained by Niko-lota, who explained what Donoway had tried to do against impossible odds. As the fires died, Delaware death chants were sung, Christian prayers were said, and Evangeline cut off her hair in Indian mourning.

The next day, disheartened, empty, Sutherland was taken along the trail south, to where he had left his canoe —but if ever he marched as an enemy in this country, he was told, he would risk death at their hands.

"For such as you and I in these times," Niko-lota said, "there is no other choice, it seems."

Sutherland sighed, saying, "Perhaps, my brother, there is no other choice for you but to fight. For me, there is a choice." Evangeline, the children at her side, stood with Niko-lota as they watched him push off with his paddle. He said, "Never again, Niko-lota, will I make war on the Indian. Forevermore, I will leave the warpath."

PART TWO

The Sandusky Trail

chapter 9

CHOSEN PATH

Sutherland reached Fort Pitt two full days after the return of Williamson and his men. He expected to be arrested by Colonel Brodhead for his escape from prison, but he marched into the colonel's office anyway and cast blame for the Moravian massacre at the man's feet.

Brodhead, to Sutherland's surprise, did not deny responsibility for the massacre—which was already popular knowledge at Pitt—and did not even threaten to press charges for Sutherland's escape. Neither did he declare himself opposed to what had happened at Gnadenhutten— too many people fervently argued that it had to be done for the safety of the frontier. He would not punish, would not even rebuke Williamson and his killers. War was war, and the Moravians were unfortunate victims, but by their own fault, for remaining in that country while enemies fought over it. And were not those stolen garments proof of their collaboration with raiders?

Yet Sutherland could sense that Brodhead was shaken and full of remorse. Though privately repelled by what had happened, he dared not cause a public stir, lest the militia volunteers refuse his future musters. At the same time, he let Sutherland go free, an admission of the Scotsman's

righteous position in the tragic affair. While some settlers
were ashamed of what had been done, most whites on the
frontier viewed it as a show of strength that would have
good effect on the rest of the Indians. Between these two
poles Daniel Brodhead vacillated, to his own inner distress.

In the following days, news of the massacre spread
quickly to the East, where it was received with widespread
revulsion. Ironically, however, the decision had already
been made to remove Brodhead from command at Pitt,
where he was replaced by General William Irvine, a Pennsylvanian of Irish birth, known as a brilliant and courageous leader of Pennsylvanians in Washington's army. The
departure of Brodhead and the return of the Washington
County militia—except for Williamson and Grub—to
their farms for spring planting settled things down at Pitt
for a while.

For the Sutherlands, the matter of most immediate im-
portance was Owen's gradual recovery from the heart
spasms he had apparently suffered on the dash to Gnadenhutten. Peter Defries, postponing his return to Albany,
helped Susannah oversee much of the daily Frontier Company business, which was picking up with the coming of
spring; and Entellus Greyson, to everyone's approval, became a regular visitor to the cabin. It did Sutherland good
to see the growing friendship between the young man and
his daughter, for he had heard of Greyson's brave attempt
to prevent the massacre, and he liked the Marylander all
the more for it. Susannah's lingering infatuation with
James Morely seemed nearly over, and she made no secret
of her disapproval when there was no outcry from Cullen
and Company about what had been done by Williamson
with the company's money.

"James and Maxwell want the Washington County men
at their beck and call," Owen told his daughter plainly one
morning in April. "Should James want more lands cleared

of Indians, he'll be able to employ the Washington County men and Williamson, and they'll serve him, trusting him as a man whose plans jibe with their own."

He was oiling and cleaning his rifle, with a short-stem pipe in his teeth, as a fire crackled in the hearth and sunlight poured through the unshuttered windows. Ella was spinning, Peter Defries was sitting at the table with an ale and an old newspaper, and Susannah was working on the Frontier Company books. Her quill pen scratched as she listened to her father talk.

"Even your friend Entellus Greyson will need to have fighting men he can count on if he means to take possession of Indian lands," Sutherland said. "Congress won't send out an army, and it can't pay for one to be raised here. That will leave men like James as the prime mover for driving off the Indians, and men like Entellus will find themselves hard pressed to beat him to land claims."

Susannah understood that the settlers on small farms mostly took it for granted that the government would one day recognize their claims as squatters who had fought and died to hold their lands. Eventually, most of them hoped to sell out at a good profit to newcomers, ultimately to push on westward again and claim more country as their due by conquest and by making a primitive start at farming. This was a way of life for many, it seemed, and if a company could organize them into a fighting force—a company like James's—then they could be employed effectively against the Indians, to carry out the schemes of Morelys and Maxwells . . . and Greysons, she had to admit. She hoped Entellus would never stoop to ruthlessness. She hoped he would purchase his lands legally, not steal them from Indians.

She stopped writing, saying, "There has to be some justice, some humanity to our side, or the killing will never end!"

Defries answered moodily. "Ain't no Injuns gonna up

and tip their hat, saying, 'Here's my land, white folks, just give me a few shillings and I'll be off to make my way somewheres else.'" He gulped some ale. "There ain't no-wheres else fcr 'em, not in this life, nohow!"

Susannah protested. "Mr. Greyson told me his people will pay the Indians something—" She stopped short and stared out the window, but her eyes were blank, for she was trying to think through this puzzle that seemed to have no solution. It was the puzzle of white against Indian, in which she could make out no clear right or wrong.

Sutherland said there were plans for another private army, mostly of Washington County militia, to march against the Sandusky Indian towns, and this time they would not turn back as they had after the Moravian massacre. No other Indians had been attacked by Williamson's force, not one hostile warrior encountered during the entire campaign, because as soon as Gnadenhutten was destroyed the whites had fled back to Pitt, laden with their considerable plunder.

"James will finance the next army, too, and before long hundreds of settlers will be beholden to Cullen and Company, and will deal with James at every turn, getting deeper and deeper into his debt."

It was Cullen and Company, Sutherland said, that had purchased the booty from the returning militia, and at good prices. No doubt it would be resold to newcomers arriving in droves that spring.

"If James has his way, raiding Indian towns will become a profitable business, although there won't be as much plunder as at the Moravian villages."

Defries looked up from the old Albany newspaper his wife had sent him and said, "There'd be rich booty at Detroit! And there's lots of borderers who think themselves man enough to march up there and take it, figuring on running every loyalist and Redcoat out as easy as the Moravians was done for."

Even Ella, not especially learned in the ways of frontier war, gave a sound of derision at that and stopped her spinning to say, "This next campaign had better be two thousand strong, even just to get to Sandusky. If I know Niko-lota, every Indian in the northwest will be with him, ready to attack any invaders."

Sutherland agreed. "It's Colonel Crawford and Williamson who'll lead this one, and Crawford's asked me to scout for it."

There was silence in the room save for the clock ticking, as the others turned to look at him. He gave the rifle a final wipe with the rag and said softly, "I turned him down. I'm done with it."

Ella closed her eyes and sighed, resuming her spinning. Defries rustled the paper, saying, "Without good scouts they'll need four thousand men to get in and out again." He eyed Sutherland, as if wondering what the man was thinking.

Sutherland rose and hung the rifle on brackets over the mantelpiece.

"The next time I cross into Indian country," he said, "I'll be going in peace to Detroit." He nodded at his claymore hanging near the fireplace. "I've vowed it will stay there until I go home again."

Coal clattered and rattled down the steep slope, channeled into a trench leading to a makeshift wharf, where it was loaded onto barges for shipment to Fort Pitt and the lower Kentucky settlements. The hillsides of the Monongahela just south of Pitt were rich in coal, and as James Morely stood watching the laborers shoveling, he knew this land's bounty had hardly been touched. Some even swore there was silver in Washington County, on the west bank of the river.

He was on the deck of his keelboat, standing in the spring sunshine, watching the blackened workers shovel and pick at the vein of coal halfway up the rocky slope. The coal rumbled down the trench; at the bottom, twenty shovels worked at it, quickly filling the docked barge. Beside James was Noah Maxwell, eyes alight as he admired this primitive, promising stage of the country's development.

He said, "It's only a penny a bushel at Pitt, but down in Kentucky blacksmiths'll pay the price, and before long there'll be many a coal stove hungry for this. . . ." He spoke at length of the market for coal down the Mississippi and up the Illinois. "And if there were canals connecting the headwaters of rivers in the mountains, Pittsburgh coal could supply all eastern America, too!"

James's mind was working. "Pity that all this land is settled already. It would cost a great deal to buy the rights from farmers to mine coal and the other minerals here."

Maxwell was grinning and looked around at that, as if he had been waiting for James's lead. "We'll soon have the rights, and maybe the lands, too, in time!"

James wondered what this sly fellow had cooked up. He observed his partner, waiting for the explanation. Instead, Maxwell had called to the servingman for brandy. He had one poured for James, and with a wink, he toasted: "To the Washington County militia—long may it serve us, long may it do our bidding!"

James drank to that, but still wanted Maxwell to go on. He listened patiently over the rattle of coal and the singing of strong workmen in the background.

Maxwell spoke at last, obviously pleased with himself. "I have arranged, at small cost to us, to purchase the mineral rights of seven hundred farms, most of them in Washington County. . . ."

James was surprised and impressed. "At small cost? How so, say you?"

"By also offering to hold mortgages on those farms—

mortgages that will be paid back in five years, if all goes well with the farmers, and if they can meet our payments . . . payments that even I must admit are fair enough, seeing they can be made in commodities like cattle and crops rather than in cash."

James thought Maxwell unusually generous with the settlers, many of whom might sell outright in a few years, with the borderer's well-known inclination to develop, improve, and move on to do it again. "In five years," James said, sipping brandy, "those same settlers might be willing to be bought out."

"Perhaps," Maxwell replied, with a look of cunning about him. "But I'm gambling on . . . well, let me not tell you what I'm gambling on, because I fear you'll think me somewhat of a blackguard to anticipate certain bleak realities of life out here." He chuckled at his own words, as if knowing—but not caring—what James truly thought of him. "Bless me, James, I pray for only the best to happen to these settlers. Let's not talk further about this for the moment, if you please."

"Very well." James trusted the man's judgment. "If you have reasons for secrecy, then I'll respect them." He thought a moment, adding, "It sounds as though you've committed considerable Cullen and Company funds to this . . . this gamble."

"Indeed, James—but I thought you would approve of a certain daring. You see, the Washington County militia are almost to a man going off on this big campaign, and I feared that there was no time to waste . . . I mean, I had to get their agreements to the mortgages before they marched off, if you get my drift."

James did not, but he had other things on his mind and did not press Maxwell for a clearer explanation. Let Maxwell have his little machination. James was preoccupied with thoughts of Susannah Sutherland, as he had been for the past weeks. The last few times he had encountered her, she had seemed to want to avoid him, and he had little trouble imagining why. Ever since returning from the Moravian massacre, Owen Sutherland had kept his distance from James, as if blaming *him* for what had happened, as if proclaiming *him* the murderer. James resented that fiercely. He had no apologies to make, held no responsibility at all!

James drew away from his friend and from watching the coal diggers and walked to the stern of the boat. He stared down the Monongahela toward Pitt, where Susannah was at that moment. James had not expected the Moravian tragedy, and he would be damned if he would crawl to Owen Sutherland to beg forgiveness. Sutherland had not even deigned to come to him and accuse him to his face for his part in it!

James had first heard about the tragedy from Williamson, before Sutherland had returned. But Williamson had not gone into details. He had not told of how the Moravians had been murdered by the blows of hammers, one by one, as they prayed in their house of worship. Williamson had not told of how his men fired the village, with the bodies of scalped men, women, and children left to burn as if they were animals.

It was Entellus Greyson who had come to him and related all those terrible things, and for a while James had feared Sutherland might come and abuse him—but he had not. Sutherland had written a note, simply saying, "You have chosen your path, and you must walk it with this crime on your conscience."

Sutherland had not said that James might never see Susannah again. He had not told James never to cross his threshold again. He had not made one threat. He had simply turned his back in a gesture of finality that James knew was truly final. It still would be up to Susannah to choose for herself, James believed, but to his dismay, she was growing ever closer to that damned Greyson, and her father obviously approved.

Greyson was another starry-eyed hero, like her father, and like her father he had connections with the highest officials in the states. James Morely was a power to be reckoned with, but he did not have the social stature of Entellus Greyson. James was a wealthy man who would be invited to any household, entertained by General Washington himself if he so chose to visit the man—but would there be true warmth for him, genuine respect? Would he be welcomed only because he was master of Cullen and Company, an organization noted for its influence, brute strength, and uncompromising aggressiveness?

If men such as Washington and Franklin greeted Sutherland or Greyson, it would be with hearty, well-met good cheer, as friends or comrades. If they greeted James Morely, it would be no more than if they greeted the toadish Bradford Cullen, a man many of them had loathed to shake hands with, though they had often fawned on him and begged his indulgence in their business affairs.

James stared, unseeing, at the placid river, while within he raged with jealousy and self-doubt. He had all the power and riches he wanted, but he did not command the kind of respect his own father had earned, that Owen Sutherland received wherever he turned. Men like Williamson and Grub hated Sutherland because they feared him, but they obeyed James only because they needed his money, his backing. He had bought their allegiance, gratifying their lust for killing Indians. They might obey him well enough, but not as men would obey Owen Sutherland, and that knowledge gnawed at James Morely—that and the thought of the gentle beauty of Susannah Sutherland. Owen Sutherland called up James's fiery ambition, but Susannah made him remember the past, when he was her dearest friend but was not the ruler of Cullen and Company, and never would have consorted with men like David Williamson and Mike Grub.

It was some weeks later, and Owen Sutherland had not enjoyed himself so much in a long time, as he and Entellus Greyson, with blunted foils, face masks, and padded shirts, fenced back and forth across the yard behind his cabin.

It was a good spring day, the breeze fresh from the northwest, and the whole family, including Defries and Little Jake, were on hand to sit in the sun, eat a bread pudding and cream Ella had made that morning, and watch the two men go at it with gusto. Sutherland was not the swordsman Greyson was, but he still had the raw skill of the professional fighter, and though he would have been unmatched with the much heavier claymore, he was only very good with the foil.

Greyson clearly was in his element, and he relished the cleverness and imagination of Sutherland, whose parries and thrusts were more instinctive than trained, and whose intuition made him a vexing opponent. By now Sutherland knew Greyson was reputed to be one of the finest sword duelers in the country, and this whetted the Scotsman's enthusiasm and made the challenge all the more fun.

With whoops of glee when he took the offensive, and laughing yelps of mock anxiety as he was driven to defend himself, Sutherland made great sport of the competition, working up a sweat. It was the first real exertion he had allowed himself since the terrible dash across country to the Moravians.

Sitting on a swinging chair, enjoying the pudding from new china bowls Ella had acquired, Susannah played with the blue jay, Punch, and admired Greyson and her father. The younger man was not as muscular, but she guessed her father might have looked a bit like him at the same age, though physically stronger and more serious a person.

Greyson was still somewhat of a dandy, a purple silk scarf around his neck, his white shirt frilled at breast and cuff, his shoes buckled with silver and gold. Susannah thought he would lose that inclination with a few more months on the frontier.

Owen wore moccasins and leggins, with a linsey shirt, loose and full, revealing the green turtle tattoo on his chest, the mark of Ottawa adoption. His physique was impressive, though he was not as bearlike as Peter Defries—and the way Peter dug into his pudding while he watched the swordplay spoke of his will to keep the paunch he had acquired in his years at Albany. A native of Albany, Peter had spent much time on the frontier, and although he certainly was no swordsman, he thoroughly enjoyed the fencing match. Susannah thought the contest was fairly even, until age got the better of her father and Greyson's superior skill began to tell.

But even as his vigor failed, Sutherland found the ability to recite Shakespeare, grabbing in his left hand a chunk of wood as he did so, and fighting in Elizabethan fashion, warding off blows with the wood as if it were a dagger, and striking with his foil. Susannah laughed to hear him.

"With piercing steel he tilts at bold Mercutio's breast!"

And Greyson, panting for breath, replied, "Who, all as hot, turns deadly, point to point . . ."

"And with a martial scorn, with one hand beats cold death aside, and with the other sends it back to Tybalt . . ."

Sutherland blocked and thrust, blocked and blocked, his hand faster than Susannah could follow, the foil of Greyson just as quick.

Greyson took up the refrain. ". . . Tybalt! Whose dexterity retorts it . . ."

Then Sutherland was retreating, the wood knocked from his hand, his foil parrying, barely parrying, his guard falling—

Suddenly he gave a gasp and dropped to his knees,

throwing off the face guard. Greyson almost thrust, but held off, for Sutherland's face was pale, his eyes dark with pain.

"Pa!" Susannah cried out and leaped to his side. Ella was there at once, and Defries and Little Jake hurried up. "Pa? Is it your heart?"

Sutherland caught his breath and looked at them, the color coming back into his face, but there was the shadow of pain, the memory of it. In a moment he gave a little smile and stood up on his own power, taking long, slow breaths.

"Maybe I'm . . . just winded. . . ." He clapped Greyson on the shoulder. "You should give young Jake here a lesson or two—"

Little Jake lit up with excitement, but Ella cried out, "Owen! No! He's too young!"

Jake gave a yelp of indignation. "No, I'm not! What're you saying?"

Ella threw up her hands. "Jake, sword fighting isn't just play! Don't you know what it—"

Jake stamped the ground and whirled right around as he jumped into the air, gesticulating in excitement. "I can do it! Just watch!" With that, he yanked the sword away from Sutherland, then whirled it about his head so that Greyson had to leap back. Unfortunately, on the backswing the blunted tip caught the hem of Susannah's dress and ripped it.

Jake gasped an apology as the sword clumsily clanged to the ground, and Ella went at him, finger wagging, while he stood there, his head down. Susannah saw a tear on his cheek, and Ella suddenly caught herself, just as the boy said, "If it'd been Benjamin, you'd have let him do it!"

"What?" Ella put a hand to her breast. "Why, Jake, I—"

"It's true!" he said, lip quivering, and they all saw how painfully embarrassed he was to be unable to keep from crying.

"Why, Jakie . . ." Ella put a hand on his shoulder, and he halfheartedly tried to pull away, but Owen came up and put his arm roughly around the boy, giving a hearty laugh.

"Come on, laddie. Ella's just forgetting how big you've grown!" He winked at Ella, and Jake did not see, for he was still downcast. "You'll have a go with Mr. Greyson, and the rest of us will take care to stay well out of the way."

Greyson was there to take charge, and Ella stepped back, her hands knitted before her, while Peter Defries gave an enthusiastic shout, saying that Jake should not waste his anger on his foster mother, "but let Enty here have it, and make him skip, my lad!"

Susannah tucked away the torn part of her dress and was glad to see Jake's head come up, his eyes alive once more. Greyson handed the boy the foil and clapped a mask on his head, moving him away where he "wouldn't touché the wrong man . . . or woman!"

Susannah went to Ella, seeing her mother's troubled look as the swordplay began. While the steel clashed and Jake cried out in delight, Susannah touched her mother's hand and said softly, "It's time you adopt him, isn't it?"

Ella sighed, nodding slowly. "It's just . . . just that—"

"You can't help thinking of Ben—I know, Ma. But so does Little Jake, and he wonders whether you truly love him like a son."

Ella smiled, saying, "I love him, more like a son every day. Yes, Susannah, we should adopt him soon, while we still can."

In the next moment, Susannah thought about her father and how his heart could no longer bear such exertion. Neither she nor Ella said anything more but went to sit with Owen, one on either side, as he rested on a split-log bench and leaned back against the table. Ella took his hand. None of them spoke except to give words of encouragement to Little Jake. Susannah saw Peter glance worriedly over now and again, to see how her father really was.

The swordplay went on, but somehow the conversation was not as buoyant as before. Later that afternoon, when the others went inside to prepare for supper, Greyson took a walk with Susannah down to the Ohio. They walked all the way to the battlements of the fort, where the sunlight was red and beautiful on the grassy dry moat.

Between them passed the usual conversation of young people in search of something to say, something enjoyable that might not even be necessary to say, since the company was enjoyable enough and silence would have sufficed. Susannah started many of the subjects, most of which were soon exhausted because the couple still hardly knew each other, and their lives had been so different that matters familiar to one were often obscure to the other, too difficult to explain, or the explaining became so complicated that the teller lost the way and began to laugh, conscious of the absurdity of the situation.

In the past weeks Susannah and Greyson had spent much time together, but always in company with someone else, as was correct. Now, however, Susannah was acutely aware that her parents had permitted them to be alone, even encouraged them to take a walk. Perhaps Greyson had requested it of them. Perhaps he had something important to say. She wished, if it were so, to let him get to it then, and after a while she stopped opening avenues of conversation, hoping he would take the lead and maybe introduce a more interesting subject. A more romantic subject. As they strolled along the dry moat, where spring flowers were appearing purple and yellow, Susannah knew she liked Entellus Greyson more than she had yet realized.

But what was he thinking? Her heart hurried as she glanced at him, his gaze on the ground, so serious and so thoughtful. Was he thinking about her? He looked at her briefly and smiled, a bit embarrassed, she thought. She kept glancing at him as they walked, he half a step ahead. She bent to pluck a small purple flower and smelled it, feeling like a very interesting and graceful young woman as she did so, and noticing that he was watching her now. She smiled and returned to her flower, brushing back a lock of straggling hair and beginning to feel a bit self-conscious. His eyes were still on her after a few more paces, and she wanted to talk again but refused to start the conversation. If he had something important to.say, she would not divert it by some idle chatter. But did he? Would he? What was he waiting for?

He was still staring at her when she could not help but say clumsily, "What's on your mind, Mr. Greyson?" She smiled a bit weakly. "If I may be so bold as to ask?"

"What?" He seemed to come back from distant thoughts and put his hands behind his back, leaning over a bit and licking his lips as he sought for something to say. "On my mind? Yes . . . well, I was wondering . . . whether . . . you . . . ah—"

Now he was getting somewhere, and she continued to sniff at the flower, glancing alternately at him and it.

"I was wondering, Susannah . . . Mistress Sutherland—"

"Susannah, please."

"And call me Entellus, if you will."

"Entellus."

"What?"

"Nothing." Susannah sighed in mild exasperation. "You were going to tell me something . . . ask me something—"

"About?" He stopped, and so did she.

"About whether I . . . You were wondering, you said."

"Yes!" He walked again, leaning over, thinking hard. "I was wondering, Mistress—Susannah—whether you would like to join me tonight at the camp meeting!" He gazed at her with eyes she thought resembled those of an innocent puppy.

The camp meeting? She and everyone else at Pitt had been aware for a couple of weeks about plans for an outdoor revival meeting, starting that night and continuing for three days, at which ministers, exhorters, and traveling preachers would hold meetings in the open air. For the past few days the common fields behind the fort and reaching up Grant's Hill had been filling with wagons and tents, with people coming from as far as thirty miles away. Although the weather was not as warm as was desirable, the decision had been made to hold the meeting now before the Indians took to the warpath and made the trails and roads even more unsafe.

"I would be pleased to go with you, Entellus," she replied with a slight incline of her head, and saw he was obviously glad for it. "But do not expect me to join the masses in their fervor, or to praise the Lord in the way those preachers might want me to. And if you begin to shake or quake or get the jerks, or start shouting to the heavens the way some of them do, then I'll take myself on home and leave you to your hysteria!"

She had spoken plainly, and his answer could not have been more reassuring. With a laugh he declared, "I'm going for the amusement and to hear some of those fire-eaters exhort! Why, I haven't heard a good rabble-rousing since the Sons of Liberty raised a liberty pole in Baltimore!" He chuckled and helped her over the embankment until they were coming out of the dry moat and were looking at the river on the right and the crowded campgrounds some distance away on the left. "This country's pretty, like you, but it's all too reserved for a man from back east—"

"Reserved like me, too?" She wanted to be demure, not coy, and thought she had succeeded, as he looked so taken with her.

"I think you're not so reserved with those who know your heart."

She liked that. "My heart's on my sleeve, for all to see, sir."

Unexpectedly, he stopped, taking her hands in a way she thought brash, and yet sincere. Excitement rose in her, for his eyes were so clear, so honest, and full of feeling.

"Susannah . . ." He sought for words, taking a long breath before saying, "My heart, too, is on my sleeve . . . for you to see!"

That was not bad, she thought, although it might have been a bit more classical in its attempt at love talk. James, for example, could recite Shakespeare until it moved her to a flutter of emotion. She loved Shakespeare and would have liked Entellus to employ some, perhaps a sonnet or two. . . .

He did not. "You are wonderful!"

He might have expressed himself more poetically, as James would have, but his words had an effect that Susannah had not expected. Her palms began to sweat, and all at once her legs felt weak. Was this romantic love? It was indeed something strong and deep, that she knew, and those beautiful blue eyes of his were magical, spellbinding, and she could not stop gazing at them as if her very soul depended upon it. . . .

That last thought brought her back to the revival camp meeting that night, and it also broke the spell. It would not do for a young lady to be seen embracing in public, and she did not like it that her hands were moist as he held them so tenderly. She drew them away and put them into the folds of her dress, surprised to find herself trembling. Now she saw how intense Entellus was, and so obviously excited. Clearly he was in love with her, but she was not sure what she felt for him. Perhaps if he had recited something thrilling, had spoken a poet's words of endearment, it would have moved her with more familiar womanly feelings. Now she was simply trembling and had to look away, out at the river, down the bank . . . and there she was startled to see James Morely.

Sitting alone, casting stones into the river, he had not seen them, and was in such a position that it was difficult for passersby to see him from anywhere but this particular part of the riverside. A sudden rush of sorrow filled Susannah, a familiar and almost comforting pity and, yes, love . . . the certain kind of love she had held in her heart for James for so long—perhaps ever since she was a girl back at Detroit.

Stone after stone was plopped into the stream, methodically, thoughtfully. She guessed how downhearted he must be, and she presumed he was thinking not only of his role in the massacre of the Moravians, but also of how he loved her and had not won her. She stood there, almost forgetful of Entellus, and felt tears to see James like this, so lost, and so sadly alone in the world.

For an instant she wanted to rush to his side, but then she looked back at Entellus, feeling that it would be wrong of her to forsake him abruptly. Entellus, too, had seen James, and had seen how Susannah was moved by the sight of him.

To her surprise, he said softly, "He does not know we are here . . . but I think it would be good if you went to him, and I'll withdraw."

It was not said out of false sincerity, or to impress her with his chivalry. Entellus genuinely felt for James Morely, for of late he had come to know the man better.

He voiced Susannah's thoughts. "There is good in him that will never be extinguished." He looked closely at her, and she felt a powerful emotion, still unfamiliar, but inexpressibly sweet and warm. "Until this evening, Susannah . . ." he smiled and said with a wink. "And promise me you won't join the masses in their fervor, and won't begin to shake or quake or get the jerks, or start shouting—"

Her hand went softly to his cheek, and they both smiled. He took the hand and kissed it, then bowed slightly, and they parted, fingers lingering.

Composing herself, Susannah went to James, who needed a friend, needed someone who knew that in him was yet goodness that never would be completely extinguished.

chapter **10**

CAST THEM DOWN

The spring evening was balmy, the sun low in the sky so that the broad fields at the foot of Grant's Hill were lit with rosy sunlight, turning the tents and covered wagons there a radiant hue.

Campfires burned everywhere in a wide crescent around the base of the hill, sending up smoke that drifted over the trees on the high ground. The campground was busy with people cleaning up after dinner, changing into their best clothes, and chasing stray children down. The mood of anticipation sharpened as the trumpet sounded a signal, and folk began to gather and move toward the large wooden platform in the center of the crescent's arc. It was there that the preachers would orate, flanked by benches for a choir of at least fifty.

This would be a Methodist revival for the most part, although to keep the peace a few Presbyterian ministers had been invited. Susannah Sutherland knew, however, that should one minister or another be carried away in his sermon, others would have a long wait for a turn—unless they set up a little way off to preach simultaneously to their own flocks. No one knew how the camp meeting would end—whether the majority would sway to the Presbyterians or to the Methodists—and Susannah and Entellus

Greyson were speculating about the outcome as they strolled through the crowd toward the platform.

Susannah was dressed in a simple white linen gown, a matching bonnet with a sprig of cattail in the band, and a soft woolen shawl over her shoulders. Beside her, as handsome as she was pretty, strode Greyson, in a buff-colored waistcoat and breeches, with a dark blue frock coat and bicorne. He carried two folding chairs over his shoulder, and in his other hand was a picnic basket. His sword hung by a sash at his side, for it often happened at these gatherings that rowdies burst in and caused trouble, needing forceful ejection.

Not far away, in fact, were two dozen or more hard cases who habitually hung about the settlement near the fort—men whose bad character often had been the reason new arrivals got their families away from Pitt as soon as possible, to populate the lower valley. Susannah looked across the sunlit meadow at the rogues, hearing their coarse and drunken shouts as they danced to a twanging jew's harp. She noticed that some merchants were dispensing drinks from barrels of whiskey. She was sure that many men who came here for the meeting would also find their way to whiskey, for a dram was commonplace on the frontier, and whiskey was an accepted part of every event, from barn-raisings to funerals.

As she walked, Susannah saw a few lean, poorly dressed settlers gazing at the gang of rowdies and their devil's brew. More than one wife gave her man a tug to get him to keep trudging toward the meeting place. Susannah hoped there would be no real trouble, but she was sure some hell-raising would result from the mingling of outlaws with God-fearing folk.

As she and Entellus drew closer to the platform, the crowd grew thicker and noisier. She felt a thrill to be among so many people—at least a thousand of them, women and children, old men and young. Some were singing, others praying, many already emotionally moved by their pilgrimage here. She saw an old, skinny woman sitting on a barrel, her eyes closed, toothless mouth working, singing a psalm in a nasal, high-pitched, plaintive wail. The woman was leaning forward, then throwing her body back—craning forward until she almost fell off the barrel, then jerking back until Susannah wondered that she did not fall off and break her neck.

Greyson smiled and said, "She's got religion, all right!" Like him, Susannah rejected the generally held belief that such strange behavior showed the touch of the Holy Spirit, and that jerking, wailing, and even prostration were signs of the sinner's soul being cleansed by some violent purgative of the Lord.

Standing on another wagon, a brawny fellow was exhorting his large family, quoting Scripture copiously and calling upon them to prepare for rebirth, for the coming of their Savior, lest they all be damned. Bright-faced little children listened, their eyes wide; older children were somber; and the eldest son—it seemed to Susannah—was as grave and enraptured as his pontificating father. This was an incredibly strong man on the wagon, with a great beard and huge muscles, and Susannah knew that if the rowdies invaded, they would be up against trouble.

The din of voices rose as torches were placed at the corners of the platform. Greyson set up the folding chairs quite close to the front, but "far enough back that spittle, sweat, and tears won't rain on us." Their neighbors cheerfully made room for them. It was already fun, all this agitation, and the young couple opened their picnic basket for a supper of cider, hard-boiled eggs, bread, and cheese. They did not dare bring wine, lest people rail against them and call them sinners. Susannah hoped the sermon would be something other than a temperance lecture, and that some of the intricacies of Methodist or Presbyterian dogma would be explained or clarified through clever anecdotes. Those sermons always fascinated and delighted her, both for their sometimes illogical but passionate conclusions and for their colorfulness.

There was nothing more entertaining than a backcountry preacher in full sail, said Greyson. The first preacher, who began while they were still eating, was a young fellow, a stringbean with grave demeanor—the "five o'clocker" he was called, and considered a small-caliber gun. He was fairly restrained, but later would come the "six o'clocker," who was older, more stirring, more to the point with the need for saving one's soul immediately, before it was too late. Even by the end of the first young preacher's sermon on the wages of sin, however, Susannah could tell that many in the seething crowd were swayed by emotion, some crying out for salvation, others sitting gloomily, as if feeling forsaken.

For just a moment, Susannah thought of her encounter with James Morely by the river earlier that day, of how he had brightened at her appearance. Soon, however, he had slid back into a mood of gruff annoyance, as if no one in the world could help him, or wanted to. Though Susannah had tried to be kind, James had not responded as he used to do, and had finally thanked her and gone off, a cloud following him all the way. She suspected he was ashamed of what had been done to the Moravian Indians, but she had not mentioned it to him. Also, she knew he was aware of her deepening friendship with Greyson. She wondered whether James had given up trying to win her hand. She thought it might be for the best, for she was indeed strongly attracted to Greyson, who sat calmly but interested, listening to the "six o'clock gun" work up some women nearby, telling them "No one is good—no, not one! Not even babes in arms are without original sin, and are doomed to hell unless they are of the elect!"

That got a wail from a woman, causing a chain reaction of groans so that some husbands came over to pat shoulders and shed tears along with their women.

"Oh, Lord, I pray Thee help me," the preacher intoned, "for I am nothing, and helpless as a child! Glorify Thyself in my great weakness!"

"Amen!"

Susannah felt the fear, the remorse, the passionate fervor for salvation swell in the crowd until it touched her with its magnetic power, and chills ran up and down her back, so that it seemed her hair was standing on end. People were screaming, others were laughing hysterically and crying aloud to heaven in their thanks at being saved at last.

"Repent, ye, therefore, and be converted, that your sins may be blotted out, when the time of refreshing shall come!"

"Amen!"

It was not the religious message that moved Susannah —though she admitted readily enough to being a sinner— but it was the loud and eager excitement of the crowd, and the passionate and almost musical preaching of the minister as he swayed them right and left, called upon them to fall down—which many did—compelled them to weep, to scream in their extremity of remorse, and implored them to let the power of God into their miserable hearts before it was too late.

They wept and they shrieked, and they fell down prostrate by the scores. As yet, the entire mass was not wholly overcome, but it was powerful enough for Susannah, and she saw that Greyson, too, was agitated by it. Both felt closed in, oppressed by the crush of the crowd, which had shoved closer to the platform until no one could go or come unless able to fly over hundreds of heads.

Before the appearance of the seven o'clock preacher—
one Reverend Godspeace Willis, the heaviest gun of all—
the crowd calmed down somewhat, though tears flowed on
many a cheek, and hundreds were on their knees, praying,
as a choir began to sing a hymn by John Wesley, the
founder of Methodism. Susannah felt relieved as the beautiful, soothing music carried over everyone and laid comfort on many a repentant sinner whose head was bowed in
despair.

Greyson touched her hand then, to get her attention, and
she saw that he was nodding toward a bulky figure kneeling not far away, gazing hatless at the choir. It was Colonel
David Williamson, and his expression was as that of a
saint. His full cheeks were ruddy in the torchlight, his eyes
shining.

"Looks like he's been saved, eh?" Greyson's voice was
low and without emotion, but Susannah knew the bitter
resentment that filled her friend just then. "He's got religion, for he only killed Injuns, you see."

Just then a disturbance broke out behind the crowd, and
the voices of the choir fell as angry shouts and curses filled
the air. The people moved apart, men motioning their
women back and striding forward as if to meet some adversary. Indeed, it was an adversary, as a score of the
toughs pushed through the crowd, pistols in their belts,
knives in their boots. They were swigging whiskey and
calling out that the preachers were telling a pack of lies.

"Have a drink, like men, gents, and don't bend yer knee
to the likes of these hypocrites who only want yer collec-
tion money and don't give a damn about anybody's mortal
soul!"

The toughs were drunk and loud, and numerous enough
to give brave men among the worshipers a moment's second thought.

"Methodist fanatics!" one cried, and Susannah saw with

a start it was the huge Mike Grub, who was carrying a jug of whiskey and brandishing a club. "You won't interfere with my fun, you dogs! Come out, preacher! Step up and let me see your lying face!"

Grub stopped before the platform, as onto it climbed a squat and curly-haired elderly man—a man with black eyebrows, huge shoulders telling of much physical strength, and a fierce expression as he glared down at the thugs. This was Godspeace Willis.

"Be off, sinner, before you get more than you bargain for!" the seven o'clock and final gun said with a growl. When Grub just snorted and downed a swig of whiskey from the jug laid on his shoulder, the preacher went on: "God hath pronounced a curse on him that useth ardent spirits!"

Grub retorted, burping, "Ain't no law agin' using whiskey, and you ain't about to git one passed! I'll do as I please!"

At that, the preacher suddenly changed, transformed, as a look of serene kindness came over him. He nodded slowly, drew a breath, and said with a sigh, "Yes, my son, you will do as you please, but it would be best for you if you would do as God pleases, for God has not forsaken you, and Christ Jesus will come to you, if only you open up your heart! God loves you, my son!"

To Susannah's surprise, Grub was slightly taken aback, perhaps more by the unexpected change of mood and the powerful feeling that emanated from those surrounding him than by any eloquence of the words. A rush of pity and love seemed to have been released by one thousand worshipers, all of it aimed directly at Mike Grub, and it made him unable to take another drink, though he tried to bring the jug to his lips, as the preacher went on talking to him in a most soothing, loving voice, accented by cries from the crowd of "Hallelujah!" and "Praise God!"

"Glory, glory, glory to God!" Willis half sang the words. "For my Savior is coming, and He is at hand! He is coming for you, sinner . . . and who amongst us would not admit to being a sinner?" Willis looked at Grub as though he could see into his heart, then said in a voice that Susannah thought soft, yet which carried far over the crowd: "Jesus loves you, my son, and He will bring you home. He will comfort you and will pour out His merciful blessing on you, though you be a sinner. And, son—"

The voice was like magic itself, like silk, like the voice of a father who loves his wayward child, and Grub listened. Surely no one had ever talked to him like this before.

"—you and I are sinners, are we not? Have we not forsaken our true calling? Do you not remember why you were put here on God's earth, to do the work of the Lord, to be saved? What would your mother think of you? What would you want her to think of you now? Do you ·dare deny that you are lost without Christ? Do you believe you can be saved? Do you? Are you worthy of salvation, son?"

Grub swallowed and licked his lips, his simple mind juggling with those questions. No doubt he was thinking about the mother even a man like himself once had, and he was touched.

"Look into your heart, son, and ask whether you want to spend the rest of eternity in the hot fire of hell. The rest of the rest of forever, day after day, week after week, month after month, year after year, decade after decade, century after century, eon after eon . . ." Grub waited, hanging on the words that suddenly scorched him with their vehemence. ". . . in the hellfire . . . the hellfire that burns, that sears, that blackens, that will never stop, and will be a chastising and terrible fate, for even now the devil stands ready to spring, stands ready to claim *you* if you do not repent!"

Grub could not look away, his mouth half open. The crowd shouted in their ecstasy.

"It is only at the merciful whim of God that you do not fall into the awful flames of hell *right now,* this very moment! Hallelujah! Praise God! It is only the mercy of God that you woke up this morning still alive, my son, and not down there, burning with the unspeakable agony of hell's flames! It is only because God *loves you* that you are here now, standing before the Lord! You know that tomorrow you may die, and if you have not repented, have not been saved, have not got religion, then you will be destroyed, burned in an agony that makes me weep for you, my son! Oh, my God in heaven, my sweet Jesus, I beg of you, Lord, awaken this young man's heart, teach him to cry out in his despair, let your mighty power pour into him and awaken him from his sleep of sin that he may be saved! I pray, dear God, that this young man be saved! Be saved! In the name of Jesus, who loves him, as I love him, as all Christians who got religion must love him! Hallelujah! Praise God for His mercy! Let us pray."

And at once, every man and woman and child—except for Grub and most of his companions—fell to their knees, their shouting and weeping stilled, except for random sobs and for the few who were hysterical. Susannah was breathless, the power of what she had witnessed nearly overwhelming her as she stared at Mike Grub, his eyes wide, sweat on his brow, a look of dismay on his dark face. He had dropped his stick.

"Hell opens wide its mouth!" Willis cried in a voice so loud, so deep, that Susannah jumped when he began, and found herself trembling even after Greyson took her hand and gripped it. He, too, was shaken.

"Forgive us, Lord! You know that every natural man flatters himself that the devil won't get him. Every man, young and strong, is sure he has a way of avoiding final judgment. The young and strong think they will never die. But upon dying, they find themselves in hell. And the sinner laments, cries out with every ounce of strength, to be released from torture, to be forgiven. But it is *too late!* Dear God, make him know that to die a sinner, unrepentant, is too late! Too late! Too late!"

The minister's teary eyes were closed, head bowed, and he sobbed as Grub stared at him, transfixed.

"O sinner, consider the danger you are in! The wrath of God is terrible, greater than the wrath of a hundred, a thousand, an infinite number of cruel savages! Sinner, you hang by a slender thread, with the flames of hell flashing under you. You have no way to save yourself, sinner, no way to escape, nothing to lay hold of to prevent eternal agony in the fires of hell, nothing, my son, but repentance! Now! Repent, repent, or God will tread you in His fury, trample you in His anger, and your blood will stain His garments! Therefore also will I deal in fury, neither will I have pity, for the day of mercy will be past, and you will be damned! Damned! Damned!"

The people were gasping, many sure it was they to whom he was preaching, and they begged aloud for religion, for light, for forgiveness, and professed their faith, cried out in their awful terror. Grub had dropped his jug.

After a pause, Willis gathered himself and raised his strong arms, his huge head lifting as he looked out over the masses.

"And the Lord saith that it shall come to pass, that from one Sabbath to another, all flesh shall come to worship before me, and they shall go forth and look upon the carcasses of the men that have transgressed against me, the men who have lied, the men who have cheated, the men who have murdered, the men who have lain with whores, the men who have become drunk with whiskey! They shall look upon the carcasses of these men once strong, for their worm shall not die, neither shall their fire be quenched, and they shall suffer on and on and on, and they shall be an abhorrence unto all eternity!"

Oh, how that cast them down in wailing and terror, and even Mike Grub collapsed to his knees, his face buried in his hands as he wept fiercely, shoulders shaking with every great sob, his dirty, scarred palms wet with tears and sweat.

Struck with awe, electrified by the power of the moment, Susannah sat back in her chair, panting, and looked at Greyson, who was grim.

The voice of the minister softened, and now—following the terror—came the gift of mercy, the promise, the path of righteousness. "What those poor damned souls would give to be in your position right now, my friend! What they would do, what they would endure, what they would deny to have the chance that you have now, this very moment, right here, son, to enter through the gate that is thrown wide for you, the gate the mercy of our Lord and Savior Jesus Christ has opened so that you might repent, so that sinners might flock to him . . ."

Mike Grub was willing to flock all by himself, and in a moment he was flat on his face, pounding the ground with his big fists, begging aloud for forgiveness. And the preacher promised it in tones melodious and smooth.

". . . with their hearts filled with love for Him! Praise God!" His voice rose, becoming almost shrill, sentences interrupted by his sudden cries to heaven, cries of near-hysterical joy that cracked like lightning over the thousand penitents, who echoed him and cried out even louder. ". . . sins washed away in His own blood! Hallelujah! Make the heavens—hallelujah—ring with your joy! Make them ring—praise God—with your rejoicing! Let everyone that is out of Christ *awake!* Praise God! Awake, and fly from the wrath to come! Awake now! Escape for your lives! Look not behind you! Escape to the mountain of God, lest you be consumed!"

Had Mike Grub been able, he would have taken wing and soared to heaven right then, and he screeched, "I repent! I repent! I want to be saved! Please God! I want to be saved!" And the entire congregation cried out at the miracle of his conversion. The clamor rose like a storm at sea, and the minister was laughing, tears running down his cheeks, to see Mike Grub kneeling, hands clutched, shaking and jerking, crying out for joy. Mike Grub had been saved! Mike Grub had got religion!

The choir stood up to sing, and Susannah saw that David Williamson was clapping Grub on the back and grinning, tears in his own eyes. The hymn exploded, loud and inspiring over the crowded meadow, taken up by a hundred others who knew it well. Susannah recognized it as another hymn by John Wesley, who had translated it from the German. It was popular on the frontier.

Stirred and excited herself, marveling at the mighty force of the revival meeting, she turned to express her wonder to Greyson, but was startled to see some dark shadow had come over him, and he had let go of her hand. The song rose louder, and she leaned over, asking why he was so somber at such a thrilling moment.

His face set, he said through clenched teeth, "That's the same song the Moravian Indians were singing when Williamson's men murdered them, one by one!"

Shocked, Susannah looked over at Williamson and to her amazement saw he was trembling, staring fearfully at the choir, as if the music were gnawing at his very marrow. His laughter was gone, his whole being seemingly struck with icy cold, and slowly he began to walk backward. The music rolled on in its glory, and many people laughed and sang:

> Jesus, Thy blood and righteousness
> My beauty are, my glorious dress,

Midst flaming worlds, in these arrayed,
With joy shall I lift up my head!

Susannah watched Williamson draw back, quailing, through the crowd, turn clumsily, and stumble away into the night.

Bold shall I stand in Thy great day,
For who aught to my charge shall lay?
Fully absolved through these I am,
From sin and fear, from guilt and shame.

Mike Grub scarcely noticed the words, or even the music, so joyful was he in his newfound state of grace, and soon he and the beaming minister were shaking hands, two strong men, both certain they were on the path to salvation.

Later, Susannah and Greyson made their way home, neither talking much, but both taking comfort in the other's presence. They went arm in arm through the streets, and Susannah thought she had never before felt so akin to any man except her brother, Benjamin. The evening had moved her tremendously, and it had brought her close to Entellus Greyson. What would happen next between them?

She asked whether he was staying at Pitt through spring, or was he planning to start east and report to his company. After a moment, he cleared his throat and said, "I am going on the next campaign as aide-de-camp to Colonel Crawford. We leave in two days."

Susannah was troubled, not having expected this, not after the terrible experience he had gone through with Williamson. He assured her, however, that such a massacre would never happen again.

"No, dear Susannah, this time I believe Colonel Crawford will be elected as leader, and he is a good man, and together we will hold the killers in check."

"Must you go?" she asked, turning to him as they stood in the shadows, just out of the light of the lamp at the door. "It will be so dangerous. . . ."

He smiled, no trace of fear about him. "I have to survey those lands, Susannah, and plan my company's future here. This is why I came out in the first place, and I cannot go back unless my work is done. Have no fear—" He smiled and kissed her hand. "There will be a strong army with me, and Colonel Crawford believes we will have no trouble in reaching the Indian villages at Sandusky and destroying them once and for all. That will save hundreds of lives on the frontier, and help bring this bloody Indian war to a speedy end."

"Father says it will take at least two thousand men."

When he shrugged and nodded casually, Susannah felt cold terror rise in her, and she was so weak from the day's experiences that she almost sobbed when he casually answered, "Six hundred surely will suffice—"

"What?"

"Well mounted, brave men—"

"Please, dear heaven! You cannot! Six hundred only? But it is madness—"

Greyson simply smiled, his smile telling her that he did not know as much about wilderness war as even she did. He changed the subject, though she did not want him to.

"It has been a wonderful day for me, Susannah, and I have to tell you how I feel—"

She squeezed his hands, then thrust them back at him and said in her despair, "No! I will not let you talk to me with sweetness and . . . and of love! I will not, Entellus! Not if you are fool enough to risk your life like this!"

He was startled and almost stepped backward, stammering, "But . . . Susannah . . . you . . . you cannot presume to be a general, my dear!" He laughed lightly, but then saw how fierce she looked.

"I am no general, sir! Just a woman! And that's all it

takes to see that you and your brave six hundred will be fortunate ever to return alive! Damn this war!" She could not keep back a sob, and tears began to flow. She bit her lip, saw those beautiful blue eyes of his, and threw herself into his arms. "Oh . . . oh, why is it that men can only learn one way . . . with so much pain!" He put his arms about her and held her close.

"I will come back, dear Susannah, and when I do, I will ask you to mar—"

Again his words were stopped, but this time with her lips, and she kissed him hard before pulling away, with her eyes closed as she caught her breath.

"Dear Susannah—"

She turned away, opening the door and saying, "God keep you, Entellus. I will not let myself love you." She paused, half through the door, and said to him, "Not until you come back!"

She closed the door on Greyson and hurried through the dim common room, where the fire was dying. She went into her own room, trying not to weep, and shut the door behind her, knowing that her father had been sitting in the darkness, near the fire, and no doubt had heard it all.

That same evening, in the woods just northwest of Fort Pitt, two horsemen stopped at a lonely cabin, which had no lights and seemed deserted. The riders dismounted, and one—a huge man carrying two pistols—went to the door while his companion waited, pistols also in hand.

After opening the door and looking around, the bigger man came out again, saying, "Ain't nobody here, Mr. Maxwell."

"Damn you!" Noah Maxwell snapped and shook a pistol in the air. "Don't use my name again, Bartholomew! Can't you remember anything two minutes after you're told?"

Bill Bartholomew, former bodyguard to Bradford Cullen, apologized to Maxwell, the man who now employed him, but before he finished, the bushes nearby rustled, and several dark forms appeared, all carrying rifles. Some of them were Indians.

Maxwell gasped audibly, and Bartholomew stood fast, weapons at the ready, until a man cackled, then said in a creaking voice, "If you be the gents who summoned us, never fear. The password, then?"

Maxwell trembled as he said, "'A daring escapade.'"

The voice snorted and came back with, "Ain't you gonna demand the countersign? Do it military-like and official or don't do it, I always says."

"Y-yes! Indeed!" Maxwell's teeth might have been heard chattering all the way to Fort Pitt.

"Right!" The man in the shadows cleared his voice, but it sounded just as rusty and primitive as he said, with a mock military air, "'Can always be defeated!' There! That suit you, Mr.— Ah, but I ain't saying yer name, and you ain't saying who I be. Leave us enter this here warm cabin alone and have a chat, sir. Let your playmate out here to smoke with my Injuns . . . he do have some baccy, don't he? Wouldn't be mannerly to invite us to a parley and not supply the smoke, now, would it?"

He went on jabbering like that as he opened the door and bowed with exaggeration for Maxwell to enter. For just an instant, Maxwell got the shakes, terrified that he might be robbed and murdered, and he wished Bill Bartholomew could come in to protect him.

But that would not do, not at all. Even his trusty bodyguard must not know that tonight Noah Maxwell was conspiring with the one man rebels on the frontier hated and feared more than any other: Simon Girty—loyalist, spy, and Indian scout.

chapter **11**

TWO COMPANIES

Even though he was speaking to a man standing close by, the ringing baritone of the Reverend Godspeace Willis carried over the Fort Pitt parade ground, and many heard him.

"Is there any—I ask you any—sight more inspiring than a body of well-mounted soldiers mustering for a campaign against the heathens?"

Willis was standing in front of the Cullen and Company trading house, James Morely at his side, both of them watching four hundred and fifty Pennsylvania militiamen mount up at the command of Colonel William Crawford. There had been a vote earlier in the morning, and Crawford had been chosen by only two or three ballots over David Williamson, who now sat moodily on his mount nearby, as second in command.

The contrast between them was sharp: Williamson, bulky and hard-eyed, wore buckskin and feathers; Crawford, tall and dignified, a friend of George Washington's, and of good Virginia family, wore a buff coat of fine cut, with shiny boots and the best weapons at his belt.

Looking at him, the Reverend Willis slapped his big thigh and declared that Crawford was every bit the officer "who would clean out the nest of loyalists and redskins and make this Promised Land safe for the Israelites, the Chosen People, and cast out the British Canaanites . . ."

Willis was in high spirits, thought Ella Sutherland as she looked on from the trading house porch, where she stood shaded from the bright May sunshine. And it was no wonder, for had not James Morely invited Willis to stay with him, even planned for a meetinghouse to be built for his devoted followers? Perhaps the minister had struck the right chord with James, who seemed lately to be acting as if he were quite uncomfortable with the world. It might do James good to have a spiritual adviser at hand, as a means of relieving the pressure that surely built up in a man who had to oversee Cullen and Company.

Even just yesterday Peter Defries and James had argued bitterly at the tavern, with Peter accusing James of being responsible for the deaths of several men working for the Frontier Company back in Albany. Although Peter had no proof—as James pointedly reminded him—it was suspected that Cullen and Company agents had waylaid the men and destroyed much-needed munitions being shipped to a rebel fort on the Mohawk River, west of Albany. Cullen and Company had subsequently brought in more munitions, at a considerably higher price.

James was in a huff toward all the members of the Frontier Company, and did not even seem inclined to talk with Susannah, though Ella saw clearly enough how he looked at the young woman when Susannah was not aware of it. Or was she? Susannah was grown now, with a woman's mind and a woman's intuition, and she saw much that Ella thought she missed. Ella was glad for the bond between Entellus Greyson and Susannah, but like Owen and her daughter, she feared for the man's life on this campaign. At the moment Susannah was at Greyson's stirrup, bidding him farewell.

Ella was distracted from watching the soldiers prepare to ride out by the appearance of Noah Maxwell at James's side. Of late, the two men seemed less friendly to each other, Ella had noticed, and there were rumors that more than once they had almost come to blows over company policy. Certainly James had hardened in these past few years, but he was in no way as underhanded and heartless as Maxwell, who was well known among the town's prostitutes and gamblers, but had pretensions to good citizenship and breeding whenever he was in the public light.

"A fine body of men!" the Reverend Willis declared. Earlier, before they had mounted up, he had said a prayer for them, their heads all bowed in devotion. "Godspeed, gentlemen," he had declared, "and may you do the work of Christian soldiers, for the good of God's kingdom on earth. Godspeed!"

Mike Grub came riding slowly past Willis and leaned down to shake hands. Willis laughed and called out encouragement, and Grub's eyes shone with the gladness and confidence of a saved man. Indeed, a change had come over Mike Grub. He no longer drank, and it was said he had not gouged an eye since the night he got religion, two days back. Still, he would be a scourge to Indians, and he did not seem to have taken to the admonition that cleanliness is next to godliness, for he was as greasy and caked with dirt as ever. But Willis was pleased enough with having converted one of the hardest cases on the frontier.

Just then, Peter Defries appeared behind Ella, with an open letter in his hand. He was reading it as best he could, looking close to tears, which for him was unusual. Ella knew the letter was from his wife, whom he had not seen for months. As he finished, he cursed under his breath and looked up at James.

James was coming back up the trading house steps, Willis at one side, Maxwell at the other. The troops were pulling out, and Ella looked to see Susannah staring at Entellus Greyson, who waved and rode off to join Colonel Crawford at the head of the column. In her distraction, Ella did not see Peter stride forward and block James's path at the head of the steps.

James stopped, coldly demanding to know what Defries wanted. Seeing that Peter was about to cause trouble, Ella quickly moved to him, as the big man said in a hissing voice, "We got those dogs of yours who raided my convoy!" He mentioned two names, both of which must have been familiar to James, for he paled. "Both dead, but afore going under they confessed that Cullen and Company ordered them to hit us! What do you say, James? That I'm lying? Say it! I had good friends killed—"

Ella grasped Peter's arm and pulled him back with all her strength, but Peter was not willing to leave off, not until he had shamed James. He spoke loudly, so that many could hear. "Cullen and Company killers, James, just like ever! But you don't know 'em! Your hands're clean! Admit it! Who set 'em on us? Tell me, for if you don't know the truth about your own dogs, then you ain't a good master of hounds!"

"The testimony of dead men isn't much, Peter." James was red in the face, looking up at the towering Defries, a man who had once been like an uncle to him, who had taught him much. Now there was nothing between them, nothing but suspicion and resentment. Ella wanted it to be no more than that.

She cried out, "Leave off, Peter, for heaven's sake! In the name of God, don't fight here!"

She knew how much influence James had with the fort's authorities, and knew that Peter was already suspected of having sprung Owen from prison months back. If there were trouble, it would go hard for Peter.

Maxwell had taken a step back, but now he spoke in a

shrill voice to the gathering crowd. "Why, this is slander! Call out the watch! This man is publicly slandering Mr. Morely—"

"Shut up, Noah," James said with a growl, and kept his eyes—dark and fierce eyes—on Peter Defries. "You have no proof, and I deny everything you say! Simple as that, Peter. Now be wise and step aside."

Defries would not go. "Jamie, my boy—" He shrugged free of Ella and moved even closer to James, just two feet away, and Ella could not pull him back. "Jamie, you best get some religion from this holy man, because you go on like this and you'll be meeting your Maker afore your time!"

That hurt Ella deeply. After all the years in which Frontier Company members had been like a family, it had come to this. Peter was a bear, but a sweet and kind one unless roused to anger. Now he was ready to attack James, because justice would not otherwise be done.

At a signal from Maxwell, the bodyguard Bill Bartholomew appeared, and he was even taller and broader than Defries, whose eyes lit up to see him. Peter licked his lips as the brute came on.

Ella could not have stopped it, but the Reverend Willis —not a small man himself—leaped between the giants and held them apart with a shout that stung Ella's ears.

"This is not—this is not the way! Peace, gentlemen!"

It appeared that James had not noticed Bartholomew's approach, but as soon as he saw the man, he shouted him back, as an animal trainer would curb a beast. Then he swung on Peter, glaring without fear at him.

"I accept no blame for whatever crimes you are speaking about! None! Now, will you move aside?" Suddenly, as if something had come over him, James stepped back and, rubbing his eyes, had to steady himself with a hand on the shoulder of the minister. Ella was alarmed, aware that James was subject to bad dizzy spells and fits of epilepsy.

The old feeling of affection for the James she had known welled up in her, and in pity she stepped forward. Touching his arm, she spoke gently.

"James, won't you sit down with Peter and find out what this is all about?" He looked up at her, his eyes fogged. "You know what Bradford Cullen built, and how much evil still remains in your company."

Peter was grumbling, unwilling to give James any benefit of the doubt. "He well knows what's going on."

Ella ignored him. "James, we must not shed blood—"

Maxwell stepped up and said, "Come away, James." He reached for his partner's arm and pulled. "We don't need these people—"

James wrenched away, glaring at Maxwell with what Ella could only describe as hatred. The look set Maxwell back, and he turned away, withdrawing quickly with Bartholomew.

At last, breathing hard, James recovered and looked at Ella, his eyes clear and soft now. "I will do what I can, Ella, and Frontier Company representatives may call on me this afternoon to discuss this . . . this affair."

With that, he pushed past Defries, who let him go. Ella felt infinitely relieved, and she sighed, leaning on Peter's strong arm.

It was then that the feisty minister stepped close to Peter and stared at him for a long moment, as if trying to fathom who this giant was. Ella could tell the minister was badly nearsighted, which made him squint and peer at Defries.

"And what faith do you profess, my headstrong fellow?" Willis loudly asked without the slightest timidity.

Peter chewed his lip, then replied, "Ayrab!"

The minister was a bit jolted. "Ayrab? And what do you worship, then? Do you believe in original sin? In God's mercy? Do you believe in Christ dying so that sinners may be saved?"

Defries cleared his throat and smiled in a friendly way.

"We believe in Methodists, preacher. Methodists take all the world's sins on theirselves so there ain't none left for us Ayrabs."

"What? In the name of—"

"That way we got to keep on sinning so's the Methodists don't run out of sin to take on theirselves and get saved for it."

Willis's lip thrust out, and he said, "Likely your soul'll take a regiment of preachers to save, Ayrab!" He began to pass Defries.

Peter said, "What would preachers like yerself do if there weren't no sin? You oughta thank us Ayrabs—"

Ella yanked him away, but she could not help from giggling, though she was embarrassed and told him to hold his tongue. Her good humor was interrupted, however, when Little Jake appeared, dressed for travel, and with a small-bore hunting rifle over one shoulder, the blue jay on the other. Ella had the sinking feeling that he meant to go out with the army, and she let go of Peter's arm to ask the boy what was the meaning of this unannounced departure. It was just like the close-mouthed Jake to go off this way without asking permission, or even hinting of his plans.

Jake shuffled his feet and said, "Clemmons and Heath boys and me're going hunting . . . up by the Six-Mile Creek."

"Hunting?"

Defries looked closely and said, "You ain't aiming to tramp away with them militia now, are you? That wouldn't be smart, nohow."

Ella's heart fluttered when Jake did not immediately reply. "Hunting's all," he said, forcing himself to meet her eyes. "You don't have to worry, Ma. I'm old enough to go out."

In that moment, a rush of love, true mother's love, filled Ella, and she wanted to reach out and embrace Jake, but she did not, though her arms tingled for it. He would have been embarrassed. He reminded her so much of Benjamin, her boy now gone forever. Jake was not of her blood, but indeed he had filled an emptiness in her heart, and she did not want him to go.

"Jake . . ."

"Please, Ma. I'm old enough now, and I ain't—haven't —been out hunting for a long time!"

"Now, Jake, no son of mine would ever lie to me—" As she spoke, she was waving to Owen, who stood talking with General Irvine near the commander's stone headquarters. "Talk to your pa."

Jake flushed, his color growing as he saw Sutherland coming toward them. At first, he became angry. "He won't let me go! You think I'm just a babe, but I can take care of myself!"

When Sutherland heard what Jake was doing, he thought a moment, then said, "When Crawford's army is two or three days gone, then you can go hunting, boy."

"Aw, damn!" He threw down his cap, the bird flying off, and Ella recoiled at hearing him swear. "We want to go now, by damn!"

"Jake!" she cried.

"You can't tell me what to do! You ain't my real ma and pa! You can't stop me! They would've treated me like a man! Damn it all to hell!"

Sutherland gave him a stinging slap on the side of the head that sent him reeling, and Defries clucked, saying, "That looks like a whack from a pa to me, Jakie. That's the sort of whack my pa used to give me now and then just to show he loved me!"

But Jake was in no mood for joking. He scowled at Owen and Ella, snatched up his hat, and began to storm away.

"Be at the cabin!" Sutherland called out. "If I have to

come find you, boy, I'll give you a licking you won't forget, real pa or not! You hear me, laddie?"

Jake knew he meant it and replied with a grudging "I hear!" as he stamped off toward the cabin.

A moment later, to Ella's relief, Owen called to the boy to come back, and with bowed head Jake returned, the side of his face red from the slap.

Owen said, with a hand on the lad's shoulder, "I wouldn't want you to go with them even if there were three thousand, laddie."

Jake sobbed. "I'm man enough!"

"Aye, you're man enough." Sutherland gave him a little shake of affection. "And there's an army of good men who are man enough . . ." Ella thought her husband's voice almost broke as he said, "But I fear there are not enough men, laddie. Those militia are in grave trouble, and I fear many will never come back."

There was a gasp, and they turned to see Susannah standing close by. She had heard all this from her father before, in gentler terms, but to hear it spoken so bluntly brought tears to her eyes. Ella went to put an arm around her daughter. Turning her away, she glanced back at Jake and Owen, saying, "Hasn't there been enough heartache? Now, Jake, for the love of heaven, listen to your father!"

As she walked away with Susannah, Ella took one last look back and saw Owen put his arm over the boy's shoulders. Then Defries gave a laugh and roughly yanked Jake onto his back, making him giggle like the child he had been, not so very long ago.

"You know, James, many's the time I've sat talking across this very table to Bradford Cullen, just as I'm talking to you now, and I still don't like it." Sutherland was in Cullen and Company's spacious inner office, seated in an upholstered chair, a red-faced James Morely behind the polished mahogany table, leaning back, looking glum.

Beside Sutherland was Peter Defries, and sitting nearby James was Noah Maxwell, these two listening with scowls on their faces. Outwardly, Sutherland was the calmest man in the room, although he felt rage and anguish as he addressed James almost the way he had once addressed Bradford Cullen.

"We've just told you of a dozen occasions where Cullen and Company agents have attacked our people, bribed authorities to obstruct and harass us, conspired to cheat and steal from us . . . and now, as in the past, there have been killings." Sutherland paused to let this penetrate, sure James would recall that his own father had been murdered by agents of Bradford Cullen almost twenty years before.

Maxwell snorted and said to James, "It's all hearsay—nothing provable! Do you think they'd be here now, talking to us like this, if they thought they could make a case of it in court? Pah!"

Defries answered, "We ain't lawyers like yerself, Maxwell, so we don't need to make cases. We act, and whenever we do it'll cost you!"

Maxwell again snorted. "Your company's puny! It's of no concern to us. Why would we deign to commit crimes, when all we have to do is outbid you and undersell you? It's laughable, to think you believe Cullen and Company has the slightest fear of what's left of the Frontier Company."

"Just the same," Defries said in a voice that was as sharp as it was low, "ye're now warned to leave off bloodletting, or ye'll lose more than ye gain, and ye'll feel my hand on yer own neck, lawyer!"

The color left Maxwell's face, but he tried to tough it out with another scoff, turning to James for him to give the reply.

Sutherland and Defries had made their point, and as for

Maxwell's theories, Sutherland knew that if anyone could challenge Cullen and Company for mastery of the rejuvenated fur trade in the northwest, it would be the Frontier Company. James and Maxwell surely knew it as well. When James made no immediate reply, Sutherland spoke up.

"You have many loyalist agents, James, and though Congress does not know it, we know it—"

Maxwell began to protest, but James waved him off. It was useless to deny that Bradford Cullen had often dealt directly with loyalists and spies for the British. He waited for Sutherland to finish.

"You believe you can get rid of them in time, and that when the war ends, all your company's treacherous conspiracies will be forgotten, and your double-dealing agents will become honest men again." He sat back in his chair. "That won't happen, James, and you won't be able to get rid of them, not as long as you have knaves like Maxwell here at your side."

Maxwell blanched, but he dared not challenge Sutherland, and sat trembling with anger and fear.

James spoke up. "Cullen and Company is not what it once was, Owen, and I am not Bradford Cullen, God forgive him, and rest his black soul." He hunched forward as he spoke, as if thinking hard, one hand rubbing the surface of the desk in a mannerism that gave Sutherland a chill because it so resembled one of Cullen's own gestures.

James said, "You don't have any right to bully Mr. Maxwell, Owen." He drew a slow breath. "I'll have these instances of alleged irregularities looked into—"

Maxwell made a sound of exasperation and looked away, eyes rolling. James paid him no attention.

"But don't expect me to relent in my competition with your company. Unlike Mr. Maxwell here, I respect the Frontier Company, and well know that should I give you room to grow, you will be a genuine threat to my plans for this country."

Sutherland said, "Plans that include Congress, James? Or will they, too, simply be in your way?"

James remained cool, refusing to react to Sutherland's barb. "Let me just say, Owen, that my plans do not include in any way the success of the Frontier Company." He leaned forward a little, his eyes suddenly glittering. "But you know that it would please me if you would sell out to me, and join me as a captain in my company, as a man who immediately would have far-flung influence over a vast region, a region greater than the former thirteen colonies combined, and with an even mightier future!"

Sutherland again saw before him not James, but the image of Bradford Cullen, who had served as James's mentor for some years. Cullen had nurtured this same dream, and had made the same offer to Sutherland, who more than once had refused it.

Sutherland stood up. "I have my own plans, James, and they do not include an independent northwest, nor do they include a captaincy in Cullen and Company."

James sat back, rigid, obviously hot inside. "Let the past die, Owen! What in hell does my company's name have to do with it?"

Sutherland and Defries went to the door, Sutherland turning to say, "In this case, everything, James, though you don't seem to know it yet." He looked at Maxwell, whose mouth was turned down in anger. "Ask *him* what's behind the name of Cullen and Company, James . . . I think he knows better than you do."

Sutherland and Defries left. Out in the street they walked quietly for a while, until they were away from the fort and approaching their cabin. Defries said, "That Maxwell's a dog, but he's got James on the leash."

Those were Sutherland's sentiments exactly, and he

nodded. "When Maxwell and the powerful cronies who manipulate him have no more use for the clever James Morely..."

He need say no more.

Soon after Sutherland departed, Maxwell left James alone in the office, neither man saying anything more. James knew Maxwell would do little to right whatever wrongs Cullen and Company agents had done, so there was no use speaking to him about it. James would have to be the one who rooted out the corruption, at least as much as it could be rooted out. Last year he and Maxwell had come to power through their own corruption, secretly altering the books of Cullen and Company, forging a will for Bradford Cullen so that everything would be left to them as major partners. There were several other lesser partners of long standing, however, men back east, with whom Noah Maxwell was intimate, and these were hard, ruthless businessmen who put pressure on James to do things their way, to run Cullen and Company as viciously as it ever had been run.

James was ambitious, and he reveled in the great power he had inherited, but he was not one to employ murder and theft as his tools. More than once he had cut off Maxwell when an oblique suggestion was made as to how an opponent might be removed. At least, James thought, Maxwell had never even hinted at assassination when it came to dealing with Frontier Company principals. Obviously, Maxwell knew by now that James had a strong tie to Sutherland and the rest; it was like a family bond, and even though there had been a long feud and bitter competition through the years, they were still family. They were all touched with the influence of the far northwest, and they considered themselves "men of the North," with a high standard of honor.

Yet this very honor tormented James. Even now, as he sat gazing out his window at the parade grounds, he remembered the death of Bradford Cullen last autumn. He remembered it with a surge of remorse and shame, though he had not yet admitted even to himself the full truth of what had happened. It was said Cullen died of an apoplectic fit. Perhaps he had.

James had suffered from a dizzy spell during a heated argument with Cullen and had nearly fainted. As he had fallen to his knees, the world spinning around him, he had been aware that Cullen, too, had fallen to the floor, clutching his chest. The memory of the vision was vivid, as was the sound of loud thumping, flesh against floor, that came to him. Now, when he closed his eyes, James remembered the blurred impression of Noah Maxwell crouched over the prostrate Cullen. Was that real? Had James, in his dizziness, actually seen Maxwell force a pillow over the weakened Cullen's face and suffocate him? Or was it an illusion?

James shook himself back to the present, seeing Susannah Sutherland strolling with her foster brother, Jake Smith, across the fort grounds. James sighed. Susannah did not cast even a casual glance his way. She looked forlorn, doubtless because of the departure of Greyson. Yes, James knew, he had won Cullen and Company and all its unmatched power, but he had lost the friendship of the members of the Frontier Company, and he had lost Susannah Sutherland.

His own mother, now living down at the settlement at the Falls of the Ohio, had been full of remorse at his defection to Cullen and Company. Well . . . He stood up and poured himself a brandy, downing it quickly as he watched Susannah walk out of sight. There were more important things for a successful man than sentiment. He had the world at his feet. The northwest was ripe for the plucking, and before long he would rule it. History would remember him with respect.

He took another brandy, the heat of it and the fire of his imagination making his heart lighter. Every triumph required sacrifices, and there would be other women, other friends. Soon enough he would purge Cullen and Company, as only a man of his ability could. The third brandy went down more smoothly than the first two. He would bring even Noah Maxwell to heel, and would show the shrewd men back east a thing or two. And who would stop him?

Nothing Owen Sutherland could do would make the Frontier Company rise from the ashes of the Revolution. Too many of his people had remained loyalists, while he was a staunch rebel. Cullen and Company, however, had friends and customers on the king's side, and they would serve well when the time came to negotiate the future of the northwest.

There would be other women than Susannah Sutherland, other friends to count on—friends far better than Noah Maxwell, that was certain. James was on his way to being drunk, and was glad for it on this quiet, lonely afternoon. There would be other women, no matter if none was quite like Susannah Sutherland. A man could not have everything, though James Morely would come very close.

Far away to the west, sitting outside her lodge in the Delaware village on the lower Muskingum River, Evangeline looked up from fixing Niko-lota's moccasins and saw the white scout Simon Girty come riding in. A grizzled, black-bearded man, he had a look of excitement on his face as he sprang down from his horse with the agility of a young brave, though he was near fifty. Bandy-legged and short, he was still strong and wiry, wearing a feather in his flat buckskin hat.

Evangeline had never liked Girty, who often had come

to her native village of Chillicothe, sometimes bringing prisoners for the Shawnees to torture. He was dirtier than the dirtiest Indian, and when drunk was dangerous to man and woman. Yet he was known as a wily woodsman, perhaps the best of the loyal whites in all the northwest. So when Simon Girty came hurrying into this village, everyone knew there was something important to tell, and men and boys crowded around him as he made his way to Evangeline's lodge.

"Your husband here?" he asked in his rasping, creaky voice. "Tell him I got big news!" His eyes lit with pride and excitement. "News that'll get revenge for your people, Praying Woman!"

Evangeline feared that more killing was at hand. She desired no vengeance. Ever since marrying Niko-lota a few weeks ago, she had been living here with the Delawares— heathens all, but still good to her as the wife of Niko-lota. Although they called her Praying Woman, after her Christian practice, and did their best to get the two children, Maria and Christoph, to adopt wild Indian ways, all three of them had been treated kindly.

Had it not been for the dreadful circumstances of the past few months, Evangeline would have been happy beyond hope as the wife of Niko-lota. As it was, she accepted it that he might never come around to her Moravian faith. Still, he did not abuse her for her beliefs, and he was tolerant, defending her against slander, and taking the children in as his own.

Now, however, the arrival of Girty was about to change the tranquillity of Evangeline's new home. Soon the frightening word passed through the village that the whites were once more on the march into Indian territory.

Niko-lota came to stand above her and say, "They will not go home again, Evangeline, and I will not come back to you until they are rubbed out."

She did not answer, did not weep or beg him not to go.

It would have done no good. She wanted no blood for the deaths of the innocent Moravians, but she knew it was beyond her power to stop what was about to happen. All around, the painted men were cavorting, dancing with weapons raised as they boasted of their prowess in battle. Their war songs promised to shed the blood of ten whites for every Moravian Indian killed.

But Niko-lota did not dance. He stood watching his people, his arms folded, deep in thought. Nervously, Evangeline tried to go on with her mending of the moccasins. He would need them. In battle, they must stay on his feet, and she would see to that, because he was her man forever.

chapter **12**

SPEED AND SURPRISE

Little Jake's mind was made up: he would prove himself a man; he would learn to be one the only way he knew how—in the heat of battle, as many a youth before him had become a man.

It was three days since his foster parents had kept him from following Crawford's army, and yesterday morning, without much difficulty, he had gotten permission to hunt. By now they might have learned that the boys with whom he had intended to hunt had changed their minds and were still at home. He hoped that would not matter much, and that before looking for him the Sutherlands would give him a day or two on his own, to make up for having forbidden him to go on the campaign. Probably they had assumed he would no longer attempt to join the campaign, for the expedition was long gone. Anyway, no one had made him promise not to follow it.

Jake's mind worked over these thoughts as he paddled his small canoe downriver toward Mingo Bottom, where the troops were to have debarked for their march a hundred and fifty miles overland. He hoped his parents would not be too upset when he did not come back soon, and he believed they would be proud of him after all was said and done. He

was not a Sutherland; he was still the orphan of brave
Pennsylvanians—men such as those who made up the militia army under Crawford—and he would be campaigning
with his own kind when he caught up to them.

The journey downriver was swift and hazardous, with
water high and snags everywhere, debris and floating logs
swirling in strong currents. Jake pushed on as fast as he
could, sure he would reach Mingo Bottom before nightfall.
Twice logs nearly rammed him, and several times the
canoe spun out of control in the eddies. Darkness gathered
more swiftly than he expected, and the wind turned cold.
Mosquitoes and gnats swarmed, stinging his face and
hands, but he could scarcely brush them off, because it
took all his efforts just to manage the canoe. In time, it
seemed as if the forest on all sides were watching him,
threatening, and brooding. There were great dark avenues
in the trees, and the gullies and vales filled with the
shadows of night long before the sky turned dark. Jake was
sore and tired from paddling, but he thought he knew
where he was on the river, was sure it was only an hour or
so more.

He was in no mood to pull ashore and sleep on land
alone, and that increased his determination to reach the
army. He took one quick handful of pemmican, the fur
trader's traveling meal of cooked meat ground and pounded
with berries and sweetener. He wanted more, but it was
difficult to eat and steer the canoe, so for safety's sake he
paddled and stayed hungry. Time passed, and night closed
in. He hoped he was not wrong about the distance to
Mingo Bottom. He would get there soon, then he would
have some stories of his own to tell about this trying river
journey, stories to make the older men grin and nod ap-
provingly. His parents might be terrified for him, but the
soldiers would accept him as one of them, and he would
prove himself worthy.

• • •

Crawford's army laughed and joked around their camp-fires deep in Indian country. They were not far from Gnadenhutten, and most of the men who had been at the massacre were also in this expedition. Many had stories to tell about that first adventure, jokes and anecdotes that proved their disdain for Indians and their confidence that they had done right.

Entellus Greyson had heard them boast that they would kill every Indian they came across on this campaign, and he did not doubt they would try. As yet the army was only a few days from Pitt, but already Greyson was uneasy, almost sorry he had come, unless he and Crawford and a few of the less bloodthirsty men could do some good, preventing other massacres.

Already some men were calling this the second Moravian campaign, as if the first one had been a military triumph, an example of what to do to all Indians. There were other Moravian Indians in a village at Upper Sandusky, Greyson knew, and this place would be attacked, according to the plan, the village destroyed along with the villages of thousands of hostile Indians.

The plan depended on speed and surprise, and if any men could carry it out, these Pennsylvanians and the handful of Virginians could. As he reclined before his campfire, listening to confident, jovial chatter, Greyson observed the men nearby. There was the handsome Crawford, long legs stretched out, and beside him his grown son, John; also with him was a son-in-law who was an attorney, William Harrison, and a nephew, William Crawford. Unlike many of the backwoodsmen in this army, these four were kind and refined gentlemen, good at a game of whist, and glad for the company of Greyson.

Because of Greyson's previous defiance of Williamson and Grub, most of the Pennsylvanians avoided him, thinking him an Indian-lover. At that moment, Grub was at a nearby campfire; he and Captain Bilderback were discussing a Bible passage, debating its meaning. Bilderback had read it, and Grub was asking him to repeat it over and over so he could fathom it, could turn it round and round, and make it fit the notion he wanted it to. Every once in a while, when the spirit moved him, Grub would let fly with a shout of joy or praise, and sometimes he would lean back and laugh in his delight at being saved, at getting religion.

Greyson paid little attention, absorbed as he was with a new friend he had made, a dashing young Russian émigré and fellow aide-de-camp who called himself John Rose. Rose, who spoke French fluently and was an excellent surgeon, would not reveal the true story of how he had come to leave Russia to fight for the Revolution in the northwestern wilderness. Despite the mystery surrounding him, he had won the confidence of the men with his willingness to share their daily work, even though it was obvious he was of higher birth than they.

Tall and slender, quite dark, with penetrating eyes, Rose enjoyed studying the half-wild frontiersmen like Grub, and he would ask Greyson endless questions about backwoods American culture. This evening, while resting in his blankets, Rose observed that he could not understand a man like Mike Grub. So fierce and dangerous, but now that he had been converted, Grub hungered after spiritual enlightenment.

"Americans are turmoil of ideas, none they truly understand," he said in a rolling Russian accent. He looked at Grub and gestured with his pipe. "Who would imagine such a brute would be so enraptured with Holy Bible, would have such profound longing to understand his reason for being . . . and yet, what does he know of Christian mercy?"

Greyson took a small chess set from his pack and began

to set it up between himself and his friend. "Don't your Russian serfs wonder what God wants from them, why He set your czar over them and made them so humble?"

Rose was quick with his answer and scoffed, "What a question! The smelly ones? Wonder about meaning of Bible? Why, they don't have Bible, and could not read it if they did! You won't find men in serf's hut like that Grub there, struggling like schoolchild to read! No, my friend, I don't believe our peasants have the curiosity of yours."

After a moment, Greyson said with a wry smile, "Has anyone of your nobility bothered to ask them what they think about?"

Laughing, Rose first dismissed this as a witty joke. Then he considered it, knitting his brows. In the background, Grub cried out something about repentance, that one's sins may be blotted out.

Rose remained pensive, then after a while said, "Why, now, my dear Greyson, you have whetted appetite for my own homeland. Curiosity that brought me to America might send me home again, to learn more about my own peasants!" He moved a pawn. "Ask peasants whether they think . . . How charming a thought!"

Grub cried out, and no one dared tell him to pipe down. "The salvation of the righteous is of the Lord! He is their strength in time of trouble!" Grub's eyes shone, and he looked around the campsite as if to see who understood. Most men averted their faces, some nodding and smiling politely, a few others giving a mild supporting shout of sympathy. Grub called to the army: "And the Lord shall deliver them from the wicked! And He'll save them, because they trust in Him!" He was on his knees, hands clasped, and cried, "Hallelujah! Praise God!"

In the heavy silence that followed, Greyson could not help himself, and without looking at Grub, he called loudly, "And that same Psalm Thirty-seven of David declares that the *meek* shall inherit the earth, and shall delight themselves in the abundance of peace!"

Several score men lying in blankets nearby turned to stare, first at Greyson and then at Grub, perhaps wondering whether their rough companion had got religion and meekness all at once. Grub opened his eyes and looked at Greyson, who made another move in the chess game.

Greyson assumed Grub was thinking about meekness, and resolved to give him something else to think about. He shouted, "The wicked have drawn out the sword, and have bent their bow, to cast down the poor and needy, and to slay such as be of upright conversation!" Rose, smiling, moved a piece. "Their sword shall enter into their own heart, and their bows shall be broken!"

Silence. Trees rustled, and campfires crackled. A man coughed here, another poured himself tea that dribbled noisily into a cup—this was Colonel Crawford—while big Mike Grub pondered. Greyson heard Grub quietly ask Bilderback whether the Bible really did say such a thing. Bilderback nodded.

Then Grub called, as he sat down, arms drawing up his knees. "What you getting at, Greyson?"

The Marylander turned and said calmly, "Don't you remember that psalm, Grub? Old Brother Abraham of the Moravians recited it just before you killed him with the hammer."

The backwoodsman stiffened, fury building in him, and other men sat up to curse and scorn Greyson, but the Marylander was not finished, and he said brazenly, "Old Abraham knew a bit more of that psalm, and I have made it my business to remember it myself: The steps of the good man are ordered by the Lord; and he delighteth in his way. Though he fall, he shall not be utterly cast down, for the Lord upholdeth him with his hand. . . . For the Lord loveth judgment, and forsaketh not his saints; they are preserved forever; but the seed of the wicked shall be cut off. The righteous shall inherit the land, and dwell therein forever."

There was silence again, until Rose said cheerfully, "Amen! Your move, sir."

To Greyson's surprise, Mike Grub made no reply. He sat with his knees drawn up, late into the night, until the fire died and the camp became completely dark.

To the east, in a gloomy cove of the rushing Ohio River, young Jake Smith huddled inside a hollow tree for warmth, and for safety.

The haunting sounds of night were all around, and everything seemed unfriendly. He was alone, having been unable to reach the Mingo Bottom base camp by nightfall, and now he prayed for morning to come and wondered whether the Sutherlands were thinking of him just then. At first he wished to be home, safe, warm. But he forced the thought away. He had never been so cold before, and he shivered as much from fright as from the chill. His rifle was held close, and the little food he had brought was tied high on a tree a ways off, in case a bear or a panther came to investigate its smell.

The howls of wolves sounded in the distance, and he heard owls hoot and call back and forth. The animals of the night. Or were they Indians? Had they seen him land, and were they already closing in, watching him with their cat's eyes as he lay trembling—trying not to tremble—in that dirty log?

Morning could not come soon enough for him. He was sure he would never sleep.

But morning came, sunny and fresh, and Jake was startled to find he had slept through part of it. Stiff and filthy, he drew himself from the rotten log, gathered what little gear he had, and readied the canoe for a push back into the water. He ached and was hungry. Tearing at some jerked meat, he did the best he could to eat but did not want to waste time. In a few moments he was pushing the canoe into the cove again. The water was cold on his legs, and he quickly got into the birch craft and was picking up the paddle from the seat when he jumped in fright at the loud crack of a rifle, and a slug whizzed past. He dived forward into the boat as a dozen other rifles went off, and lead tore into the sides of the canoe all around him. He dared not move, lying there, shaking, praying the canoe would be pulled away by the current and drawn into the main stream, where he could sit up and paddle for safety.

Suddenly, the boat was jerked to a halt, and with horror he knew they had him. He was grabbed by the hair and yanked painfully up. He went for his knife at his belt, but he stopped when he saw the fierce, savage face of a Pennsylvania scout.

"Blast me if you ain't white!" the bearded fellow declared. "You with the Injuns? Eh?" He gave the boy a shake by the hair, and Jake cried out his name and that he was from Pitt. Just then the others came down to the water's edge, and among them he recognized several young men, a few years older than he.

"Why, Smith," one yelled, "you come down for the fun? Come to join up with the campaign? Well, you're done too late, boy! They's gone!"

The older man let Jake drop into the canoe, which now had taken on considerable water. Jake was rattled, but he refused to show it.

"I come to go along with Colonel Crawford," he said bravely.

The old man cackled. "Like the fella said, boy, you done come too late. The party's gonna be a hundred mile from here by now. But you kin set with us, guarding boats and supplies—we're jes' down the river there—and thank yer lucky stars that a white man's bullet didn't put an end to yer adventure right quick!"

Jake had slept just a hundred yards from the base camp! He had missed the expedition, but he dared not set out alone overland. He swore and pounded the bottom of the boat with his fist, springing a larger leak, and the boat proceeded to sink as the men pointed and laughed. Jake despised them all just then, for they thought him just a fool boy. He could not deny it, either, and that galled him all the more. Maybe he would go off anyway, and let them think about that!

Not long afterward, Crawford's expedition arrived at the ruins of Gnadenhutten. The men were silent at first as they rode in and gazed on the destruction. Some of the Pennsylvanians were unrepentant and cursed the Moravians as loudly as ever. Many, however, did not say much, and only a few wanted to go to the blackened church to see whether the charred bones were still there. They were.

There had been an attempt to cover the foundation and basement with earth and rocks, and the walls had caved in for the most part. But Greyson could tell that no Christians had been here, not even the missionaries now still in exile. Only Indians had come to hastily bury the dead in the ruins. They did not know how to bury Christians. It was an eerie, doleful place, with few tracks, as if the Indians shunned it as somehow cursed, or haunted.

Greyson realized that the entire journey so far had been through an abandoned land, not one Indian being seen, not one run-in with any of their scouts, and no prisoners taken. It was as if the army were advancing through a forbidden country, desolate of human life. The massacre here at Gnadenhutten could have scourged and terrified all the Indians, of course, causing them to avoid the area. This was what some of the more callous whites declared during the afternoon meal on the edge of the village clearing. Greyson did not believe it, and neither did Colonel Crawford.

Shortly after dinner, before moving out, Greyson took one last visit to the ruins, where some of the whites were poking around for cast-off tools and equipment that might be of use to them. By now it was not exactly looting, for the village was given up to the weather and wind.

Greyson felt the need to stand at the place where the dead lay. He walked over, and found Colonel Crawford there ahead of him, with his relatives and John Rose, all of them with heads bowed, silently praying. When they were finished, they turned and greeted Greyson.

Crawford put his hat back on his head, saying in his deep but gentle voice, "You should be honored for having tried to prevent this, sir. I would have done the same, but I fear with similar results."

Greyson nodded, not knowing how to answer.

Rose and Crawford's three relatives walked away, and the colonel looked back at the devastation. "I hope this expedition of ours throws a shock amongst the Indians, so that the war will come to an end and they will sue for peace. This, however . . . this sort of tragedy will only make them fight harder, and want to do the same to us."

Greyson said, "Many of the men believe this massacre has terrified the Indians and made them run. They think we won't meet any opposition at all. Do you think so?"

Crawford was looking over Greyson's shoulder, obviously staring at someone. Greyson turned, surprised to see Colonel David Williamson, leaning against a maple tree, close enough to have heard everything. Williamson's chin jutted out, and his eyes were hard. He was struggling with some inner conflict.

Crawford asked, "What do you think, Colonel? Have the Indians turned tail and run because of this?"

Williamson's jaw worked as if he were chewing something, and he stood up straight, hitching his buckskin jacket over his shoulders.

"They might," he said, turning partly away. "And they might not. I ain't no prophet, but I ain't worried, neither. They ain't men enough to stand against us." He strode off, head high, arms swinging in an exaggerated way.

Greyson said, "I thought he might have been with Mike Grub, both of them praying here." He gave a little ironic laugh but stopped short when Crawford spoke.

"Grub came by before you did, but I've no idea what he was thinking. He certainly did not give out with any shouts of religious jubilation."

Greyson looked closely at this man, at the wrinkled, weathered face, the lean and strong features. Crawford was the cream of the frontier folk, and it was no wonder George Washington had chosen him as a companion to journey with down the Ohio in search of good land. Colonel William Crawford was no David Williamson, and that gave Greyson hope that one day this country would be settled and developed by the best men of the northwest.

Crawford then gave Greyson something to think about. "Do not condemn these folk too quickly, sir; you do not know their trials, and you cannot know what they have suffered at the hands of the Indian." He cordially touched Greyson's arm, and they turned to rejoin the army to continue the march. "We are riding today to put an end to this horror, but mark me, sir, there is only one way that it can end: the Indian must surrender, and the white man must reign supreme."

Greyson slowly nodded.

Crawford said, "After all, sir, that's why you have come out here, isn't it? You want Indian country for your own. You fought, and your men fought in the Revolution without pay, and Congress and Maryland promised to grant you this country for your very own." He let that sit a moment, and they went on toward the men, who were striking camp and dousing fires. "Very well, Mr. Greyson, if you want this country, then you had better be prepared to fight for it, and to kill for it, or you will come up empty-handed. Maybe dead."

Greyson finished the thought in his own mind: *And if I fail, some other white man will step into my place, to go on fighting until the last Indian is beaten down and his race crushed forever*.

He glanced one last time over his shoulder at the ruins of once-lovely Gnadenhutten.

The army had not gone far past Gnadenhutten when, during an afternoon rest, forty horses took fright, spooked by something unseen, and broke away from the herd. They escaped so quickly that it was as if they had vanished, scattering into the woods along unknown trails and disappearing.

This serious setback dampened the spirits of some, many of whom saw it as a bad omen for the campaign. The men who lost their mounts were compelled to turn around and trudge back to the base camp, thus weakening the army considerably.

As Greyson rode along with John Rose later in the day, he noticed that the mood of the army had indeed changed. It was as if the dismal scene at Gnadenhutten had unnerved them, made them feel less enthusiastic about what was to come. That place had truly seemed haunted, and now the dark woods hemming in the trail were equally doleful, silent, and watchful.

Rose said, "We need action, good chase, or few shots exchanged to give confidence to men." He rode on, looking intently into the shadowy woods, a green, shimmering wall of spring leaf crowding out the sun. "The men want fight, and first blood will give heart!"

Greyson agreed. "They expected the Indians to fight us

and get beaten and run off . . . then more of them to stand
and fight and get beaten, and so on." He thought about
that, and how there was not the slightest sign of Indians
anywhere. The few lodges here and there were abandoned,
fires long cold, not even a stray dog left behind. The trail
was steep and winding, the sun hot in open spaces, and
mosquitoes and gnats plagued men and horses without
letup.

That evening, after making good distance, the army
camped along the trail, with their horses picketed close by
and extra guards put out. There was still no sign of Indians, not even moccasin tracks or hoof marks to warn that
an enemy scout was dogging them. In camp, the men
spoke little, and seldom sang; everyone seemed deep in
thought—thought colored with worry. Greyson knew these
were brave men in a fight, men who would give their lives
for friends and family, men who had seen much of Indian
warfare. But they did not understand this long march without a shot being fired. They had not expected it, and they
did not like it.

Fires were lit, dinner eaten, and the weary troops lay
down as night fell. Greyson was saddlesore and pensive, as
full of anticipation as the rest. At any time, he knew, the
Indians might ambush them, might strike in force, kill, and
flee to return again, as a wolf pack attacks a bull elk.

The evening was soft and beautiful. Nearly every man
puffed on a pipe and sat close to the fire so the smoke
would keep off the terrible mosquitoes. Just as dark settled
in, the horses grew nervous and whickered. At once Greyson sat up, as did all the men.

"Indians!" said Bilderback, standing nearby.

Grub declared, "They're after the horses! Let's go!"

He and at least two hundred men leaped to their feet and
snatched up weapons, their voices growling and cursing,
everyone ready for a battle.

Greyson and Rose looked at each other, knowing there

had to be discipline, that the men must not dash off without order. Colonel Crawford appeared at that critical moment and shouted for officers to restrain their men. Greyson and Rose drew swords and tried to get to the front of the troops, who were already pushing into the dark forest.

"Stand fast!" Greyson yelled. "Assemble in companies! Muster, gentlemen! Do not run off—"

Few listened.

"Injuns! They're going after the horses! . . . Let's get 'em! . . . Come on, Marylander, this is how you fight redskins! . . . Where are they, the red skunks? . . . Over by the gully there! . . . No! Down by the stream! . . . No, that's our boys! . . . Come on! . . . Hey, I forgot my ammunition! . . . Stick to me! . . . Watch yerself! . . . Here! Down here!"

The dim forest filled with men eager to fight, men prowling through the dark, their eyes glittering; men whispering and calling softly, alert for the enemy. They were determined not to lose their horses, and not to miss this chance for a scalp.

"We'll get 'em afore they sneak off with our mounts! . . . Come on! I'm ready! . . . I'm loaded for bear!"

Greyson looked to Crawford, who remained with his three relations in the camp, assembling as many of the men as he could.

"We'll wait to see what develops, and then go to the sound of shooting." Crawford gave orders for some men to protect the other side of the camp and for a reserve to wait for further commands. "Three hundred men are beating the bushes; I pray there are no Indians out there, or they will have us!"

Crawford's eyes were hard, his face red with anger in the light of the fires. Greyson saw he was the best of men, an excellent commander, but his troops were undisciplined for all that they were brave and otherwise good in the forest. They were used to fighting in small parties, slipping

through the woods like Indians, and outwitting their enemies, killing and dying in single combat among the trees.
Crawford needed a fighting force, however, if he was to
advance deep into Indian country, carry out the devastation, and withdraw in good order. He needed men who
would restrain their instinctive fighting habits and operate
in concert with many others.

The colonel called out for David Williamson and swore
when he heard that the man had gone off with the others,
scouring the woods for Indians. Soon Crawford himself
entered the woods to assemble the men, leaving Greyson
and Rose in command of the reserve protecting the camp
and horses. As he and Rose lay behind a clump of bushes,
watching the darkening forest for sign of a counterattack,
Greyson felt they were extremely vulnerable. Only thirty
men remained to guard the supplies and horses; they
would not be able to hold out long if the Indians struck in
force.

Rose, too, must have realized the gravity of the situation, for he slipped from man to man and instructed them
on what to do if they were attacked. Greyson would guard
the mounts with a few men, and Rose would coordinate a
defense of the camp and supplies.

Crickets, which had been silent, began their chirping
again. The night deepened, and the flying insects buzzed
noisily, feasting and stinging. Owls hooted, but the woodsmen said they were indeed owls. After a while the horses
settled down, and that was a comfort. Frontier folk knew
horses sensed Indians and would always give warning if
the enemy were at hand. This time, it seemed, the horses
had been worked up by something else, or perhaps there
had been only a couple of Indian scouts who had eluded
the swarm of whites who had gone to do battle.

Within an hour, men drifted back in twos and threes,
annoyed and grumbling. Some were embarrassed at seem-

ing so alarmed when there was no one to fight, but few could have anticipated the wrath of their commander when he had them all assembled again, mustered in a loose crescent around him as he stood on a boulder and shook his fist at them.

"This is an army! Four hundred men! Not a pack of coon hunters or a few rangers taking their chances where they may in the woods! By God, you men had better understand that the Indians are out there, all around, and that there are hundreds of them! If they see they can start you up like a covey of quail, they'll find a way to do it again, and then they'll be on our asses thicker'n flies and biting hard and fast!"

He did not single out Williamson by name, but everyone knew he meant the militia colonel when he said, "Your officers are to be obeyed, and they are to obey me! We're fifty-five miles into Indian country, and by God I won't have you free-lancing or coon-hunting or chasing shadows, whether or not your officers get the itch to skirmish! You'll damned well listen to me first, and I'll say whether you go off more than five men at a time! Is that clear?"

He looked directly at the glowering Williamson, who jutted out his chin and said, "We ain't no covey of quail, Colonel."

The men began to grumble agreement, but Crawford's voice lashed above the sound.

"By damn, you'd better not be, for I'll court-martial and shoot the next man that sprouts wings!"

Some of the men chuckled at that, saying, "Well said, sir!" and "Them's the right words, Colonel! I'll pull the goddam trigger!"

Most of the woodsmen were insulted, however, put out by the rude treatment of their hero Williamson, and sure they had done the right thing by charging off on their own to fight. That was the way they knew best, and their folk had been fighting Indians for nearly a century.

Mike Grub called out, "Got to fight like a Injun to beat a Injun! They ain't gonna come at us rank and file and exchange volleys . . . sir!"

Crawford was ready for that, too. "They're not going to get the chance to pick us off in the woods, either! We're not going to piss away our strength because you men think this is a weekend scout alongside your farms! This is an army, damn it! And you signed for it! Now, you'll obey me or turn around right now! Which is it? Go on with me and risk being shot for insubordination, or turn around and tell your wives you didn't fight like soldiers, but knew better than your commanding officer! Decide! Which is it?"

Greyson almost smiled as he watched the men shuffle and saw Williamson flush and clench his teeth in resignation. Beside Greyson, Rose rocked on his heels, nodded toward Crawford, and spoke softly.

"He could be captain of cossack horse!"

"Only a captain?"

Rose grinned. "If he learn to curse in Russian he be general! Look, they listen to him, and they hold their piss, I think."

"That's hold their water, Mr. Rose—and I think you're a good judge of men, sir."

Rose winked. "Our cossacks just as pigheaded as your backwoodsmen, and I see officers like Colonel Crawford before." He listened as Crawford changed his tone and spoke to the men more gently, instructing them on how they should behave if there was another similar alarm. "They listen to him now, but when lead start to sing, he maybe not manage them."

"And Williamson?"

"He's the one they hear, and I worry . . . maybe he be too much wrong more than right."

Greyson agreed, and saw how Williamson's face was

set in a sneer as he listened to Crawford's speech. When
the time came, the extent of Williamson's loyalty to Crawford might decide the success or failure of this campaign.
Not for the first time, Greyson felt in his bones that all was
not well, and that his own life hung in the balance, ever
more in danger with each mile they advanced into enemy
country.

The next day was a long, fast march, and they reached
the prairie at last, riding out of the dismally dank forest
into a sunlit world of birds and wind and low ground-
cover. The flowers of early June were everywhere, many
trees in blossom, and the sun was soft and comforting after
all those miles in near darkness.

For most of the men, this was their first time on the
plains, and they marveled like little children on an outing
with their families. For a while the silent threat of the wilderness was forgotten, for here they could tell that no enemies were near. They could see for hundreds of yards, and
scouts were sent in all directions to find some trace of
Indians. There was supposed to be a large village at a river
not far from here, and it was all the more surprising that no
tracks had been seen, not a hostile shot fired at them.

That afternoon they camped in bright sunshine, eating
boiled venison and partridge. Now they were more enthusiastic, more sure of themselves. So many soldiers out in the
open, mounted and well armed, could handle three times
their number in Indians, perhaps more. No one deluded
himself into thinking they had the element of surprise anymore, for the enemy obviously was withdrawing westward
before their advance. Still they were confident, exhilarated
by the wide-open grasslands, and ready for the fight that
surely would soon come.

As Greyson drank from a stream, shouting broke out
among the troops, and he got up to see some men chasing a

frightened fox, which scampered for its life through the camp. Men were laughing and shouting, diving and missing, throwing knives and tomahawks at the unhappy creature, its tail high and ears back as it twisted and zigzagged, now between legs, now among the startled horses. After two or three minutes of this, the laughing changed a bit as men became more determined. Some of them were made to look like fools as the fox kept eluding their best efforts.

"It's a curious scene," Greyson said to Rose as they watched. "A little critter raising a commotion with dozens of full-grown men, all of them fine hunters." There were even a few hunting arrows shot at it, and Greyson was glad to see that no one fired a gun in the general eagerness to get the fox. The amazing chase went on for ten minutes or more, and it became apparent to Greyson that the soldiers were actually growing angry that the fox was escaping them. He knew that many of them were superstitious, and the incident with the lost horses had already boded ill.

By now well over a hundred men were involved in the chase. They crashed into one another, their joking becoming annoyance, their fun turning into anger. Two men came to blows when one accused the other of causing him to miss a knife throw, and several men cursed and threatened when they were nearly stuck by arrows or thrown blades.

Greyson was dismayed at the turn of events. That amazing fox would not be caught. He scampered among the baggage, darted under a stack of firewood, raced back toward the horses, setting a hundred of them kicking and neighing, then found himself in a tightening circle of thirty hard-bitten men with glaring eyes and fixed jaws.

But they could not do it. The fox dodged a blow, squirted through a hollow log, sprang at Mike Grub's face, bounded over his head, and succeeded in getting away into the woods.

When the cursing died down, the men became very

quiet, some wiping noses self-consciously, others making up excuses why the critter had escaped, and all of them wondering the same uncomfortable thought.

It was Charles Bilderback who put it into words, his voice low as he walked off, shaking his head, to settle down his horse and put the saddle back on.

"If an army of four hundred men can't catch a goddam fox, then what'n hell does that mean?"

What it meant, Greyson knew, was that the troops were sure this was a bad omen, an unnerving portent of disaster. There was no room for error or failure out here, not if a man meant to live. They resumed the march, and now even the stillness of the open grassland oppressed them. Many had lost confidence, and no one boasted that as soon as they got into battle they would fight off this bad luck and make their own good fortune.

Somewhere ahead was a large Wyandot village, where the enemy surely was waiting in force. Bad luck or no, the troops would strike hard, Greyson thought, and a little blood and courage should be enough to right things for them. The sooner the better.

chapter **13**

RED CHILDREN'S AFFAIRS

Late in the afternoon, Owen Sutherland was sitting with Ella in their common room, reading a letter recently arrived from Benjamin Franklin, who was at the peace negotiations in Paris.

Franklin knew Sutherland well and for years had kept in close communication with him regarding developments in the northwest. Sutherland felt certain that if any man could win the northwest for the independent states, it was Franklin. The old statesman knew the intentions of France, and he had friends among the British, influential men who would do anything to prevent France from getting a foothold in North America again. If France and Spain were to combine to wrest control of the country west of the Appalachians, both America and Britain would be faced with prolonged Indian wars, perhaps ultimately another worldwide conflict with those nations, and probably a complete loss of Indian trade for many years.

Sutherland was reading the letter aloud. "' . . . and so, my friend, we who view the northwest as America's future are doing our utmost to see that the treaty will give that country to us. As indebted as we are to France for having supported our Glorious Cause, we wish earnestly to remain friends with her, and with this object in mind we can best eliminate any possible conflict by assuming full possession of your beloved northwest.

"'What will your red brothers say about it, I wonder? I, for one, feel certain that you will best be able to lay Congress's case before them, for they trust you more than any other white man we could send as our ambassador. Tell them we will honor all their treaties with the former colonies, and that we will place you at the forefront of our embassy to them. Tell them we will reopen a favorable trade with them as soon as hostilities end, and that their great white father across the sea has given it into the hands of Congress to manage his red children's affairs and to see to their welfare. . . .'"

Sutherland looked over at Ella, who sat in warm sunlight. She was thoughtful, gazing out the window, and after a moment she turned to look at him. Sutherland wondered whether her mind was full of the same misgivings as his.

He said, "Dr. Franklin still speaks as if the Indians were no more advanced than they were twenty years ago." Sutherland knew that the leading Indian chiefs, such as Nikolota, were no longer flattered to be addressed as "children of the great white father." Many Indian leaders, including Joseph Brant and some of the Creek and Cherokee chiefs to the southwest, had been educated in white schools, were half-breeds themselves, and had no illusions about the ambitions of the independent states as soon as peace was declared.

Ella said, "The Indians will fight on, because they will have to defend themselves against us until they are rubbed out."

Sutherland heard the Indian influence in Ella's choice of words; she had spent much of her life in their country, and she felt as he did about their bleak future. It was indeed bleak, unless enough influential whites stood up for them.

There was little time between now and the next great invasion of white settlers. In a year or two, thousands of rebel soldiers would be given Indian lands as a reward for having fought for independence. They would come out well-armed, with their officers, likely organized along the lines of their former regiments. They would be impossible for Indians to stop, and eventually they would be supported by regulars from the states.

Sutherland read on: "'I have used what influence I have to arrange for you to be named an ambassador to the king's lieutenant governor at Detroit—an American from New York Town, one Colonel DePeyster, with whom I understand you are acquainted, and I hear his wife is a Scotswoman. I do not know when hostilities will cease sufficiently in your country for a delegation from Congress to pass safely through, but I know there are others in Congress who have their own ideas about who should represent us to the British army in the northwest, and with these I fear you will have sharp disagreements. We shall see what will come to pass. Await word from my friends in Philadelphia.'"

Sutherland was at last assured that, contrary to popular belief, the northwest would fall into American hands. He wondered aloud as he put down the letter, "What will our former Frontier Company partners and friends at Detroit think if they see us again at the straits?" He truly did not know whether those staunch loyalists would welcome him or shun him.

Ella said quietly, "I wish we could go up there tomorrow." She looked at Owen, a serious expression on her face. "When the fighting ends here, won't you try to have some of your Indian friends escort us to Detroit ... to Valenya?"

Sutherland was surprised not so much by the question as by the intensity of Ella's tone. She was well aware of the risk involved in such a journey, even if peace were made with the British. Yet it was obvious she was willing to take that risk, just to get back home to Valenya again.

Before he could reply, there was a knock at the door, and in came Peter Defries, in company with the beaming minister, Godspeace Willis. Rising to greet them, Sutherland saw that something was on Defries's mind, and even before the men took off their hats and sat down at the table, Defries was voicing it.

"Why, Owen, laddie, the reverend here wants to talk to you about our . . . our acquaintance, James Morely, knowing as how we and James ain't on such good speaking terms these days."

Reverend Willis gave a smile that lit his broad face, and he nodded as Defries went on hastily, "The minister says we ain't right in thinking the worst of James, because the good fellow and his company really got the best interests of this country at heart. Ain't that right, Rev? See, there! Now listen here, Owen, so the Rev can tell you what he was telling me about our good, gracious Cullen and Company. You've got the floor, Rev."

Willis cleared his throat, obviously aware that Defries was making light of him, but apparently determined to press on.

"Now, Mr. Sutherland, I've spent some time of late in the house of Mr. Morely, and I can tell you from many a conversation with him over supper that he in no way wishes you ill and does not want to continue the course of hostility between you and him." He looked closely at Sutherland, smiling warmly again. "While he did not ask me to represent his case to you, I've taken it on my shoulders to express my concern that Mr. Morely's reputation is being sullied by your continued shunning of him, and your public unwillingness to associate with him—"

Before Sutherland could remark that he did not like the

company Morely kept, Defries interrupted. "Get to the heart of it, Godspeace! Get the numbers and figures out so's you can show my friend here what a saint Morely is."

Shrugging, the minister said, "Well, it's clear Cullen and Company has great interest in the welfare of the settlers here, for the company has executed many generous mortgage transactions with a large number of farmers—"

Defries pressed. "Tell how many."

"Several hundred."

"And where be them several hundred now?"

"Why, many are out with the army, and Mr. Morely's money has been a true godsend to the wives and children, who can use it to buy whatever they need while their husbands are off in service to their country."

Now there was no jovial look on Defries's face. He was scowling at Sutherland as he said, "Maxwell's taken out mortgages on seven hundred farms, Owen! Near five hundred of those settlers are with Crawford right now!"

At that, Sutherland gave a start. He knew just what Defries was getting at, though the minister did not. Uneasy, Ella came to the table and touched her husband's shoulder. He turned to her and answered her unspoken question.

"Maxwell has loyalist allies. It's not good."

As the minister sputtered an exclamation, there was a shout at the door, and Susannah ran in, her eyes wide and her voice breathless. "Jake's gone down to the army!"

Sutherland sprang to his feet in disbelief, and Ella gasped, "No! Little Jake!"

Susannah blurted out that a message had come with the daily courier from the base camp, saying Jake was down there but would not return to Pitt until he had seen some action.

"They tried to force him to leave, but he kicked and fought them, and then went into the woods with the scouts."

Sutherland's mind whirled with both the thought of great danger to the army and the knowledge that Jake was at the base camp. Who knew what could happen? If Maxwell had indeed conspired with loyalists and Indians, as old Cullen had often done before him . . .

"I'll go now for him," Sutherland told his wife, and Defries said he would go along too.

Ella took her husband's hands. "I'm going with you."

Sutherland saw her determined expression and knew he was in for trouble. She had made a bad decision, and he shook his head. "No, Ella. We'll be back in a few days—"

She gripped his hands fiercely and looked at him with a fear that was impossible to allay. "I'm coming! He's my son now. I'm coming with you, Owen, and you can't tell me no."

The minister gave a cluck, saying something about the woman's place being in the home, but he soon found himself alone in the cabin, the Sutherlands and Defries hurrying away to arrange for their journey downriver. As he closed the door behind him and trudged back to James's house, the Reverend Willis thought about the possibility that Cullen and Company actually could have conspired to destroy an army in order to acquire vast landholdings. It was too horrible a thought, too cruel. Not James Morely! Then he thought of Noah Maxwell and cold gripped his spine. Perhaps. Perhaps it was possible after all. . . .

James Morely was at his desk, examining the books of his barge-building company, which had constructed forty new vessels during the winter and spring, all of them already sold to settlers traveling downriver. There were orders for at least twenty more, and they would sell for high prices, for no other company was left at Pitt to underbid him. He had driven them all out of business.

James felt satisfied at what he read, and he looked up

pleasantly as the Reverend Willis came in. Willis greeted him uneasily and asked for a private conversation. James gestured him to a seat across the table and offered a glass of cider, which was accepted with gratitude.

The sun was warm, the room bright and cheerful, matching James's own feelings just then. The butler was gone for the afternoon, and Maxwell was in his own part of the house, likely entertaining one of the many loose young women for whom he had such a predilection—a weakness, the minister had said more than once.

"It's about these mortgages, Mr. Morely, the ones on the Washington County militiamen's lands." Willis tried to begin gently. "Now, it's been suggested, in my hearing, that . . . Ah, dear heavens, this is difficult to express, quite difficult!" He took a deep gulp of cider and stared at the floor, trying to find the right words.

James paced casually, enjoying his own glass of cider, wondering what could be troubling his friend. It had done James's soul good to make Cullen and Company the benefactor of the minister, and plans were well under way for the new church near the settlement.

Willis tried again. "Lord knows I'm not a man who has difficulty in putting words on a string, but I confess I cannot say bluntly to you what it is I have heard about this matter. I—"

The door abruptly opened, and Noah Maxwell entered without excusing himself. James realized he had been outside listening, for he was glaring at Willis and his words cut the minister off.

"Is Owen Sutherland perpetrating rumors that Cullen and Company might be doing something underhanded, again?"

James wished the word "again" had been placed after Sutherland's name—a more discreet meaning. Willis was blushing with embarrassment and made no reply as Maxwell went to the sideboard and poured himself a glass of brandy. It appeared to James that Maxwell was already affected by strong drink.

Maxwell spoke again. "In this country, Reverend Willis, a man of honor must learn to discount Frontier Company rumor and to recognize Sutherland slander without hesitation. Whatever it is you've heard, be assured that it is a lie, and that Cullen and Company has only the welfare of its friends and neighbors in mind at every turn." He paced, ranting on like this while James sat on the edge of the table, sipping and listening. James wondered why Maxwell was so worked up, and why Willis was troubled.

Cutting into Maxwell's speech, James nodded to the minister. "Please, Reverend, go on with what you were saying."

"James!" Maxwell protested. "You'll not, surely, deign to hear this slander—"

"I'll deign as I please, Noah."

"What? Damn my eyes, Morely—"

"Then damn your eyes and be done with it!" James shot back. "Get out if you don't want to hear what he has to say!"

"By God!"

"Enough!" Willis, clearly upset by the repeated swearing, leaped to his feet, his hands spread. "I'm likely sticking my nose in where it doesn't belong—"

Maxwell grumbled, "Precisely!"

"But, nevertheless, I think it my duty to Mr. Morely to say that there are some who believe—"

"Frontier Company bastards!"

"Shut up, Noah!" James stepped threateningly toward his partner, who was no fighting man. "Shut up or I'll shut you up!"

Maxwell snarled and turned away, hurling his glass into the fireplace. He leaned against the mantel as Willis, after several apologies, finally unburdened himself. "I have

heard that . . . Cullen and Company agents . . . may have arranged matters with loyalists to have the army wiped out so
you can . . . can take over the mortgaged farms. There! It's
said, and you have my regrets, but it had to be said!"

There was a long silence. James thought hard about this
unexpected development. While thinking, he stared at
Willis, who grew more uneasy by the second.

Then James looked at the back of Maxwell.

Though he did not turn around, Maxwell said, "All
right, Willis, it's said. Now forget it, and don't believe
those goddam lies . . . not if you want a goddam church
from us!"

"Mr. Maxwell! I resent this! I—"

James shook his head in apology to the minister, who
was on the point of replying with anger to Maxwell. James
showed him to the door and thanked him for his candidness
and concern. Then, when the door was closed, James
stepped toward Maxwell, seeing now that the man was
even drunker than he had first realized. Maxwell glanced
around, his eyes moist from liquor, his mouth turned down
in his bitterness.

"What you looking at?" Maxwell demanded and gave
the unlit logs of the fire a kick, sending up a mess of ash
and soot. "Damn my eyes, Morely. . ."

James crossed his arms. "Just tell me the truth, Noah.
Have you done anything wrong in this?"

When he turned again to face James, Maxwell was all
astonished indignation. "I'm no Bradford Cullen! I
wouldn't know how to do it if I wanted to! Can you imagine me in a conspiracy with the enemy?" He turned to
begin pacing again, arms flailing to express dismay. "I try
to win the affection and loyalty of those settlers to our
company, and you listen to lies from Sutherland!"

"Swear to me!" James demanded.

Maxwell whirled. "Get me a Bible! I don't care!" He

raised his right hand. "May lightning strike me now if I'm lying! By damn, I'll never take an initiative like this again for the company, if this is how it turns out! By damn!"

He pushed past James and went to the door, flinging it open, and James listened to the unsteady clatter of his shoes on the floor as he retreated to his chambers. From down the hallway Maxwell cried, "If they get their backwoods arses kicked it's their stupidity, and nothing to do with me!"

James felt a great weight just then. He had tried hard to right this company, at least as much as was possible in the short time he had been at its head. But there were so many others, so many who had the use of Cullen money and Cullen connections. Maxwell, for one. The man was a danger, James knew, but was he capable of a conspiracy of this magnitude? It was painful even to contemplate. It would mean the ruin of the company if word ever got out. If it were true. Was Noah brave enough to go into the woods and deal directly with loyalists? Was he that ruthless? James poured himself some brandy, confusion and anxiety tormenting him.

Then the vision came back, blurred and painful, of Bradford Cullen lying on the floor of this very room, and Noah Maxwell leaning over, smothering him with a pillow.

James cursed and clenched his fists, shaking them at the ceiling as he began pacing. Why was it all so complicated? Why could he not enjoy the power and wealth he had always dreamed of, without such haunting visions? He cast aside the awful image that had awakened him more than once, which he had been unable to forget since Cullen's death. Noah had denied the reality of that image, too, saying Cullen's heart had simply given out . . . but James could not believe it, though he wanted to so very much. Just as he wanted to believe Noah now.

•   •   •

Sutherland decided Ella and Defries had better stay at Pitt, and that he should take this journey alone. At the same time, it would be impossible to argue them out of coming. So he made his preparations accordingly, and by five o'clock his canoe was loaded and ready, and he was on the wharf with Ella and Peter, about to depart. Susannah was to stay behind, and she came to the river to see them off, tears in her eyes.

As Ella and Peter said good-bye to Susannah, Sutherland took the opportunity he had been waiting for. Quickly he stepped down from the dock into the canoe and pushed the craft off with his paddle. The others turned to look down at him as he waved, and he was a bit surprised they did not protest at being left behind. He was about to shout back something encouraging when the canoe gave a sudden wrench and came about, as a thick rope cable yanked tight. Fixed to a thwart, the cable was tied to the timbers of the dock, and Peter quickly drew it in until the canoe was back at the wharf again.

At first Sutherland was angry, but he accepted it as they clambered down into the birch boat. Ella did not speak, did not even laugh—neither did Defries—for this was too serious; they merely nodded to one another in acknowledgment, then away they went with the stream, hoping to reach Mingo Bottom without further delay. As he paddled in the stern, Sutherland kept thinking over and over that they must not be too late.

Stay with the men in camp, Jake, he thought time and again. *Stay in camp, laddie, for the love of God!*

But Jake was already out of the base camp, having spent the day with scouts patrolling the trail of the army. By now the army should be attacking the Sandusky villages, and if all went well it would be on its way back tomorrow. In a couple of days a hard-riding courier would probably come in with news of the victory. Crawford was supposed to have sent couriers back each day and receive news from the base camp in return. It was strange, some of the men had remarked more than once, that couriers went out daily to find Crawford, but none had come back. There had been no news at all for six days.

Jake was out with fifteen men on this patrol, and he felt good in their company. They did not treat him as a child, although he had the responsibilities normally assigned to the youngest, fetching water and seeing to the fire. It was exciting, and he felt freer than ever before. Often he spoke with the men about the part of Pennsylvania where he had been raised, before his family was wiped out by marauding Senecas who had taken him captive to Detroit.

"Don't you want to get yer teeth into some Injun meat, boy?" a man asked, showing him a tobacco pouch he said had come from the leg of an Indian. "Don't you want revenge? A scalp, a bag out of Delaware hide? Would be a trophy a man could be proud of, and your folk'd be proud, if'n they was alive."

But he did not want to kill Indians. He had learned too much about them from the Sutherlands and from his stay at Detroit. Indians taken one at a time were not so different from whites, when you got to know them. Sure, he would fight and kill if he had to, but he did not hunger after it, or boast about what he would do, like some of the others. He just wanted to be a soldier, to march and patrol and talk of warfare, and so grow to be a man, like the rest, like his father and brothers had been. Jake Smith, Pennsylvania ranger and Indian spy. One day he would be good . . . but he had no thirst for blood, and surely would never make a tobacco pouch of Indian skin!

He just wanted to be a soldier, that was all, and then the Sutherlands would see he was man enough to be their son, man enough to take the place of Benjamin, whom he had loved so much, and still missed so. Even Benjamin's death had not made Jake hate all Indians—just the one who would line up in his sights. That would be enough. He would need hate then, if he was to be able to pull the trigger.

Late the following morning, Mike Grub was praying again, and Greyson wished he himself could find some comfort in the way things were turning out. The army was in the middle of a huge Wyandot village, where at least two hundred lodges stood—all abandoned, unused for months. Grass grew in the doorways, and it had been ages since the cooking fires were used. The scouts apparently had made a grave mistake, leading them to the wrong place.

An hour earlier, the army had formed into columns and galloped screeching and howling like terrors across the grassland, thundering into the village, expecting to find it defended by warriors who would be cut to pieces at the first onslaught. The noise and fury of the attack had been fantastic, and Greyson had felt for the first time the raw power of this fighting force. But there had been no one here to fight.

One of the scouts, a man who had been a captive of the Wyandots for years, said the people surely had flocked upstream to a larger town, known as Upper Sandusky. There had been a quick and heated council of war, with Williamson and some of the other militia officers declaring that they ought to turn around now and withdraw, because they felt a trap was being laid. He was not afraid, he had declared, but there were only five days' provisions left.

Now the war council was drawing to a close, with opinions flying fast and thick, but Crawford had made no decision yet. He was studying a rough map of the region with his scouts. Not far away, a surprising number of men were listening to the harsh but plaintive voice of big Mike Grub, as he called upon them to repent, before it was too late.

"We be doing thy work, God, of conquesting the Canaanites, and driving the heathen from thy Promised Land. We know that, God, and we ask you that you show us thy way, and help us who are sinners and can't rightly find the way you want us to go. We ain't saintified, but we're trying, and we're trying to do your holy work, God, so this is a good time to look down on us. Hallelujah! And help us, because we know you'll help your chosen people! Hallelujah!"

There was little left of the strong, passionate conviction that had sprung from the camp revival at Pitt some weeks ago. Grub was trying, though, and Greyson thought it pathetic. Yet it seemed that the frontiersmen kneeling around Grub did indeed take comfort in the prayer. They were not afraid to face death, but they needed to be reminded that God had chosen them to rule over this land, that they were in the right, and that the redskins were Canaanites.

"Read us a psalm there, will you, Cap'n Bilderback?" Grub asked, and the other man rose, clearing his throat, letting the Bible fall open. It appeared he wanted the choice of verse to come at random, as if it were God's inspiration.

Crawford was dismissing his scouts and about to turn back to the gathered officers as the sound of Bilderback's wavering but determined voice rose above the prairie wind.

"Psalm Thirty-eight. 'Lord, Rebuke me not in thy wrath! Neither chasten me in hot displeasure . . .'"

"Amen!" they shouted, Grub the loudest.

"'For thine arrows stick fast in me, and thy hand passeth me sore . . .'"

"Goldurn it, Cap'n!" someone shouted, as others groaned. "Don't read that one, will you?"

A prickly uneasiness came over them, and Greyson felt

it too. He was glad when Colonel Crawford spoke to his
officers and came to a decision to which Williamson reluc-
tantly agreed: they would march to where the suspected
main town was, eight miles upriver, and there join battle if
the enemy awaited in any force. If Indians were not there,
then the army would turn around and withdraw. No one
liked the idea of withdrawing without a battle, because two
years earlier the Pennsylvanians had been humiliated in a
similar large campaign, which had had to be called off
because of high water. Only one prisoner had been taken, a
squaw, and ever since that, the failed expedition had been
laughingly called the Squaw Campaign. This time, said
Crawford's son, John, as he walked past Greyson, "there
isn't even a squaw in sight! What'll they call this march,
then?"

The troops were glum, but word was passed that Indians
likely would be at Upper Sandusky, and then they would
have some excitement. A few men were confident again,
almost jovial. But many—including Greyson—were worried that it would go hard if the army had to retreat now,
especially if the Indians were determined to cut them off.

chapter **14**

GOOD LAND

Rose and Greyson rode ahead with several scouts, leaving the main body and its packtrain behind. They galloped over rich, windswept plains, and Rose commented on what fine farmland this would be. The country was flat, with scattered islands of trees along the way. They paused at a large grove and enjoyed the scenery a while. The wind was fresh in their faces as they let their panting horses rest, and Greyson found the view distractingly beautiful, as if there were no danger or war out here. It was easy to see why the Indians loved this land and were determined to fight bitterly to hold it. But when would they fight this army?

It was then that one of the scouts gave a shout. "There they be, lads!"

Across the grasslands, about a mile off, was a mass of Indians, on foot, running directly toward them. "Now we have them!" the scout cried. The Indians were obviously intending to take this grove, which offered relatively good cover on the open plain. One of the scouts took the fastest horse and galloped back to Crawford; the rest, with Greyson, withdrew slowly, watching the swift approach of the warriors. Shortly, the Indians had possession of the island grove, but Greyson knew that the whites would have no trouble dislodging them, for there were no more than two hundred enemy in all.

The whites soon appeared, and at first Greyson heard more than saw them. As the ground trembled under their charge, his sweating horse whickered nervously, excitedly. The riders came pounding across the prairie, looking like the approaching shadow of a cloud on the grass, then taking form as individual horsemen, waving and yelling. The Indians in the grove began to fire at them, but without much effect. Riding in the space between the two groups of fighters, Greyson waited until his men neared, then he drew out pistol and sword, leaned forward in the saddle, and spurred his horse to a gallop in the lead.

Bullets whizzed and sang past. The Indians in the trees could not resist the charge, and the ragtag horse soldiers burst in among them with incredible fury and courage. The Indians showed their own mettle. They fired and withdrew, slowly driven from the grove. They retreated into the long grass, where their gunfire became hotter and more accurate, cutting down a few whites. Greyson soon found himself on the far side of the trees, but few of the enemy came close to him. He fired his pistol and missed, slashed at a fleeing Indian with his sword, but the man eluded him.

In a few minutes, all the Indians had withdrawn in good order. The weary horsemen dismounted, collected their animals in the center for safety, and took firing positions. They exchanged long-range shots with the Indians in the grass while the officers decided the next step. Greyson joined Crawford and Rose, while Williamson brought a few other officers in with a report of one killed and eight wounded. The losses were not serious, but Williamson showed considerable worry.

He pointed across the prairie in the direction they had come from, and there was another mass of Indians, even larger than the first. They were positioning themselves across the route the whites would have to use to withdraw.

Gunfire became more rapid between the whites and Indians as they settled down to a test of marksmanship. The firing was so loud that Williamson had to shout to be heard. "These here redskins be Wyandots, and them back there be Delawares! I don't see no Shawnee, but you can be sure that if we stay here long enough, they'll be coming to the party, too."

Crawford did not say it, but Greyson thought, *We're surrounded, and the Indians have plenty of guns and ammunition.* Just then bullets spattered around them, as if a volley had been carefully aimed their way, and one of the officers went down, a bullet in his leg. The rest took cover, Crawford pulling the injured man to shelter in the middle of the grove. Greyson ducked low, amazed now at how much lead was in the air, rattling against trees and wounding horses, which screamed and bled and broke away in their agony. All around, gun smoke rose white and blue from the grasses, and a column of smoke hung over the grove as the militia kept up their own fire.

In the middle of the grove the wounded lay, moaning in pain and thirst. There was no water here, other than a small, stagnant pool, and most of the men had already exhausted the supplies in their canteens. The roar of gunfire rose to a crescendo, and Greyson saw a body of Indians come charging through the long grass, as if mocking the marksmanship of the Pennsylvanians. They ran and whooped, not one hit, until after forty yards they dived for cover in the grass and among a tumble of brush and logs, to open a wicked fire from this protected position.

Crawford and Rose seemed to be everywhere at once. Williamson was more caught up in the firing than in playing the role of officer. The sun rose higher, and the air became heavy and sultry as the breeze failed. The sour stench of smoke and the smell of blood filled Greyson's senses. He was dirty and tired, thirsty beyond belief, and was beginning to see that the Indians were doing just what they wanted to do: hold the whites at bay, protect their village, and wait for the arrival of reinforcements.

"We are losing fight," John Rose said as he moved to Greyson's side. "They got us in place they want, and those there good shots!"

He pointed at the band of Delawares who had rushed up so boldly to take positions close to the whites. They were difficult to see from the grove, and some whites had climbed trees to snipe at them. The exchange was even at first, but the hail of Indian bullets was so dense that leaves shredded and fell, and the white marksmen became exposed. Just then, one screamed and dropped from his perch, holding his bloodied face, landing heavily near Greyson and Rose, who dragged him to cover, but it was too late. Immediately, a second marksman was hit, and he managed to claw his way down the tree, only to collapse at the bottom, dying with a slug in his stomach.

Heat and thirst and bullets and exhaustion, and the knowledge that death hung ever lower over their heads, made the whites angry and fierce. They fought furiously, but it was not until dusk began to fall that they had any cause for cheering. It was then that Greyson and Rose, with another dozen men, charged fifty yards in the dimness to attack the warriors who had taken close firing positions.

Greyson threw away all caution, and with drawn sword and a yell of battle-madness rushed upon the enemy. The Indians had just fired, and the whites took the opportunity to go for them. It was suddenly like that bloody, desperate charge at the Battle of Long Island, when the Delaware and Maryland troops lowered their heads, presented bayonets, and assaulted the cream of the British army, only to be driven back, shattered and bloodied. They had re-formed and come on a second time, striking the Redcoat line with courage and tenacity, but they were outnumbered, shot to pieces by massed volleys, and met by bayonets, ten to one.

As Greyson now charged, bullets slicing his clothes and striking his sword hilt, he recalled that third mad rally, that final attack against the Redcoats. It, too, had crumbled, but the British had been delayed, and Washington's beaten army escaped to fight again. The entire British army had been jarred, expressing admiration and surprise, for who would have thought the Americans could fight like that? Now, on a distant prairie, Greyson ran through long grass, hunting an enemy he could not even see, knowing he was there—but where?

A man sprang up at his left, and another two in front, all of them dark and painted wildly, feathers flying as they screamed at him, tomahawks flashing. He took the one on his left first, parrying a blow, knocking the tomahawk away, and driving the sword into the man's belly. The two before him leaped. The sword was caught in the first man's body. He had his pistol. It went off, but misfired. One of the Indians was on him, a tomahawk slashing past his head, a powerful, tawny body landing on him and throwing him back.

Greased and painted and smelling foul, the Indian scratched and stabbed as Greyson fought to get the knife hand. The other Indian must be there, too. Screaming words his mind did not register, Greyson threw the warrior off and rolled over. The second Indian struck, and the tomahawk hit the earth where Greyson had been, and hit again. The other Indian was struggling to rise. Greyson had his sword free. The tomahawk was blocked, but a knife blade stabbed down. Greyson slid to the side, kicked, and smashed with his sword hilt, crushing a jaw, felling his attacker. He spun to the other, who should have slain him by now, but saw that the man was crumpled, blood pouring from a bullet hole in his back.

There stood Rose, panting, gasping for air, face dirty and streaked with sweat and blood, smoking pistol in one hand, broken sword in the other. Whites were cheering, and Greyson struggled to clear his mind. The Indians had been given a licking and had recoiled. Suddenly the firing died down, and night came on swiftly. In the gathering darkness, Rose and Greyson were joined by a hundred others who ran out to recover the wounded, scalp the Indians, and pile up heaps of firewood.

Across the grasslands the Indians also were constructing a line of bonfires to prevent a surprise night counterattack. Soon the prairie blazed with red and yellow flame, as the grove was ringed with two lines of fires, one from the whites, one from the Indians.

Dragging and sore, Greyson wandered back to the command post and found Crawford in council with Williamson and the other officers. Rose came from tending the wounded, and the Russian and the Marylander were congratulated for their courage. They were given a place as Crawford spoke.

"Five killed, nineteen badly wounded, and dozens of men sick from drinking bad water they found here!" Crawford was weary, as dirty as his men, but his eyes gleamed with fierce courage. "Equal number of enemy out there, I'll guess, but they've suffered heavily this day!"

The officers talked of their chances, and they sounded uneasy. Greyson agreed with Crawford, who said, "Before dawn, we attack."

Williamson and the others were not so sure. "Too many sick," he said. "Too weary from the march. Men need to tend the ill and wounded, guard the packtrain. We don't have enough to attack."

"But we must attack!" Greyson declared, ignoring the look of hatred Williamson shot him. "We can't let them have the initiative! We have to—"

Williamson broke in. "Not during the day, man! They'll cut us to ribbons!"

"Then before dawn!" Greyson almost shouted.

"No!" Williamson said. "Maybe tomorrow night—we'll see what can be done then!"

Silence fell, interrupted by the occasional vulgar insult shouted by Indians, and the equally vulgar replies of tired militiamen. The officers looked to Crawford, who was well aware he would not have the men behind him if Williamson did not agree with his plans.

Finally, Crawford said wearily, "All right, Colonel. Will you back me in an assault tomorrow night, after we rest?"

Williamson grumbled something about doing his best, and that was all Crawford would get. After final instructions for the evening and morning deployment were given, Greyson drew off with Rose. Neither had drunk water for twenty hours. They dared not touch the foul pool that had sickened a hundred men already. They sat against a large tree and listened to the taunts of enemies back and forth between the lines. The fires roared, sending sparks up to the starry sky.

Rose said, "Don't we get good-night prayer from Grub?"

Greyson felt like shouting Grub's name and demanding a loud and moving prayer, but he stopped himself at the last moment. It would do no good to mock religion at a time like this. Nor did he feel any particular hatred for Mike Grub right then. After all, Grub was a good fighter, and they needed every man. Maybe now they needed his prayers for salvation most of all.

The morning of June fifth was warm and beautiful, and when the firing of the Indians continued only fitfully throughout the day, many whites began to take heart, thinking the Indians had lost courage and were breaking off the battle.

For hours Greyson and Rose tended the wounded, who lay in the center of the trees. At midafternoon Greyson overheard Mike Grub and David Williamson discussing the situation.

"I was up in that tree," Grub boasted, "and I don't know how many redskins I kilt, but I never saw the same head rise again after I shot at it."

Williamson cast a glance at the wounded, ignoring Greyson, and spoke slowly, thoughtfully. "Seemed to be a passel more Injuns than I thought they could muster, but I reckon we gave 'em what for yesterday, and they're sitting out there wondering when we'll come chase 'em."

Williamson's confidence had returned with the apparent reluctance of the Indians to resume the attack; but he gave no credit to the gallant charge of Rose and Greyson that had cleared out the nest of Delawares from a threatening position.

"A Pennsylvania rifle," Williamson snickered, patting his weapon. "Near as effective as a cooper's mallet, eh, Mike?" He cackled and glared at Greyson, who stood up, fists clenched.

Greyson spoke coolly. "You're a bag of shit, Williamson."

Nearby, Rose said something that sounded like *"Oy vay!"*

Riled, Williamson came on then, and Greyson moved toward him.

Suddenly, there was a shout from a sentinel, and men hurried to their feet. Crawford called for Williamson, and the Pennsylvanian held off, then shook a fist at Greyson, saying with a hiss he would get him when this was over.

"I'll be waiting!" Greyson replied, and buckled on his sword, about to follow Williamson to Crawford's command post.

Rose came, too, and winked at his friend. *"Oy vay,* my people say! You got *chutzpah!"*

Greyson did not understand, his anger surging as he

stared at Williamson's broad back. He was distracted by the chattering of the soldiers all around, many of whom were pointing across the field.

"White men!" Rose cried. "They be Butler's Rangers! Look there! They come help redskins!"

It was a strong body of reinforcements from the loyalist camps at Detroit, at least fifty whites in the green uniforms of rangers—wilderness fighters driven out of New York and Pennsylvania for siding with the king in the rebellion.

Matters now had turned grave. Not only were the Pennsylvania militia outnumbered, but they were up against a tough and determined enemy, loyalists who hated white rebels more than the Indians did. Immediately, Crawford called for a council, but just then there was a shout from the southern positions, and the men looked in that direction. It was a bad sight. In full run across the grassland came hundreds of Shawnees, painted and feathered, to support the fight against the invader. There was no hope now of a militia attack.

Rose said softly, "It be a long way home, friend."

The men hurried to ready their horses, to see to their weapons, and to await instructions from Crawford. They worked almost without talking as they prepared themselves. The officers decided quickly that they must retreat that night by fighting their way out between the Delawares to the southwest and the Shawnees to the south. It would be hard going, and the Indians likely would attack them all the way back to the Ohio.

"We'll form a strong rear guard and vanguard, and keep the main army, the wounded, and the packtrain in the center," Crawford declared decisively as he pointed to a map on the ground. "Colonel Williamson, you command the skirmishers on our flanks, and—"

"You're dead wrong, Colonel." Williamson stood up, and the other officers waited for his intentions. "Only way to get out of this is to divide up, scatter in bunches of twenty or less, and run like hell—"

"You're mad, man!" Crawford cried, smashing the map with his fist. "We have to stick together, or we're all lost!"

Williamson shook his head slowly, hitching his pistol belt. "My men and me been fighting Injuns all our lives, and in a tight spot you got to scatter, and them that gets chased is outa luck."

Crawford stood up, quivering with anger. "Your orders are stay with the main body! You have a hundred or more men who'll listen to you, and if you take them out, we're done for!"

Williamson made no reply but stared without emotion at the ground.

"Well?" Crawford demanded. "Will you obey?"

Slowly, Williamson answered. "This expedition's whupped, Colonel, and you led us into this. . . . I aim to get my folk out, however it's gotta be done."

"Damn! Now listen, at nine tonight, we begin our movement, retiring to the abandoned Wyandot town, and there we'll re-form for the march. We can fight our way through, and Colonel Williamson is put on notice that if he disobeys me, he'll be prosecuted when we get back!"

Williamson said nothing but just stood there as Crawford dispatched aides with orders to the men. The wounded were to be put on litters, and maps were to be prepared for the captains so that if the army did get divided they all would know how to get home. The dead were to be buried, fires burned over the graves, and the horses run across them to prevent detection and desecration.

"More coming in!" someone shouted, and Greyson saw groups of five and ten warriors, some of twenty and larger, come trotting across the plains to join their fellows.

When all preparations were made, there was nothing to do but wait out the rest of the long, hot day. Men and horses were in an agony of thirst, but there was no help for it. The enemy was willing to sit it out, and did nothing more than fire random shots into the camp, although a few found their mark.

As night began to fall and bonfires were again lit, Greyson stood with Rose by a huge elm tree. They had just laid a wounded man on a litter that would be pulled by a horse. The Marylander offered his hand to Rose, who accepted it and grinned.

Greyson repeated the advice he had been given by one of Crawford's friends. "If you get separated from the main army in the confusion, you'd better not follow its trail, for that's where the Indians will be thickest; and if you happen upon what appears to be an abandoned hunting camp with food cooking, don't eat any, for it could be a trick, and the food poisoned." He was about to say more, but Rose interrupted.

"You know, sir, I have not told even one American why I came to this country, why I left Russia. . . ." He smiled at Greyson. "I like to tell you, so someone knows, at least."

With utmost seriousness, he explained that he had challenged an enemy of his aged uncle's to a duel, a man who had inflicted a blow on the old fellow. To Greyson's amazement, Rose casually said, "I killed the gentleman in a fight in an apartment in the royal palace. . . ." He shook his head. "You know, the czar did not like that, because the man was a favorite, and so I had to get out—"

"The palace?" Greyson almost laughed. "How the hell did you get into the czar's palace? You mean in Saint Petersburg itself?"

"Of course!" Rose stiffened and seemed to grow taller, pride filling him, pride and an air of nobility that made Greyson step back in amazement. "I am Gustavus H. de Rosenthal, baron of the empire, of Livonia, and if I live, I will go back to Saint Petersburg and beg the czar's pardon.

After all, he has plenty of favorites and won't miss just one. Maybe he misses me, too!"

Greyson laughed aloud, a strange and uplifting sound in that dismal place. Men turned to look at him, some smiling themselves, admiring such recklessness in a man facing death.

"Well, Baron de Rosenthal, I'll take you home to Maryland if you one day take me to Russia!"

"Deal!" They shook hands again, both grinning, until something whacked Greyson on the left thigh, spinning him around and throwing him heavily to the ground.

Greyson had been shot before and was not surprised that there was no pain as yet; but he knew it was serious, even before Rose ripped apart his breeches and exposed a ragged gash in the muscle. Greyson felt suddenly dizzy from the shock.

"The bone's all right," Rose told him, as other men hurried over. "Bullet's gone through, but you can't walk on it. Damn! Damn! Damn!"

Shaking with fear for his friend, Rose looked closely at Greyson, who knew there was good reason to worry. A wounded man was in grave danger here and would not get far on his own. Yet to ask others to help him would risk their lives as well. Pain was rising now, sharp and laboring, making Greyson woozy as Rose quickly bandaged the leg.

Suddenly, men were busy all around, and there were shouts that someone was coming in to parley under a flag. Greyson asked Rose to help carry him to hear what was being said. In a few minutes, Crawford, Williamson, and the other officers were gathered at the edge of the camp, and before them stood several green-coated loyalist troops, a few Indians, and a bearded man Greyson heard others whisper was Simon Girty, scourge of the frontier.

Girty was squat but powerfully built and stood out

against the glare of the bonfires. Greyson and Rose watched, but they were too far away to hear what was being said. After only ten minutes, the meeting broke up and Crawford stamped back, cursing.

Williamson was following, saying, "Girty was once a friend of yours—maybe that's why he's giving us this chance!"

"Not so!" Crawford said with a growl. "We campaigned together for years, but I don't believe he's giving us any chance at all! He's trying to trick us!"

Suddenly Williamson cursed foully and threw down his hat. "Don't be a fool, Crawford!" Them Injuns want plunder and want us out; they don't want to get killed by going up against us full sail! Girty gave us a chance, and I say we take it!"

The grim-faced officers gathered round, and so did dozens of the men, many asking aloud for an explanation. Williamson shouted, "Girty says the Injuns ain't defending a swamp to the southwest, and that if we're quick we kin head through there and make a break for it! I say we go! What about it?"

Many voices were raised in agreement, and Crawford waited for them to quiet before he said, "It may be that Girty doesn't want us to stand and fight, because the Indians don't have the stomach for a full-scale battle. It may be they just want our plunder, whatever that's worth, which isn't much. It may be this swamp is clear, and we can get through tonight. It may be! But it smells like a trap to me."

The men grumbled among themselves, and Greyson found himself agreeing with Crawford. He felt weak, however, and could say nothing in the officer's support. It appeared that the volunteer army was as divided now as it ever had been over obeying Williamson or Crawford.

Crawford raised his hands, the firelight playing across

his weary face. "We march at nine, and we avoid the swamp. We march in four divisions, with the wounded in the center, and if we're attacked, we throw out skirmishers who will later join up with the rear guard! Those are the final orders! Stay out of that swamp, I warn you, or you're lost!"

The army broke into loud arguing and cursing, but Crawford ignored it and began to organize the officers who would listen to him. After another hour, he came to Greyson, who was weaker now and lying on a litter that had not as yet been hitched to a horse.

Crawford patted Greyson's hand, and the young Marylander looked up, lightheaded from loss of blood. In the dimness, his ears ringing, he saw Crawford smile, and he tried to shake hands with him.

Crawford said, "It's almost time, Colonel . . . I'll look after you—"

A terrific roar of gunfire suddenly erupted. The Indians were attacking, rushing through the space between the bonfires. Crawford leaped up, ordered a man to take care of Greyson, then rushed away to organize the defense. Hundreds of men and horses began to mill about. Men were falling, shot, and animals screamed in terror and agony. Confusion and panic gripped the army. The man assigned to Greyson came over, pulling a balky horse, and tried to hitch the litter to the animal's harness.

There was a thud of lead striking flesh, and the man fell to his knees, his eyes open—but he was already dead. The horse reared and plunged away. Men were running everywhere. The unearthly wailing and shrieking of the Indians rang through the grove, and Greyson knew he must get away. He tried, but could scarcely move. He raised a hand, calling for help. The gunfire was like a storm. Greyson had to get out!

The grove was rapidly emptying, horses without riders dashing off, men scampering away, some even dropping rifles in their fear. Greyson saw a big man at hand, who stopped and fired at the Indians. His silhouette against the firelight told Greyson who he was.

"Grub!" he croaked. "Help me! Grub!"

Mike Grub heard, and as he reloaded, he came and saw who was lying wounded. His face was stained with powder burns, and sweat poured down his savage brow.

"It's you, is it?" He rammed the bullet home, pulled out his ramrod, and fitted it back in the stock. "Looks like you's in trouble, Marylander." He aimed the rifle at Greyson. "Best I put an end to it now, afore they catch you and skin you alive."

There came a terrible shriek nearby, and Grub whirled, firing at an Indian bolting through the camp. The Indian fell, and Grub ran away, leaving Greyson behind. Now the firing drew off and slowed.

"Help me!" Greyson called out, his throat dry, eyes fogged; but there would be no help. Grub was gone, and for some time the campsite was quiet, except for the kicking of a dying horse and the groan of other wounded men who had been left behind. The battle seemed to have moved into the distance. Or perhaps it was that Entellus Greyson was losing consciousness, dying. The bonfires were burning out, their glare softening, leaving the grove dark and hushed. Through the trees the stars were sharp and cold in the night sky. They grew ever brighter, and Greyson lay watching them, thinking how magnificent they were, how heedless of human suffering.

He thought of Susannah Sutherland then, and a rush of warmth filled his heart. How he would like to see her again! How he loved her! Just once more, to see her...

Sounds of movement distracted him. Greyson could make out figures drifting back and forth, finding something, bending over, and moving on to something else. There came a cry of agony as a white man was killed. Indians. They would find him soon. He was ready.

chapter 15

CAPTURED

Some days later, with the weather turning rainy and cool, Jake Smith was camped miles northwest of Mingo Bottom. He had not gone back to the main base camp, having heard Owen and Ella were looking for him. Eventually they would track him down, he knew, but until then he would stay with one patrol or the other and make the most of this adventure.

So far there had been no sign of Indians, and still no word from the missing army. His patrol was the farthest-flung reconnaissance group sent out from the base camp, and they ought to be the first to hear any news. Everyone was worried that there had not been a courier from Crawford in all this time. Some even talked of abandoning the base camp if there had been a disaster and if it seemed the Indians were coming to attack.

It was nearly dawn when Jake took his turn on guard duty, walking the perimeter of the patrol's camp, which lay astride the trail taken by Crawford. The troops would likely return this way if they were not lost.

Before daybreak, the woods were coming alive, birds chirping, a thin drizzle misting and dripping from bushes and branches. Jake kept his rifle's firing lock wrapped in oilskin, and he moved silently some distance from the camp, listening and alert. He was a good sentry, dependable, and the men trusted him. Perhaps, he thought, he might soon rejoin Owen and Ella after all. He had proved he was capable, and although he had not been tested under fire as yet, at least he could say he was learning to be a soldier, the beginning of manhood. Now he could go back to them, he decided, and that gave him a good feeling. It would be fine to sleep in his warm bed. Chill rain ran down his back, and the wind picked up, cold on his damp leggins. He thought of Ella's buckwheat cakes with applesauce and Indian sugar. He could almost taste her raisin cake, and a cup of mint tea would do him good—

There was noise in the bushes ahead, alongside the trail. It sounded like a bear barging through the woods, making no effort at concealment. He brought his rifle up, feeling himself tremble unexpectedly. He cocked the weapon, hoping the bear would not charge. The bushes shook and parted, and through them burst a huge figure—but it was a man, not a bear. Half naked, cut and bruised, eyes wild with terror, it was Mike Grub, and he ran to Jake, crying out, "Save me! In the name of God, save me! They're coming! They're coming! Help! Please!"

Grub nearly knocked Jake over, falling at the boy's feet and grappling at his ankles, blabbering in terror. Startled, Jake kicked him away, dropped to one knee behind a bush, and took a close look around. If the Indians were near, they would have heard just where Grub was, and they would get them both. He was not sure whether to fire a warning shot for the camp or to save his bullet for an Indian. He did not want to run off and leave pathetic Grub lying here where the Indians might come and kill him, but the decision was made for him as several Indians came running down the trail, shadowy forms against the gloomy morning forest.

Jake raised his rifle and fired. The Indians dived for cover. He tried to reload, but Grub clambered against him in panic, trying to get away.

"Stop!" Jake cried, and pushed at the man, getting his powder out, struggling to shelter it from the rain with his cloak as he primed the pan. "Damn you, Grub! Get off!" He somehow knocked Grub aside, stood up, and got a cartridge down the muzzle and rammed home. Grub whimpered and cried out that he was sorry for what he had done and did not want to die.

"Dear God, I'm a sinner! Don't take me yet! Devil, leave me! I'm sorry! I'm sorry!"

"You ain't dead yet!" Jake snarled, his heart pounding, and tried to see whether the Indians were any closer. He was sure his friends at the camp had heard the gunshot and would come to help soon. Meantime, he had to protect Grub, who had gone half insane.

The rifle was charged, and Jake readied behind the bush again, listening for telltale noises, but the water dripped loudly, striking wet leaves, and a man could not tell the sound of a footfall from the sound of a drop.

Jake did not hear the Indian coming up behind him until a gnarled hand went around his mouth, yanking him viciously to the ground, and a club came down hard, though he managed to avoid its full force. Dazed, he scrambled away, only to end up in another warrior's arms. Held fast, he could not move, and they laughed and pointed at him. There were at least six, two of them taking hold of the whimpering Grub. Jake saw now, in the growing light, that Grub must have been their prisoner and somehow escaped and fled after surviving brutal torture. His face was blackened with soot, in the way of a condemned prisoner, his body lacerated and burned. If they got him to a village again, he would die horribly. Jake felt sick, knowing the same fate might be his, but he did not cower.

He struggled, giving a kick, but the Indians only laughed harder. An old, wrinkled one stepped up and slapped his face.

"No fight!" he spat out at the boy, and leered in an expression of hideous glee. "You mine! You come! Or fight and die now! You want to die?"

The old warrior's craggy face was close to Jake's, their noses almost touching. Jake shook his head, desperation turning into cold fear. The whim of this aged man would decide whether he lived or died.

A shout came from somewhere, and rifles went off. The men at the camp must be attacking other members of the war party. The Indians tensed, spoke quickly among themselves, then called out to one of their number, who came hurrying through the woods from the direction of the camp. The decision was made to go, and Jake's wrists were roughly bound with rawhide and he was pushed onto the trail. As he stumbled away, he saw that they had no intention of taking Mike Grub, who was shoved to the ground, begging and pleading for mercy.

Jake ran and closed his eyes, pursued by an awful shriek of terror, and then there was no more, only the whispering, rainy forest, and the thud, thud, thud of moccasins on the beaten trail.

Owen and Ella and Defries had to wait at the base camp for word of Jake, because the commander of the camp did not know where his patrols might be just then, nor which one Jake was with.

Patrols roved the woods however they saw fit, and could go as far into Indian country or down the Ohio as they pleased. These were Pennsylvania rangers, the commander reminded an agitated Sutherland, and they needed no orders when on a scout. That was all well and good as far as Sutherland was concerned, but he wanted the boy back soon, and every hour lost dallying in the camp made him that much more uneasy. His instincts told him Jake was in trouble, and if not for the possibility of wasting precious time going in the wrong direction, he would have plunged into the woods himself to find the boy.

Ella's presence at the camp also reined Sutherland in, for he knew the place might come under attack, and she would be in danger. He did not want to leave her, and so they lingered two hot and rainy June days, tormented by anxiety and by stinging mosquitoes and horseflies.

When Jake's patrol returned at last, it was not alone. With the scouts were nearly a hundred survivors from Crawford's army, who trailed in, exhausted, defeated, bloodied, and ragged. But there was no Jake Smith. The patrol had gone out in search of the boy, trying for most of a day to catch the Indians who had taken him, but instead they had run into the leading elements of the battered, retreating army.

The Sutherlands were badly shaken, and at first Owen did not know what to do. Ella fought with her misery and recovered well enough to agree that if he had to hunt for their foster son, he had best go alone. The wilderness would be alive with war parties cutting off survivors and stragglers from Crawford's army. Sutherland would be at risk with every step he took, and if quick escape became necessary, he could not be encumbered by either Ella or Defries.

They learned what had happened from the doleful Pennsylvanians. After the standoff near Upper Sandusky, the first night of the withdrawal had become a panic. The surprise Indian attack had caused scores of men to become separated and lost in the swamp, where their horses had to be abandoned. Many fled on foot until the Indians caught them. The main army had held together, however, thanks to the courage of John Rose, who was still out rounding up small parties of men and forming them into larger fighting units that could break through the Indian web.

Some of the survivors declared bitterly that Williamson and his militiamen had forsaken the main army and divided up into small groups and scattered, as Crawford had commanded them not to do. How well they had fared no one knew, but the main body of the troops had fought day and night to get back here, and many friends and relations lay dead in the forest or had been taken.

Tears flowed as men told their stories, and Sutherland listened all that day, trying to piece together what had happened. Nothing was known of either Greyson or Colonel Crawford. As it was, the army intended to abandon the Mingo Bottom base camp as soon as enough time was allowed for the last of the survivors to come in. Until then, the camp would be fortified, and Sutherland said Ella and Defries must go back to Pitt before it was too late.

"I'll find Jake, and see what I can learn about Greyson," he told Ella as they walked away from a bivouac of wounded survivors. He put his arm about her and said, "I have friends among the Indians yet, and if I can, I'll get word to them. Meantime, we'll send a message down to Colonel Clark at the Falls of the Ohio, and he'll pass word on to Jeremy in the Illinois."

Sutherland wanted to give Ella some hope, but as she looked at him her eyes were tearful, and he could see she was prepared to lose yet another son to this war. Dr. Jeremy Bently, Sutherland's stepson, had many trusted friends among the Illinois Indians, and others at Detroit and on the Miami River would take up the search for Jake if Jeremy sent word to them.

Ella caught her breath and sobbed, "He's just a child. . . . "

Sutherland held her close. "Not anymore; that's what he wanted to prove to us." They walked to their tent near the river, thinking about parting once again, knowing that this time Owen would be entering a world more dangerous than ever for whites. Sutherland wondered whether he should ride north to Wyandot country, or if it would be best to go on foot. As they approached their tent, which was set apart from the rest of the camp, Peter Defries stuck his head out the flap. Defries looked around, as if hoping no one else was near, then beckoned for them to come quickly.

Something was up, and Ella hurried to the tent, Sutherland glancing around to see if they were being watched. Defries almost dragged him inside, where Ella was already on her knees by the cot as she cried, "Mr. Greyson!"

There, lying pale and weak under a blanket, was Entellus Greyson, alive and recovering from his ordeal. He tried to sit up, but Sutherland held him down and motioned him to be still. Greyson smiled and lay back.

Defries said, "He's shot up some, and had a bout with fever, I reckon, but he's going to be all right."

Ella asked what was going on. "Why the secrecy, and how did he get here?"

Defries grinned and declared, "An old friend brought him to the edge of the woods and come to find me when I was out . . . ah, answering nature's call . . . and, well, it was worth being interrupted, as you see!"

"Who?" Sutherland asked, kneeling beside Greyson.

The Marylander said weakly, "Niko-lota. It was he who found me, just when we were overrun . . . and he saved my life. Evangeline nursed me back, and they protected me, though there were some others of us—" He began to tremble and looked away, a tear running down. "The Indians killed almost all they captured—"

Ella gasped, thinking about Jake.

Greyson said shakily, "I was in their village when the Delawares brought in Colonel Crawford. He had become separated from his men, looking for his son and other relations, but they were all dead, too. . . ." He made himself go on, saying, "I don't want to have to tell this again, Owen, so pass it on to the officers here. The colonel is dead. He died at the stake."

"Dear God," Sutherland said, and gripped Ella's hand. There was silence, except for the sound of sobbing. After some time, Greyson touched Sutherland's arm and said that Niko-lota was hiding in the forest, and that was why they had tried to keep the troops from learning of Greyson's arrival.

"He's waiting for you, Owen. He says he'll help you recover your boy, if he can."

The Sutherlands met Niko-lota a mile from the base camp, on a wooded ridge overlooking the river valley. There, after sharing a pipe of tobacco with his old friend, Niko-lota told about the defeat of Crawford's army, and how so many of the troops had foolishly split into small parties and tried to flee that way.

"We caught many," Niko-lota said in Delaware, which Ella understood. "And we learned they were Williamson's men. But Williamson, the murderer, we did not catch."

Jake, he said, had been brought through his own village by the Wyandots, and Greyson had recognized him. That had been some days ago, and the boy had not yet been harmed, because they liked his courage and his defiance of them. Also, Niko-lota added, "The warriors have drunk much blood, and this young one did not interest them." He added that the old man who had taken him prisoner had twice refused to give him up to the squaws, who would have beaten him, and that was a good sign. "The aged one has lost many sons and grandsons in the fighting, and it may be he will choose your boy as his own."

Ella's heart wrenched at that. Once adopted, Jake would surely be killed if he tried to escape. And if the Wyandots did adopt him, that would mean he would have to stay with them until he was grown—that or risk escape. Chances were slim that the Wyandots would give him up peacefully in exchange for trade goods. When Owen said he would go with Niko-lota to seek out the old Wyandot, Ella again insisted she would go, too. Her husband shook his head, saying it was simply too dangerous, even with Niko-lota as his escort.

"The journey's hard, lass, and there are plenty of bad-hearted Indians out there—"

She cut him off. "If you take your woman with you, they'll know you come in peace! What do you say, Niko-lota?"

The Delaware was sitting cross-legged, refilling the pipe he and Sutherland had smoked earlier. After a moment, he looked up and spoke.

"It may be good for your squaw to come, Donoway, because this Indian is thinking there is something else you can do for my people." He pondered a moment, then said, "We have won a great victory, and we will win others, and maybe we will keep the whites out of our country for many winters. The British are still at Detroit, and they still have much to say about what will happen to the red man, but we know that the British have lost this war." He looked down at the camp in the valley. "The Indian has to talk to Congress, Donoway, but we have no friends in Congress."

Waiting the appropriate few minutes before replying, as Indian custom required, Sutherland said, "If your people will treat with me, I can speak on their behalf to Congress when peace is made."

Ella listened, realizing how wise Niko-lota was. He was fully aware that his people's fate lay in the hands of the rebel victors. Ella knew that the Indians respected her husband enormously, and if he came to them with offerings of peace, they would hear him out. Like Niko-lota, they had no illusions about how long they could stave off the white invasion from the East.

Niko-lota said, "We will go from village to village, seeking your boy, and as we go we will talk to them, and you will speak for your own kind, Donoway. We need to understand what will happen, and what Congress means to do with us."

After a pause, he went on. "I fear our time is short, Donoway, and that this land will pass to a stronger people." His eyes were hooded as he spoke, his voice soft. "I have seen Philadelphia."

"Sold! To Mr. Morely for five hundred and fifty!"

That was the end of the day's bidding at the massive trading house in Fort Pitt's settlement, and James was satisfied. Owen Sutherland and Peter Defries had not yet returned from wherever they had gone off to, and James had just purchased every fur that was to be had, good or bad, during a session of bidding in the dim, smoke-clouded trading house. His only real competitor had been Susannah Sutherland, bidding in her father's absence.

Somewhat tired, he got up from his bench and glanced across the crowded room at her; she looked back and nodded. He had outbid her every time, but he had spent far more than he wanted to. Still, the Frontier Company must not be permitted to enter the peltry market easily, even if he had to pay dearly to assure it.

James went to Susannah, bowed, and said, "You were quite daring on those last pelts; you would not have been happy with such poor stuff had I let you have them."

She stood up, inclined her head slightly, and replied with a smile, "I knew you would not let me have them, flea-ridden and bald as they are, James. I achieved what I set out to do, as you'll see when you total up what all that peltry cost Cullen and Company."

James grinned. "You won't break our treasury that easily, Susannah; and with the war, furs are so dear in Europe that I'll make a profit on these yet."

They went outside, James greeted by nearly every man in the place, all of them obviously uneasy to see a woman doing a trader's job, a man's job, even though they had seen Susannah here many times before as her father's assistant. It was a fine, brisk day, the sun bright and cheerful, and James offered to walk Susannah to her cabin. He would have wanted to walk with her even had the weather been bad, for these days he was finding himself able once again to think of courting her. Now that Greyson was gone, James looked forward to seeing more of Susannah, and today, as usual, she was charming to be with. As they strolled, they spoke of what Fort Pitt could be one day, of how a great city could grow up here. Reaching up to let the bird, Punch, land on her finger, Susannah said she longed for some theatrical performance, for nothing had been presented since Christmas, and everyone would be glad for a Shakespeare play. James agreed, offering to finance one should Susannah wish to organize the production.

As they chatted idly, shouting rose behind them, and they turned to see Maxwell and Willis hurrying along the street. In fact, many people seemed suddenly agitated, and there were angry exclamations and even screams.

Susannah tossed away the jay and put her hand on James's arm, her other going to her mouth as she said with a gasp, "Is it the army? Oh, no! Please no!"

Indeed, word had just come in with the arrival of the first boatload from Mingo Bottom. Maxwell yelled as he approached, "Wiped out! They're wiped out! The rest of the boats are almost here!"

Susannah nearly began to faint, and James caught her, feeling how warm and soft she was in his arms, the scent of rosewater heady in his mind. He so wanted to crush her against him, to hold her close.

But the disaster was foremost, and as James helped Susannah recover, Maxwell blurted out what he had learned, telling of the great loss of life, at least two hundred men missing and presumed dead, another hundred badly wounded.

Seeing Susannah's distress, James quickly asked about Greyson, and it was Willis who replied that he was in one of the boats that had not yet landed.

Willis touched his tricorne to Susannah, saying, "I asked right off about him, mistress, knowing as how you'd want to know."

"Is he hurt?"

James felt pained to see how anxious she was, to see how she loved Greyson the way he wished she would love him. He scarcely heard Willis's reply, but caught the gist that Greyson was all right, though wounded. James was startled when Susannah threw herself suddenly into his arms, whispering her relief that Greyson was alive. Absently, James patted her back. He wanted to stroke her hair, but he forced away his desires and gave his attention to Willis, who was saying something about mortgages.

"What's that?" James asked. "Oh, yes, the mortgages on their farms . . . of course. Now, that will be a problem."

James felt Susannah stiffen and look searchingly at him. Maxwell was clearing his throat, waving a letter, attempting to change the subject by saying that some other extremely important news had just come in. "Listen, James—" he began.

Cutting him off with a wave of the hand, James said, "Cancel all those mortgages, Noah."

Maxwell's eyes went wide, his mouth falling open as he stammered, "What? Cancel? Good God, man! Do you know what you're saying? You're talking about thousands—"

"Cancel them!" To James's surprise, he felt Susannah grip his arm, and at the same time Willis gave a yelp of glee and clapped his hands, even doing a little jig and clicking his heels.

"By damn!" Noah cried, and then glanced uneasily around at the many people who were taking note. He dropped his voice. "I will not, James! Don't you know what you've got there?" He glared at Susannah, then said, "We have to talk in private!"

James had made up his mind, the very touch of Susannah telling him the rightness of what he was doing. "Every mortgage, whether the man of the house is still alive or not! Cancel them! I don't want any part of it, whether there's silver or gold in their lands or not!"

Noah made a noise like a beast and clenched his fists, as if to strike James. "You're blinded by this woman, blinded like a fool by this—"

After James hit him, Noah appeared to be running backward, and he crashed into Reverend Willis, whose back was turned while he did his jig. The two of them went down in a heap, the crowd gawking at the tangle of legs and arms and the flurry of Noah's curses and Willis's admonitions against cursing.

Susannah embraced James. "You are indeed still a man of the North, James!" He did not let his own arms go around her, for he knew there was no hope for him. Her face radiant, tears in her eyes, she said, "There is good in you, James, good that will never be extinguished!"

He felt his heart skip at her words, and his arms almost held her as she pressed against him, not caring about the gawkers. But before he could embrace her, before he could savor that moment, Susannah spoke softly. "Entellus said that about you, James, and I always knew it was true."

The wind left his sails, and he struggled inwardly with a

fury of emotion. Just then another shout came from down the street, and the crowd parted to let a horse cart come clattering through. Peter Defries was sitting in the back, waving to Susannah and calling out that Greyson was with him, lying on a stretcher. The cart rattled by, on its way to the Sutherland cabin, and with a quick farewell to James, Susannah lifted her skirt and sprang lightly aboard, Defries catching her and pulling her up. Then she was gone from him. James knew it was for good.

He was downcast, and he paid little attention as Willis helped the bloodied, sobbing Maxwell to his feet. Then James saw, on the ground, the letter Noah had been trying to show him. He picked it up, surprised to see the seal of the Congress on it. Noah had opened it already and now stood a little way off, sulking, watching to see how James would react when he read it.

James was amazed. It was an appointment for himself and Noah to serve on behalf of Congress as ambassadors to the British commandant at Fort Detroit! Despite the Indian fighting, the war between loyalist and rebel was virtually at an end now, and the British had agreed to safe passage for Congress's ambassadors to make arrangements with the western posts for the formal cessation of all hostilities. Thanks to the powerful influence of Cullen and Company friends among the new rulers of the independent states—and to allies among important loyalists—James and Maxwell had been put in a perfect position to map out the future of the northwest.

He looked at Maxwell, who was holding a handkerchief to his nose. "You do have the knack for arranging things our way, Noah. My congratulations."

Maxwell turned in a huff and strode away, and Willis hurried down to the docks to help see to the wounded. James stood a moment, alone in the street, the letter in his hands. Now, he knew, there was no way to prevent Cullen and Company's ultimate triumph. He was almost shocked by the magnitude of his success. The vast northwest lay at his feet, just for the taking.

chapter **16**

THE SCIOTO

The July afternoon heat lay slow and heavy on the valley of the Scioto River, and as the Sutherland party members paddled their canoes upstream, they saw that the Indian cornfields were empty, that squaws and children who should have been hoeing weeds were all home, or swimming somewhere nearby.

Ten canoes were in the flotilla, heavily laden with all the goods Sutherland had been able to borrow or buy on credit from traders based at the Falls. A fortune equivalent to everything he owned was in those canoes, but he was not sure it would be enough to give as presents on his way through Indian country, to buy back little Jake. With Niko-lota and Evangeline in one canoe and thirty Delaware warriors as the escort, Ella and Owen had been traveling for ten days since leaving the base camp at Mingo Bottom. They had gone down the Ohio to a rendezvous at the mouth of the Scioto with packers up from the Falls, men sent by Colonel Clark at Sutherland's written request for all the trade goods that could be spared.

It had been strange the other morning, to see the surly, restless Virginians from the Falls together with close-mouthed Delawares of Niko-lota's, all of them loading and unloading Sutherland's trade goods. Had they met on the trail, these men would have fought to the death, but now they were cooperating in a strange expedition to which Colonel Clark had given his blessing.

Up the Scioto, past the lookout rock where Niko-lota told the Indian sentry all was well, and beyond into Shawnee country, the flotilla paddled in the baking sunlight. At first they were too hot to sing, too anxious about what was to come. It was Sutherland, then, who touched their proud hearts, breaking into a Chippewa paddling song he had learned from his old friend Tamano. The Delawares liked the song, added their own, and showed their prowess in a birch boat. The current was strong against them, the heat oppressive, but the Indians drove on upriver, singing and chanting, even racing one another at times.

As they approached a large Shawnee village, the first on their route, Ella leaned back to her husband, who was in the stern of his canoe, and said, 'Owen, I don't want them to see I'm afraid when we come into this village." She bit her lip. "How . . . what can I do?"

He stroked with the paddle, changing sides while he looked at his wife, then smiled, saying gently, "Spit in someone's eye, preferably the wife of the chief."

That settled her, and with a laugh she punched him on the knee. He saw that she felt better, but she was right to worry. He did not know what would happen, what these Shawnees would think, and whether they would even allow Niko-lota to introduce him. Before this day was done, Sutherland might have to do more than spit in an eye.

Even before the canoes drew alongside the landing place, the village of bark-and-hide lodges erupted into life, mobs of children and packs of dogs first, yipping and howling as they came running toward the newcomers. Sutherland climbed out and pushed the canoe into shallow water so that Ella could get out, and as he did so a half dozen curs came snapping and growling, to be kicked and cuffed away by him and Niko-lota.

As Evangeline moved close to Ella's side to comfort her, the children came in next, prodding and plucking at the white woman, circling Sutherland, pretending to shoot him with imaginary guns. Older boys approached, eyes alight with anticipation and excitement, thinking these were prisoners to be abused. Already, many of the squaws were forming up into the two facing lines of a gauntlet, expecting the prisoners to be forced to run between them and to be beaten as they ran.

But Niko-lota and his men made a protective wall around the Sutherlands, and when the village elders arrived, they recognized Donoway and, despite their surprise, welcomed him as if he had come on another trading journey. In years past, before the war, he had visited these lower Scioto towns and done a good business here, and now the chiefs and headmen greeted him as if he were an honored guest. Wrinkled old warriors and handsome war chiefs in their prime came to shake the hand of the famous Donoway, and it appeared all would be well, for now.

Niko-lota introduced Sutherland to the gathered crowd, shouting, "Donoway has come to do you honor, to speak to you of peace and of renewed trade!" He motioned at the bales of goods in the canoes, some now being unloaded and unpacked to the wondering eyes of these miserably poor Indians, who had not seen decent trade goods in years.

Eyeing the ropes of tobacco and bags of trinkets, the chiefs did not hesitate to invite Sutherland to smoke with them at the council fire. "It has been too long since we made a good trade," one grizzled chief said. "It is too long since Donoway has come in peace," said another, and many voices—men and women—spoke in agreement. Sutherland had hope now that he could persuade them to listen and to help him find Jake. As he moved ahead, glancing back to see Ella and Evangeline fall into line behind, he said loudly in Shawnee, "It has been too long since you have heard words of peace spoken by my people."

There was silence for a moment, until Niko-lota said as he walked, "I have heard Donoway's words of peace, my cousins, and they are good."

They walked on, everyone in remarkably thoughtful silence, as if each person there were thinking of the weight of this amazing moment, with Donoway coming among them, as of old, and behaving as if there were no danger to him. Sutherland knew they had been well satisfied with the recent victory, and that they were confident, proud, sure of their strong bargaining position in any peace talks.

His speech had been well prepared, and he knew they would be content to listen, for a good speech pleased the Indians, especially if it were preceded by tobacco and many presents. They arrived at the council grounds, in the midst of three hundred Shawnees, the sun boiling, the air thick and dulling the senses. Normally they would have waited until evening, when it was cooler, to council, but the Indians were very interested and eager for the gifts carried by Niko-lota's Delawares.

Ella stayed close behind her man, ignoring the nosy, touching squaws and poking children. She was sweating, and it was hard to breathe in the close-packed crowd. For a moment she wondered how much of this they would have to endure before they finally rescued Jake. Her weary mind almost thought the words *rescue Benjamin,* but she shook her head and imagined Little Jake, his fine, handsome face and those cool, gray eyes of his, eyes that never seemed to miss anything.

"Ma!"

"Jake?" she asked aloud, and tried to see through the

crowd, which had also stopped, watching Sutherland suddenly pushing through them. Ella felt a thrill. "Is that Jake, Owen?"

Her voice was louder than she meant, almost a scream, and she began to follow her husband, knowing she must not lose control, must not lose her head.

Evangeline was beside her. "Steady," the young Shawnee woman said, touching Ella's arm. "Be careful, please. . . ."

"Is it Jake?"

The heat, the pressing crush of sweating, smelly bodies, the fear, and the desperate need to find the boy overwhelmed her, and she forced herself through, even roughly pushing at a big warrior, who did not like it. Owen was up ahead, but not yet out of the crowd. Niko-lota moved swiftly, coming between Ella and her husband. Ella's heart thundered. Could it really be?

"Pa! It's me! It's Jake!"

He was there! "Dear God!" She saw the boy through the crowd, which just then dispersed to let her through, and she almost ran, seeing Jake tied up near a lodge, a rope around his neck as if he were a dog on a leash.

"Jake!" she screamed, and dashed forward, but she was grabbed roughly, lifted off her feet, and thrown off balance by a huge Indian—the man she had bumped earlier.

She was caught by Evangeline, who whispered, "He will fight! He is Wyandot! He must be with the man who has taken the boy prisoner!" Evangeline held Ella, but not tightly enough. Ella broke away, but the big Wyandot warrior stepped in her path again. At that moment, the old man emerged from the lodge, squinting at Sutherland and back at Jake, who was calling out and frantically waving, jumping up and down. Ella saw that Owen was surrounded by three Wyandot warriors, and the Shawnees had drawn off a little, as if to watch the intriguing little melodrama. There seemed to be five Wyandots in all.

Ella could not get around the man in front of her. Owen hesitated, making a plan. The Wyandots, with the fresh scalps on their belts, their war paint still smeared from the earlier campaign, were ready for trouble, it seemed. The old chief shouted something to them, and hands went to the knives at their belts.

"Owen!" Ella cried, her voice rising above the excited chatter of the Shawnees. "Dear God, Owen! Jake! Jake, you'll be all right now!"

The old Indian leaped into the air with a shriek of fury, and the man in front of Ella moved a step toward her. Niko-lota said something to his own men, who began to throw down their burdens. The big Indian reached out to push Ella, but she slapped his hand away. He grunted and advanced, and with all her might she kicked him between the legs. He went to his knees with a moan of pain, helpless, his forehead touching the ground, and Ella ran toward Jake. The Shawnees screamed in delight at her audacity, but another Wyandot came at her, this time with a blade in hand. He made to stab, but Owen was there, bare-handedly chopping the knife away, smacking the man down with the back of his other hand. Then the other two Wyandot sprang at him, and Ella ran on toward Jake. But the old man grabbed the boy by the hair, putting a knife to Jake's chest. Ella stopped short, terrified.

Sutherland sidestepped his first attacker, taking the second by surprise with a punch to the throat, cutting him down. The first spun at Sutherland, diving, knife slashing. Sutherland ducked under the blade, caught the man by the body, and threw him several yards into a cooking fire. Stunned, burned, the Wyandot leaped up with a yelp, thought about trying again, but saw Sutherland standing there, legs apart, fists clenched. The Indian moved toward his old chief, and Sutherland turned to Ella, who was just a few feet from the man and Jake.

To Sutherland's dismay, the old man had pulled back the boy's head so that Jake's eyes were wide, the knife tip almost breaking the skin of the throat.

"Hold!" Sutherland said in Wyandot. "I, Donoway, come to buy him back, not to fight you, old one!"

Eyes darting, the Wyandot looked from Sutherland to the Shawnee headmen, who were standing beside Nikolota and the Delawares, listening.

The old Indian was nervous, and Sutherland feared that the man might slip, or might in desperation kill the boy.

Ella pleaded: "Don't move, Jake! Please don't move, my son! Oh, we love you so!"

The Indian snarled, as if too confused to know what else to do. Sutherland drifted closer, one hand out, slowly coming up in the greeting of peace.

"We mean you no harm, grandfather," Sutherland said calmly. "We will pay you much for our boy. . . . Put the knife down, grandfather."

That did not work. The Wyandot snarled again and gave Jake's hair a tug so that Ella gasped in terror. Jake, however, just swallowed and said, "Go for 'im, Pa! I'll get loose—"

"No!" Sutherland said quietly. "Don't move boy, not now." He stepped forward, but the old Indian spoke, his voice rasping and tense.

"Stand back, Donoway! Stand back, or the young brave dies! I will not give him up, not for all your riches! I have lost many sons and grandsons, young ones tough and full of fire like this one! I will have him, and he will be my son! The father of my grandsons!" He yanked the hair again, moving the knife slightly. "He will be mine—or he will die! Now!"

Sutherland licked his lips, suddenly feeling the sun's terrible heat on his head. He drew a long breath, glanced at

Ella to steady her, certain now that nothing could be done yet. He expected it when, a moment later, the Shawnee chiefs and several leading warriors came up, saying that this Wyandot was their guest and so must not be harmed.

Sutherland explained that the boy was his son, and the Shawnees thought about that a moment before one of them spoke up.

"It is not your wish to have him slain, Donoway, and it is not our wish to demand that the old one surrender him to you." The chief looked at the determined Wyandot. "We would not dishonor you, grandfather, but we think it best that you depart for your own country now, and take the boy, alive, if you care for him."

Ella groaned.

Sutherland knew that anything rash could kill them all. He contained himself and softly told Ella to show only strength, adding, "This Indian will not hurt the boy unless we force it."

Ella wanted to cry in despair, but she drew herself up and said in a determined voice, "Jake . . . be strong, my son. We'll come for you. Be strong! Be strong!"

The Wyandot withdrew the knife when Sutherland gave his word to let him go in peace. Trembling, Ella moved to her husband's side, and they watched, helpless, while the Wyandots gathered their belongings and horses and took the courageous Jake away, northward, into the deep forest and out of sight.

"My Jake!" Ella whispered, hands moving to her face, but then she dropped them, held her head high, and turned to walk with Evangeline and the villagers toward the council grounds.

The Shawnees were gossiping and laughing, not having had so much excitement in ages. It had been a remarkable summer, with a great defeat of the white enemy, and now today's adventure. They would talk about the visit of

Donoway for weeks to come, and one day they would learn
how his story ended, and whether or not the old Wyandot
gave up the boy. Many Indians were sure the Wyandot
grandfather would kill Jake, but others shook their heads at
this, saying, "You do not know the one called Donoway.
He is a man among men, and he will win his son back one
day."

It was several weeks later, and drums beat an excited
pulse as the canoes of Sutherland's party drew up at the
landing place of the Upper Sandusky village of Wyandots
—the original objective of the doomed militia expedition.
It had been a slow, wearying journey, with stops at fifteen
smaller villages along the way. Everywhere Owen had
made a long speech about the independent rebels, a subject
that was not always received kindly by chiefs and warriors
glutted with the pride of their own triumph.

The presence of the famous Donoway in their villages
brought honor, however, and the subchiefs and headmen,
the war chiefs of the Delaware, Shawnee, and Wyandot
greeted him as an equal. They accepted him as a spokes-
man for Congress, and listened patiently as he told of his
wish for peace, for new treaties, and of his desire that old
treaties be honored, the rights of Indians protected. He
even said—as Franklin had promised by letter—that Indians would be permitted delegates to Congress, and that
made even the most cynical of them take note.

Still, there had been no more word of Little Jake, except
that it was known the old Indian who had captured him had
fled rather than face Donoway again and perhaps be forced
by his chiefs to give up the boy. Sutherland dared not pursue the man, lest in his jealousy the old warrior murder
Jake instead of surrendering him.

Now, in this mobbed, raucous village, at least a thousand Indians were on hand to greet Sutherland's entourage

as they climbed out of their canoes. Already the great council fire burned high, the drums racing in excitement, and young warriors showed off by galloping their horses back and forth over the plains, firing rifles in the air, and whooping ferociously as they came back full speed into the village.

By now Sutherland knew that most Indians were anxious for peace. The defeat of Crawford had left them with their honor intact, and they were prepared to make terms with Congress. It was the British and loyalists, not the Indians, who had lost the war against the rebels. Time and again the northwestern Indians had defeated white invasions, although the powerful Iroquois had been run off their lands eastward in New York, and the Delaware villages near there were in constant danger of attack. Yet the northwest tribes had held, and the British could not give up what had not been won in battle.

As in every village, the people mobbed Sutherland and shouted in greeting, and he recognized many a familiar face from his trading days. He had to grin as he walked, jostled by well-wishers, shaking hands with acquaintances, and nodding to squaws who, at their husband's or father's bidding, had happily kept him warm on a winter's night long ago. These women were all fat and toothless now, it seemed, but they looked at him with the eyes of youth, and he smiled to let them know he had not forgotten them. He would see they received special presents from the bales and boxes being unloaded from the canoes.

Before long, stew from great, simmering pots had been served on bark plates, and everyone had smoked his share of tobacco as the pipe was passed around the concentric circles of elders and warriors ringing the council fire. Sutherland was formally greeted with a long speech from a chief, and after waiting some time he arose and, with solemn ceremony and flowery words, laid gifts at the feet of the elders. Though he did not have his famous claymore, he still impressed them, as ever he had. More ropes of tobacco, fine silk hats with feathers, a few blue frock coats, bags of beads for their women, and an assortment of colorful shirts for the children.

Sutherland knew that the British at Detroit were being stingy with presents now that the war was ending, and their licensed traders were charging exorbitant prices for what they sold.

"There is much more to come," Sutherland said in Wyandot. "The Frontier Company will return again to you, stronger than ever before, more generous that ever before, and your children, who have forgotten the name Frontier Company, once again will learn that we are the friend, the partner of the Indian, and will always be."

This got the Indians clapping and cheering, whistling and shouting. All talk of peace, all promises of treaties and good wishes were as nothing compared with the prospect of the essential trade with the East being reopened. And the notion of Sutherland's Frontier Company once again taking the lead in the fur trade delighted the Indians.

"The sun is returning to our land, my brothers, and when the British depart from Detroit, turning over their forts to Congress, the Indian will prosper as never before!" As Sutherland said these things, he prayed inside that he would indeed have the influence with Congress that Ben Franklin said he would. At the same time, he knew that these Indians and thousands like them would support him, and he would fight for them when Congress took control of the northwest. The sun, indeed, was returning—but before he could leave Indian country, he must find Jake, and that loomed ever more difficult before him.

As he talked, Sutherland stole a glance at Ella, probably the only person in this jubilant crowd who was not happy. He saw the haggard sorrow that had overtaken her, and knew that she would not truly be happy again until she had Jake once more in her arms.

"... no more will we take up the red tomahawk of war, no more will we cast our sons into the cauldron of death! It is for you and for us to find the path to peace, for we all know too well where the path of war will lead us!"

The Indians became thoughtful, until a voice suddenly rose above the silence—a familiar, creaking voice, sharp and strong, speaking English.

"Reckon we all know where the warpath leads, Mr. Sutherland. But we can't be sure where Congress'll lead us, can we?"

Sutherland knew who it was, even before the Indians parted to let the man enter the circle.

"How, Girty." Sutherland had expected this eventually, but he had said what had to be said, and the Indians here had heard him and knew he was right in calling for peace.

Simon Girty stepped forward, rifle resting in the crook of one arm, his right hand raised in greeting. "How, Sutherland. That was a mighty speech you gave, pretty and inspiring."

A hush lay over the thousand, except for the whispers of those who knew English and were giving the translation. Sutherland knew the moment of truth was at hand, and he was not surprised at what Girty said next, almost with an apology in his voice.

"Don't want no trouble with you, old hoss." The grizzled scout glanced toward Niko-lota, who was listening with intensity, then turned back to Sutherland. "I got orders from the commandant to arrest you. You got to come back to Detroit with me."

Sutherland saw at least twenty whites and loyalist Chippewas waiting just beyond the outermost council circle— Girty's escort. There was no telling what the rest of the Indians would do if Sutherland decided to resist, but he had been prepared for this to happen. Anyway, it was time to go to Detroit.

Looking over at Ella, whose eyes were alight with fear and excitement, Sutherland knew she wanted to go to Valenya, and also that she had the faith that something good would come of this in the end.

To Ella he said, "We're going home, lass,"

She drew a quick breath and said softly, "At last."

chapter 17

VALENYA

Word passed quickly through the villages that the British were preparing to give up the northwest to the forces of Congress, and the Indians were bitter. After all they had sacrificed in battle, they felt betrayed that their so-called great white father, King George III, was forsaking them. They deserved better than this, they said, and they would have it. British traders and soldiers, volunteer militia and loyalist regulars, felt the threat grow day by day.

Now that Owen Sutherland had come to them and spoken of a promising future, they looked to him and believed that he could help them in the coming negotiations with the American rebels. But the British had arrested him, and no one knew what they would do to him. As if a new call to take the warpath were being passed through the villages, runners brought the message far and wide that Donoway had been taken captive and was in danger. From the Delaware lodges on the Susquehanna to the Sioux tepees in the Wees-kon-san, from the distant fur grounds on the shores of Rainy Lake to the Shawnee villages in the Ohio Valley, the word traveled fast, and it was heard with great concern and anger. Donoway was the one white man, above all, on whom they could depend. They would not let him be imprisoned.

It was the middle of August when the flotilla of canoes rounded the bend below Detroit and came in sight of the settlement ahead on the left-hand bank. The morning was bright and warm, the breeze fresh and the smell familiar. Owen took Ella's hand where they sat in the center of the huge canoe.

Girty was in the stern, and twelve Indians and half-breeds paddled strongly, anticipating a large audience on shore when they returned with the famous Donoway. In the distance, bathed in sunshine, was the new stone fort, occupying high ground beyond the settlement that once had lain within the walls of the original Fort Detroit. The new post looked formidable, and Sutherland thought it would not have been taken easily. He saw the string of *habitant* houses all along both sides of the river and knew the name of every family. Here and there were clusters of Indian lodges, and between them were green fields of corn and orchards and vineyards. People waved from shore, and the closer the flotilla came to Detroit, the more apparent it was that today the straits were incredibly crowded with Indians of nearly every nation.

Girty gave the command, and the men laid down their paddles, loaded and raised their firearms, and at a word fired a greeting to the fort. In all the canoes following, the paddlers did the same, simultaneously, and the memory of many a "fire of joy" at a fur brigade's homecoming came back to Sutherland. He had no idea what faced him at Detroit—perhaps imprisonment as a rebel agitator—but whatever came, he was excited to be back here again.

Girty said, almost to himself, "Lotsa Injuns . . . Wonder what's up."

Sutherland replied, with a wink to Ella, "Probably here celebrating the seventh year since our Declaration of Independence, Girty, don't you think?"

Girty gave him a sidelong glance but said nothing. Soon canoes full of Indians and French were pushing out from shore, at first five or ten boats, and then thirty, forty, and by the time the flotilla was half a mile from the fort and heard the dull boom of the cannon's salute, there were at least a hundred loaded canoes swarming all around. Indians were shouting Sutherland's Ottawa name, waving and grinning. Many of them he knew well.

"Look!" Ella cried out, pointing at a nearby canoe. "It's old Mawak! And see, Little Hawk is with him!"

The Sutherlands waved at the grinning, toothless Ottawa medicine man, Mawak, who was as old as he was fat, riding like some Turkish pasha, and bedecked as usual with several brightly colored trade shirts and strings of charms and beads. In contrast to Mawak was the Sioux war chief Little Hawk, a tall and handsome warrior in his prime, a friend of Ella's son Jeremy, and the finest horseman Sutherland had ever seen. He and Mawak had six women and several children in their birch boat, and Sutherland saw that one was Little Hawk's wife, White Dove, while the other squaws—all young—were presumably Mawak's wives. They waved and called and shouted in happiness to see the Sutherlands again, and it was obvious that hundreds of these Indians wished Sutherland well, and had come to Detroit to welcome him. There were at least three thousand Indians here, however, and surely not all of them were a welcoming party. He would find out the answer when the boats pulled into shore.

More surprises awaited the Sutherlands on the gravel beach, where they were met by long-lost friends and partners in the Frontier Company. Rushing to embrace them was the French scout and trader Jacques Levesque, as robust and powerful as ever. With him was his lovely wife, Angélique, who hugged Ella and exchanged joking comments with her on how they both had managed to remain attractive in their advancing age. Angélique's merchant father, Jean Martine, came trundling through the crowd, carrying above his portly belly black-haired twins, his grandchildren, to show off to the Sutherlands.

It had been six years since they had been together like this, although Sutherland and Levesque had met as enemies—an incident neither man cared to recall just then. The pushing, surging crowd laughed and shouted, long-forgotten friends shaking Sutherland's hand and pushing to the forefront other old friends from the company to say hello. For the moment, the war was forgotten, all of them weary of it. These folk of the north were determined to get on with life, with trade, and with profit, and to see Sutherland like this again gave them hope that their old ways might be renewed.

It was an emotional, overwhelming moment, and Ella began to weep with Angélique, while Sutherland himself felt deeply touched and was very happy. How well he knew this place, for all that there were changes! Once again he was among the people who loved him most, whom he loved in return. They would not let politics or blood stand between them just now. They all embraced and wept, and some broke into a familiar *voyageur* song. The bewildered loyalists who had come recently from the eastern regions stood in amazement, not understanding what was going on, or how Sutherland, the notorious rebel, could be treated with such affection.

Then, at the tapping of a side drum, the crowd quieted and opened to let a troop of soldiers from the fort come marching up, to halt in unison on shouted command. The Sutherlands turned from their friends to face the commandant of Fort Detroit—the rotund, red-coated Colonel Arendt Schuyler DePeyster, a loyalist American from one of New York's most outstanding families. As DePeyster approached to within a few paces of Sutherland, everyone was hushed and expectant, waiting to hear the colonel's orders. Even the normally noisy Indians became still, though many whispered questions to those who could understand English or had a better view of what was going on.

Sutherland knew DePeyster well, for they had campaigned as ensigns in the British army in Europe in the 1750s. Sutherland knew the man was brave and honorable, kindly and intelligent. In fact, they had both written poetry back then and exchanged critical opinions on the other's works. Sutherland had heard that DePeyster still composed poems to deliver to the Indians in the form of long and melodious speeches, and the Indians reportedly loved it, even though the translations may have left something to be desired.

DePeyster, ruddy-faced, did not let the uncertainty last long. He took another step forward and shook hands with Sutherland, saying, "We may forgo the formalities, Owen, but understand that you are charged with all the usual offenses—agitation of the Indians, inciting to rebellion, and so on. Nevertheless, it does my eyes good to see you again, sir."

Sutherland smiled at his old friend, saying, "Of course I plead not guilty to those charges, Arendt, and have to say you fit the role of colonel well. Allow me to introduce my wife. . . ."

While these pleasantries were going on, the crowd broke into chattering banter again, most of them delighted that Sutherland apparently was not to be clapped in irons. DePeyster assured them of this by raising his hands and calling out, "You will have plenty of chance to hear from Mr. Sutherland, my red children, but first it is my turn to talk to him!" Girty loudly interpreted that, and DePeyster led the Sutherlands away, to be joined by his petite Scottish wife and several other officers, many of whom shook hands with Sutherland. The war might not yet be over at the treaty table, but these men were eager that it be ended out here, or at least a truce established for old time's sake.

In that warm July sunshine, away from the crowd of Indians and well-wishers, Sutherland and DePeyster strolled around the new fort. The colonel would not let him inside, of course. "For security reasons, Owen; one never knows when you might be in an army attacking it."

Sutherland pursed his lips and looked with longing across the straits, in the direction of Valenya. "I don't think so, Arendt." The riverside was packed with Indians and their canoes, and he gazed down upon a seething mass of humanity, bright colors swirling back and forth, a steady roar rising up from them.

"Can you afford to feed them all?" Sutherland asked. "Or is that a military secret, too? You must intend to hold a great council with them soon, I presume."

DePeyster, hands behind his back, glanced at Sutherland and then at the ground. He thought a moment before saying, "No, I cannot feed them, Owen. I cannot give them a ration of rum, and I cannot supply them with presents, ammunition, or even hope."

Sutherland was about to ask why they were there, then, if not at DePeyster's invitation; but before the words came, the Redcoat said grimly, "I worry for my people, Owen, if these Indians turn on us, as you know they will do once they are sure that the king is abandoning them. . . ." He paused and licked his dry lips, a harried look of helplessness coming over him. "Pontiac's uprising will be nothing by comparison, and every Englishman in this country will be slaughtered."

Sutherland did not have to be told this. In fact, he had

intended to say the very same to DePeyster, so he played his own card next.

"They will listen to me."

DePeyster nodded slowly, as if he had expected as much. Casually, he looked back at the women, who were talking with the junior officers, out of earshot. "Then I ask you to give me your word you will not set them against us, Owen. If so, you may talk to them when you are ready, and make them keep the peace."

Sutherland again stared down at the mass of warriors and their families gathered along the shoreline. Now he understood that they had come here for him, to see he was not harmed, and that gave him pause to think and to wonder. After all these years, after all the fighting and hard feelings, he was yet one of them, and they had come to hear him tell them that they were still his people. Inside, Sutherland trembled with emotion, and he drew a shaky breath as he looked at the thousands down there, so dependent on him for their future. But could he really guarantee anything? Perhaps. He had powerful friends back east. If he failed, the Indians would be on their own as soon as the British abandoned this country. Then they would be doomed.

DePeyster said, clearing his voice, "If, sir, you can manage the Indians and speak to them on our behalf, I can offer you the permanent return of your home, Valenya."

The thrill of it shocked Sutherland, and jubilation rose in him. He reached out to grip DePeyster's hand, and the officer added, "And you may have a trading license for as long as I have authority here!"

Sutherland was overjoyed and he laughed, saying, "Of course the Frontier Company will be fully recognized again, all our former rebels licensed as well!"

"You are indeed a Scotch trader, sir," DePeyster chuckled. "You'll have to compete with Hudson's Bay and the Northwest Company, but consider the deal made. Now, in a couple of days tell those Indians the king still loves them, and keep them from lifting our hair. And if you can do that, then God bless you, Owen Sutherland, and may you grow as fat as I am, and as rich as a—I can't say 'king' to a rebel, can I? What can I say?"

"Banker! They're the kings to be, I'll warrant. Bankers will be richer than kings, and the builders of new empires. But me, I'd rather do it the old way." He observed the Indians below and felt a rush of good feeling. "With them."

Late that afternoon, the Sutherlands went alone across the straits to Valenya, excited beyond words at what was happening to them. They would be home at last, and they could stay, rebuild, and renew their past lives.

From out on the choppy water, the house looked proud in the changing light of clouds and sunshine. Ella was sitting in the bow of the canoe, and a thousand thoughts and images filled her senses. She could not help but laugh, and reached back to take Owen's hand as he paused in his paddling. The wind was fresh, the air warm and clear, and she breathed deeply, sweetly, and cried out in her happiness.

"Valenya! Valenya! We're back! Look here! We're back!"

Tears ran down her face, but she did not care and did not wipe them away. When she looked at Owen again, she saw the emotion in him, too, and he grinned, paddling harder across the current.

To herself, Ella whispered, "I promised I would return!" In her hand was the door key, for years the last token of what her life here had been. Often she had looked at this key, and now at last she would use it once again. She recalled that dreaded night long ago, when she had fled this place under cover of darkness, lest she be arrested as a rebel by the loyalists and Redcoats. It seemed so long ago, so very long ago.

"Valenya's still ours, lass," Sutherland said, and she

nodded, closing her eyes. She knew, however, that it would never be the same again.

As the canoe drew alongside the landing, Ella felt a pang to see how empty the house looked, so lonely and in need of paint. In need of everything. With its foundation crowded by overgrown weeds, the house seemed to have lost its former dignity and beauty. For at least three years it had stood untended, and weather and wind had taken their toll. Some shingles were warped or missing, and windows were broken here and there. Still, it was Valenya, and Ella stared in near disbelief actually to be home again.

The downstairs sash windows that faced the straits reflected the afternoon sun, and the smaller upstairs windows in the shade of the eaves seemed like eyes, gazing down at them, as if wondering why they had been away so long. Ella took Owen's hand, and they began to walk up the gravel path that once had cut through a well-trimmed, broad, and grassy lawn. The grass was hay now, but wildflowers were everywhere, and the grounds were still beautiful in this more natural state.

They stopped and gazed, and Owen said, "Is it as you expected, lass?"

Ella shook her head, staring at the house. But how had she expected it to be? She had only remembered it trim and white, filled with children and music and friends. It used to stand overlooking the water as if it were the sentinel of the straits, the lord of all its domain. Now Valenya was a rundown house, large and familiar, but without life, without a soul.

Owen said, "We can make it home again!"

As Ella's heart pounded with a swirl of emotions, she noticed that Owen was looking off to the right, at the seven huge standing stones down by the water, a hundred yards away. She knew he was thinking of the grave there, of his first wife, the Ottawa squaw Mayla, who had died with his unborn child in her womb. Giving him a push of encouragement, Ella guided Owen down there, and they knelt by the grave for a while, silent and full of memories.

After a time, they went to the house, and the key still worked, though the lock was stiff. The door opened, and the wind blew into the hall. As Ella stepped inside, she was overwhelmed by a rush of happiness and sentiment. It was the same place, all right, though it had suffered from neglect these past few years. Dust was everywhere, and the stairs leading up in front of them were cobwebbed and dirty.

They went to the right, into the huge common room, with its timbered ceiling, the fine brick oven in the back toward the kitchen, and, in another wall, the fieldstone hearth that Ella had always loved. There, in one corner, was Ella's spinet, and she went tentatively to it, touching the keys and sending a sweet melody through the house. It was in fairly good tune, still, to her amazement.

Sutherland stood before the hearth, as if imagining past evenings here with his family. Now he felt almost like a stranger, and yet it was all so familiar. When Ella stopped playing, he asked her to continue. She sat down and slowly began her favorite piece, a soft melody by Couperin that drifted, hauntingly beautiful, through the house. Then, as if it were all too weighty, she changed into the lovely *voyageur* song, *A la claire fontaine,* and soon she and Owen were singing it, taking heart, and feeling happy at last.

> At the clear-running fountain,
> Sauntering by one day,
> I found it so compelling
> I bathed without delay.
> Your love long since overcame me;
> Ever in your heart I'll stay!

Then Ella was in her husband's arms, holding him close, the joy and melancholy, the years of struggle and the longing for peace mingling in their hearts and making them one.

Your love long since overcame me;
Ever in your heart I'll stay!

The afternoon drew on, and the sun began to go down. Ella lit a whale-oil lamp against the gathering darkness, then sat on the settee. Clouds had come in from the northwest to dim the sun, though there were still some hours of light left. Sutherland was uneasy and went to the window to stare at the straits. Lights were twinkling on in cabins and lodges across the water.

There was something he had to say, and he turned to his wife, who appeared to be anticipating it. "Ella, I feel very . . . strange, because it's as if, after all that has happened, that we . . . we almost don't belong here anymore." He looked closely at her. "Don't misunderstand me—"

"No," she said, and got up to come to his side, putting an arm around him and leaning against his shoulder as she looked out the window at the scene they knew so well. "I do understand you, dearest. When Benjamin and Susannah and Jeremy were here, and . . . and things were different . . ."

"And we were younger," he said with a smile.

"And that, too," she sighed. "I still have a feeling for this house, but something sticks in my mind, something that Dr. Franklin's letter told us—"

"I know." There was quiet for a moment, and Sutherland absently watched a whaleboat approaching, not thinking anything of it. "He said Valenya will likely remain on British soil after the treaty is made."

Ella sighed again. She need say nothing more.

After a little while, Owen knew he could not rid himself of that same troubling thought. This would be British territory, and for all that he loved the place, he had fought too long and hard for independence . . . too long, and too hard!

Unbidden, an old thought came to him, of the mysterious mountains to the west, the ones the Indians called the Shining Mountains, and he suddenly felt the urge to talk of them to Ella.

It was then, however, that he noticed the whaleboat was full of Redcoats, and it was pulling up to Valenya's landing. He and Ella went to the door, wondering, and saw that it was Colonel DePeyster with some officers, accompanied by two civilians. The Sutherlands went down to meet them and were astonished to see it was James Morely and Noah Maxwell.

DePeyster looked troubled and nervous, and he kept rubbing his chubby face as he came toward them. Owen said, "Something's up, Ella. Be ready for anything."

She took his arm. "I am. Don't worry about me."

James and Maxwell bowed as DePeyster said, "I believe you are well acquainted. . . ." James removed his hat in courtesy to Ella, and he, too, looked troubled, as though he were under considerable strain. Maxwell, on the other hand, could not have seemed more pleased with himself, and he neither spoke to the Sutherlands nor removed his hat.

DePeyster said they should go in the house, for he had some disconcerting news. Leaving the other officers outside to allow for privacy, the five of them walked up the path to the front door. Owen glanced back once, puzzled at the sight of many boats out on the water, but he paid it little more attention, deciding it was a group of Indians looking for a place to camp. He went to Ella's side, expecting the worst, wondering what Cullen and Company had concocted now.

Inside, the house was bright with the orange glow of sunset breaking through the clouds, and the lamplight seemed pale in comparison. DePeyster asked them all to sit, then began to pace while he sought the right words. Ella and Owen were on the settee, James on a chair by the hearth, and Maxwell pulled up a seat near the entrance to the kitchen, looking around cheerfully, as if inspecting the house and approving of what he saw.

DePeyster cleared his throat and finally seemed ready to speak, but James saved him the trouble. "Owen, Congress has named us their representatives out here, and it will be up to us alone to speak to the Indians on Congress's behalf."

Sutherland felt that clutch at his heart, but he did not show his feelings, though the blood suddenly raced through his body. Certainly James had the experience to deal with Indians.

"You know how to talk to them, laddie, and I wish you well."

DePeyster broke in, raising a hand, his face pale with what appeared to be embarrassment. "There's more, and although it's not official as yet, I have to tell you, Owen, that these gentlemen have spoken with my superiors at Montreal and have been told flatly that my government will not surrender the northwest immediately, no matter what the treaty terms say." He removed his hat and wiped his face as he paced a moment. "You must understand that our entire fur trade depends on peace with all the Indians, and there are many men of influence in the British empire who depend upon the fur trade for their fortunes . . ." He made a swirling motion with his hand. ". . . and so on, you understand." He kept pacing.

Staunchly, Sutherland waited, almost expecting what was next, and it was James who said it, again bluntly. "Colonel DePeyster's superiors have forbidden the Frontier

Company to have a trading license, and you will no longer be allowed to trade here, Owen."

James's face was drawn, though he was resolute. His business triumph obviously was not giving him the same pleasure it gave to the grinning, supercilious Maxwell. Ella began to protest but immediately stopped herself; like Owen, she would not show the disappointment they both felt. Sutherland knew the British might hold on to the northwest for many years. DePeyster was about to speak again, but Sutherland stopped him with a shake of the head. He rose and walked to the hearth, knowing what had to be said. "I see Cullen and Company has more influence than ever with the Montreal loyalists."

"That's uncalled for!" DePeyster declared.

"Not so," Sutherland answered. "But I'll have my trading license soon enough, though it might not be for this side of the river." He stared at James, still no emotion showing. "And the northwest country will belong to the independent states, no matter if the British army and your loyalist trading allies start a war again to prevent it!"

DePeyster grumbled but said nothing more. Maxwell looked sour, his jaw working in his agitation.

Sutherland said, "James, I wish you the luck you deserve, but I tell you that the Frontier Company will rise again, and again, and you will not have the power to stop it!"

"There's still more, Sutherland!" Maxwell suddenly squawked, though he did not dare stand up and challenge the man face to face. "This house is no longer yours!"

DePeyster turned and walked away, obviously distressed, but James spun in his seat, as if he were surprised to hear it. Owen gave a start, but once again he was prepared for anything. Even this. He saw Ella, too, was in control, though her hands trembled in her lap.

Maxwell's skinny face was contorted as he said with a

snarl, "I've bought this house from British authorities in Montreal, and you've been officially dispossessed as a rebel, Sutherland! As of this moment, you're trespassing—"

James shook a fist. "Hold your tongue and behave like a man!"

"He's trespassing!" Maxwell shrieked and pointed at Sutherland.

Sutherland looked at Ella, a warm rush of love passing between them, love that could rise above even this and see them through whatever faced them.

James cursed under his breath. "Why didn't you tell me this before? Damn you for a snake, Noah!"

DePeyster interrupted quickly. "I want no part of your bickering, gentlemen, so I'll be on my way; I'll send another boat back for you two gentlemen." While Maxwell and Morely glared at each other, DePeyster turned to Sutherland and spoke with feeling. "I am deeply sorry about this." They shook hands. "It would honor me if you would spend some days at my quarters, Owen, before you depart for your . . . chosen home."

Sutherland thanked him, seeing DePeyster to the door, but not following him outside or even looking down toward the landing, for his mind was racing with other thoughts. He turned to James, who was standing with Ella, holding her hands in apology.

James spoke to them both, as Maxwell turned away in disgust to stare at the hearth. "I had not intended it to go so far that you would lose Valenya, I hope you know that." James looked so sad, so utterly lost, that Sutherland truly pitied him.

Ella nodded and squeezed his hands, then went to her husband. James said quickly, "Owen, I wish you good fortune, wherever you go, and I hope we meet again in a better time."

Sutherland shook his hand. "You've won after all, James." He did not add what he—and perhaps James—was thinking: *But can you take pride in what you have won and how you have won it? Which of us will be truly happy after all?*

James said, "Yes, this time I've won," and he tried to smile, but it was impossible.

The Sutherlands turned and went to the door, to be unexpectedly confronted by burly Simon Girty, who was grinning, hat in hand. Instead of greeting them, Girty said, "You got company, I reckon!" and moved aside to let them see that the entire shoreline for a hundred yards in every direction was filled with people, many of them laden with food, kegs of drink, even musical instruments. Already someone was throwing logs down for a bonfire, and a fiddle squealed as it struck into a dance tune. They had come, all their friends, for an old-time celebration at Valenya!

Sutherland laughed and gave a long Highland battle yell that carried across the river and back again, a yell answered by a mighty chorus of voices erupting into cries of joy and pride and affection.

"Come, Ella!" Sutherland exclaimed, embracing her. "We'll dance our way out of here, and tomorrow we'll go find—"

She suddenly screamed, "Jake!" and tore herself away from him, dashing down through the grass, her arms wide.

It was Jake! The boy came running out of a crowd of Indians, hurling himself at his foster mother, and spinning in circles with her as they met in a tight embrace.

Sutherland threw back his head and gave another great shout, and as the crowd again answered in their jubilation, he ran down to Jake and Ella and into the arms of a hundred well-wishers. To his astonishment, even his old Chippewa friend, Tamano, was there, and Sutherland was overjoyed. Someone yelled for a song, and *A la claire fon-*

taine echoed above the straits, with no one singing louder
than Owen and Ella and Jake.

> Your love long since overcame me;
> Ever in your heart I'll stay!

On the porch of Valenya, James Morely stood smiling
and shaking his head, a tear coming, and he did not care.
Who had won? Who had won after all?

Just then Simon Girty gave a great laugh and entered the
house, and James turned to see him throw his bearlike arms
about the startled Noah Maxwell.

"Dear old conspirator!" the smelly, bedraggled Girty
cried out, as if with much affection. "I heard you say you
got this house! Well, congratulations to you!" He gave
Maxwell another tremendous bear hug, so that the man's
protesting became a breathless gasp.

Girty let go and slapped Maxwell on the back, winking
at James and saying, "If anybody deserved a reward, it's
old Max here. He's sure one slick hoss, I'll say!"

Maxwell flushed, stammering that he had to be off; but
before he could go, Girty grabbed his arm and declared
loudly, "Yes, sir, Mr. Morely, this here hoss is some spy.
Thanks to him, we got the word about Crawford's army!"

Maxwell pulled free and hurried to leave, but this time
it was James who clutched his arm. His face pale and grim,
James demanded that Girty speak on.

"Why, as I was just saying—"

"Shut your mouth!" Maxwell cried out, but his voice
was half drowned as a great shout of celebration went up
from the crowd outside.

Girty chuckled and said, loud enough for James to hear,
"This hoss gladly betrayed his own kind, and I reckon you
best watch yer back, Mr. Morely."

With that Girty strode from the room, stopping on the

porch to give his own shriek of excitement, then scampered down to the party, yelling, "I got me a awful dry!"

Cringing, Maxwell backed away as James let go of his arm. Circling behind the table, Maxwell was close to the oil lamp, and the light revealed the stark fear in his eyes. James stepped forward, hands on hips.

Maxwell cursed. "The men back east are against you, Morely! They want you out of the company! So touch me and it'll go bad for you! Keep away! I warn you! They won't stand for it!"

James approached, and Maxwell backed off, moving awkwardly, like a cornered animal. James felt a great inner calm rise within him, for he knew now, at long last, what he had to do. He pointed at Maxwell.

"Tell them, Noah, that I'm finished with them, and I'll send them all to the devil, and you, too!" James swung around, his heart suddenly seeming to fly, and with a laugh he walked toward the door. He did not know that Noah carried a small pistol, not until he heard it cock.

James sprang aside, but not in time. The gun went off, the bullet crashing into James's upper back, and he fell heavily.

But he was not finished yet. He rolled over, trying despite his wound to get to his feet to go after Maxwell, who was hurriedly reloading. Surely no one had heard the single shot down at the noisy shoreline. James rose, fighting against the shock of his wound, and staggered toward Maxwell, but he was too slow to ward off a stinging whack on the head from the pistol butt. He fell hard, his face thudding against the floor. Dizzied, with warm blood soaking his clothes, he tried again to get up, but he was too weak. All he could do was roll onto his back. He saw Maxwell standing above him, a look of wild ecstasy on his face, the pistol aimed.

With a low laugh, Maxwell said, "Now *I* am Cullen and

Company, and the world will learn what I can do—"

James scarcely saw what happened next. It was as if a shadow passed between them, and Maxwell was suddenly gone. The pistol banged, and there was the sound of fighting. The table tipped and fell, the oil lamp shattering on the floor. A blaze burst up, and even in his woozy condition James knew it could not be stopped. Smoke billowed over him. He did not have the strength to get out, and the heat scorched his face. He was helpless. Then he felt himself dragged up and hauled swiftly outside into the cool evening air.

It was Owen Sutherland, of course. With a short laugh of irony, James reached up weakly to give Sutherland his hand.

"My friend," James said, his voice soft and humble. "Can you forgive me before I die?"

Sutherland, kneeling at his side, saw that the wound was nasty, but not necessarily fatal. There were doctors at Detroit who could tend to it. James would live.

"Och, James laddie, that pal of yours used a cheap Cullen and Company trade pistol, and it wouldn't kill a man of the North. You'll be all right soon enough."

He gripped James's hand and grinned. James understood, at last, what really mattered. As for Maxwell, he had fled into the night, and to hell with him!

Ella hurried to Owen's side, and then someone came to do the doctoring. James was carried away, and Sutherland thought he heard him laughing in spite of his pain. Ella wrapped her arms around her man and squeezed. The flames of the burning house became stronger, warming them, but neither of them turned to look.

They walked away, arm in arm, through the singing, clapping crowd and toward the standing stones, where they could be alone. Behind them, Valenya burned, sending all its glory to the starry heavens in one last, triumphant roar.

There would never be another Valenya—but then, its time was passed. Tomorrow, from the east, the sun would rise and another day begin anew.

Epilogue

Great Britain did not give up the old northwest to the United States until 1796, but long before that the Sutherland family was happily reunited in the Illinois country, a country where British troops had no control.

Susannah married Entellus Greyson, who became a partner in the Frontier Company. Rebuilt, with James Morely as one of its new, young leaders, the company became the most important trading firm in the region for many years. In time, powerful financiers such as John Jacob Astor organized even stronger firms, but the Frontier Company continued to thrive. By 1790, Cullen and Company was near bankruptcy, rotted from within by its own corruption.

Owen and Ella Sutherland lived long, contented lives, surrounded by people they loved, and who loved them in return. Yet, come springtime, there was always a restlessness about them, a yearning during those greening, bursting months. Their family well understood, and so it was not surprising that even in advanced age, Owen and Ella Sutherland one day departed with an old friend, Daniel Boone. They were last seen traveling by wagon, west, toward the distant, beckoning Shining Mountains.